# Three Nights in 1923

William Currie

This is a work of fiction. Names, characters, places, and incidents either are the product of the author's imagination or are used fictitiously. Any resemblance to actual persons, living or dead, events, or locales is entirely coincidental.



Front jacket photograph: Mississippi Encyclopedia

ISBN: 979-8-218-85671-7

First Edition

This book is dedicated to all those murdered because of the color of their skin.

You are not forgotten.

# Part I

"Whoso neglects learning in his youth, loses the past and is dead for the future."

Euripides

# Chapter 1

The Mississippi Delta lies at the feet of pine tree-covered hills to the east and the Mississippi River, historically slithering like a black snake, seventy miles to the west at its widest point. The south and north ends are where the river and hills meet, from Vicksburg to the Tennessee state line two hundred miles to the north. Once a thick and menacing wilderness of hardwoods, dark sloughs, and canebrakes; the home of bears, panthers, snakes, and massive alligators; now mostly vast farms that stretch across the flat land to beyond the horizon.

Remembrances of forests remain, some small protuberances trying to hold back the farmland that, once cleared, will remain so forever. A few large tracts are protected though, either through the good fortune of being too low and wet to farm, or through government acquisition to hold on to patches of what used to be. The two largest of these tracts are in the south Delta – the Delta National Forest and the Panther Swamp National Wildlife Refuge, both expansive and wild river bottom forests with only a few muddy tracks that pass as roads. Outside those tracts, however, proper dirt roads were built as land was cleared for farms in order to move crops to rivers for eventual shipment down the Mississippi River and to the world.

Of secondary importance was the benefit to kids, black and white, to get to a river or slough for swimming and fishing on a Sunday afternoon, to go somewhere other than the fields to work, and to forget how hard their lives were. For others, especially those who needed no escape from the rigors of poverty, it afforded a place to push boundaries, to feign bravery against danger, and to have a tale to tell for the rest of the week.

One summer day, heavy with oppressive heat and age, dust devils swirled off those lonely roads and disappeared into the expansive forests with their deep shadows. Darkness was never far away in the Delta, waiting to smother life with a tale that would last generations.

There are almost as many versions of this tale as people in the Delta. A handful know the true story, but only one knows every detail—Charlie Neely, the one who made it happen.

## Chapter 2

1956

My little brother stuck to me like Delta dust on wet skin. That was about to change. It was Sunday, it was hot, it was the day that started it all.

We were walking home barefoot from the river, kicking up knee-high dust on Sones Road that ran dead-ass straight through the hardwoods from the river to the farms that spread across the Delta like a coffee stain. The gray dust clung to us like it did to all the boys who played in the shallows of the Mississippi.

Every step we took was toward tragedy that shouldn't have happened, if only. If only the keys weren't in the ignition of the farm truck. If only Carl Allen had been raised on hard work and taught boundaries. If only he wasn't an undisciplined and reckless teenager bathed in the freedom of wealth and wrapped in the center of the universe—himself. And, to own the pain of Tucum's decision that day, if only he hadn't folded to peer pressure and gotten in the truck, finally swayed by the pleading of his older brother, Dozer, saying, "C'mon, Tucum, don't be a pussy." But then this all had to be, or else Tucum's life and mine would have turned out some other way, and that would have been a damn shame.

Carl was showing off to Dozer, who was whooping with joy, wedged between Tucum and Carl, begging Carl to go faster. As the speed and onslaught of gravel hitting the undercarriage rose, Tucum slunk down in the seat, hanging on to the tattered armrest, becoming scared of this new experience.

Dozer saw them first.

"Hit those niggers," caused Tucum to look up in time to see two black bodies leap off the road. An instant later the truck smashed the boys' shadows. Tucum spun to look out the back window, to see only dust billowing like dragon fire behind the truck.

"Turn around and chase em!" Dozer screamed.

"You ok, Isaiah?" I asked between rapid chest heaves. Dread pressed on my racing heart as I heard the truck spin around, the sound of slung gravel piercing the opaque clouds of dust like bullets.

Isaiah coughed up dust even as more settled on us in the ditch.

"I guess so," he answered, followed by a gag and a spit that was mainly dirt.

"Why they done that, Charlie?" Isaiah pleaded for understanding between coughs. I looked down at my little brother. He was full of hate, but I wasn't going to be the one to poison Isaiah's young mind.

"Cause they stupid. Stupid white boys, Isaiah, that's all," I answered, trying to sound convincing, but falling short.

"What we gonna do?" Isaiah pleaded, sounding younger than his eight years.

"We're gonna sit right here in this ditch where they can't see us. When the dust settles enough to see, we'll climb out and slip into the woods behind us," I answered, trying to sound confident in my plan.

"But I don't wanna go that way. That way be my way home," Isaiah said, pointing across the road so shrouded in dust he couldn't see the other side.

"We gonna stay in the woods for a long time befo we cross the road. We'll make damn sho they gone before we show ourselves," I told him.

Isaiah was momentarily relieved by my plan. He thought it must be a good one since I cussed, but his relief was short-lived.

"I wanna get to the other side so I be on the right side to go home through the woods," Isaiah pleaded.

"Sit tight, Isaiah; here they come again."

I put an arm around Isaiah and shrunk us down into the ditch just before the Chevy roared by, hugging the edge of the road, splaying gravel on top of us.

Some fifteen or so years later I asked Tucum if they ever saw us in the ditch, since it seemed they must have, because they came close to running off the road where we were. Tucum told me it was damn luck; they couldn't see any better than we could. And damn luck delivered fear to the brim of my young brother's heart, God rest his soul.

Certain he was well beyond where the boys had dove into the ditch, Carl stopped the truck. Dust covered them like a breaking wave.

"Well, what you wanna do?" Carl asked Dozer.

Tucum knew better than to throw a word into the older boys' conversation, so he held his breath hoping to hear they would head home.

"Let's cover them niggers with gravel real good one more time!" Dozer screamed.

Tucum told me years later that if he gets old and his long-term memory catches a bus south, that line will be the last thing left behind in his brain, like an aggravating splinter surrounded by putrid pus.

"They turnin around, Charlie. They turnin around!" Tears began to roll, pushing channels through the dust on Isaiah's cheeks.

"It's ok. They can't see us. We'll let them have their fun and then they'll get tired of it and leave," I said, but with less conviction than before.

"I wanna go home, Charlie," Isaiah pleaded.

"We will, Isaiah. We will," I answered, distracted as I pulled with two hands on a root poking into my calf.

When I took my arm off Isaiah and messed with that root, well, that sealed the deal for the boy. As the roar of the oncoming truck built in his head, the thought of getting to the right side of the road, the side where home was, became too much for him. Before I could react, Isaiah clawed up the ditch and began a sprint across the road. Before the sound of the truck impacting the boy and before his mangled body made a thud hitting the ground forty feet in front of the truck, and before the thud, whap, thud, of Isaiah's body being run over reached my ears, I knew Isaiah was dead.

Tucum hadn't seen a thing, slunk down in the truck seat with his eyes closed, wishing it all away. He felt it, though; felt it in every part of his body. The slight and momentary jolt of the truck when they hit the boy. The vibrations matched with the sounds of running over the body rushed into every cell in his body, never to leave. Carl and Dozer knew what happened since they saw the boy a split second before they hit him. This was no longer a kid's game; this was real.

"Holy Shit, Carl. You killed that nigger kid," Dozer screamed.

"Oh, shit. Oh, shit. Oh, shit," Carl stammered as he braked the truck to a sliding stop."My dad's gonna kill me," Carl said, beginning to weep.

They sat in silence for a long moment, staring into the dust cloud and a scary future. Tucum finally glanced at Dozer and his mouth was forming words without sound until he spoke in a whisper.

"You…you tell him we were mindin our own business. You tell him we changed our minds about swimmin and turned around to head home. Tell him the dust was so thick there was no way we could see that kid runnin across the road. You tell him you never saw that kid before that and it weren't your fault."

Carl raised his head from his hands and looked over at Dozer, considering what he said. Tucum, too, stared at Dozer, surprised he came up with a rational thought and one so quickly.

"He's not gonna give a rat's ass about whatever I say. He's gonna beat me for fuckin up his truck!" Carl covered his face as more tears came.

It took a while for Carl to compose himself, long enough for the dust to thin out. When there were no more tears to wipe on his arms, Carl put the truck in gear and went down the road to a wide turnaround spot. As they cruised slowly back toward where they thought the boy lay in the road, the only thing Tucum could hear was the pounding of his heart and the slow crunching and gnashing of gravel under the tires. Finally, like ghosts in the dust, came the dark outline of a body on the road and another kneeling next to it. Carl pulled the wheel to the left to pass by as far to the side as possible, but slowly enough to see the repulsive yet irresistible sight of a dead body.

Clutching Isaiah, I looked up at the truck as it eased by. Tears were streaming down my dusty cheeks that were hard as rocks from anguish. Tucum's eyes connected with mine for a moment, his dry from emotions in shock. My eyes pleaded, "Why?", followed by a flash of clenched teeth and hatred that screamed, "Why, motherfucker?!"

That was the first time I saw Tucum, and he saw me.

# Chapter 3

The deputies didn't question me, the young black boy who was the best eyewitness. I guess the first attribute canceled out the other; besides, the fewer answers they got, the better. The white boys told the same story, the one they made up. The deputies went with it because it sounded possible and a story that wasn't open and shut would've been inconvenient.

My family felt their hearts were cut out by the white kids who got away with murder, then cut in pieces to feed to the dogs by the Washington County Sheriff Deputies who let them get away with it. My grandmother screamed and cried for days, but my father said he didn't want to hear another word about it; said talking bad about a rich plantation family like the Allens would only bring no good down on us; said there's only one side of the story, and that's the white side; said that was the way it is and "no mount of cryin's gonna do a damn bit of good."

And he was right. It was just an episode one summer day quickly forgotten by the white folk, and an everlasting pain choked and stuffed deep into the aching hearts of the Delta blacks. Life went on for everyone, and for the poor, both black and white, nothing changed.

## Chapter 4

We buried Isaiah in the black cemetery on the Tate Plantation, planting another generation of Neelys next to old family headstones, the oldest now unreadable after well more than a century. I've heard people say they will remember So-and-So forever, but on that day, standing under the broiling sun, the tall corn listless in the smothering stillness, I realized I didn't know who all was buried under those stones and when I'm planted, no one likely will remember Isaiah anymore. My ten-year-old brain didn't know what to do with that thought, but as certain as the Mississippi will flow today, tomorrow, and beyond, that thought found a place to hunker down in my head for the long haul.

By the time October had broken the months of heat and another summer was slinking south, I had learned where the face that belonged to the boy in the truck window lived. I was free to roam on Sundays, and twice I had walked four miles to see the home of the boy they call Tucum.

We lived in a two-room shack with four windows and no insulation. Tucum, however, being white, undoubtedly lived in a house not resembling a shack, or so I imagined. What I could see through the trees, though, while standing in the muddy lane carved through the deep woods, was a shack, bigger than ours, but a shack nonetheless. Much nicer was their own smokehouse instead of our communal one, and the same for their outhouse. Sharing an outhouse with a few family members instead of twenty neighbors seemed luxurious, out of reach, and while not at the level of indoor plumbing, still privileged.

Privilege is relative and after much thinking over many miles walked, I concluded Tucum and his family were closer to dirt poor like us than they were to privilege. They didn't live on someone else's land, doing someone else's bidding, but we both sure as hell shared the lack of freedom to walk away from where God or chance decided we deserved. Unlike us, they sharecropped a couple of hundred acres, which felt like it should be a good thing, but I couldn't see much of a difference it made in how they lived.

On the walk home the second time, I realized how they lived really wasn't important. What mattered was I hated that boy with a heart that turned black the moment they hit Isaiah, and I was determined to hate him until it killed him or me.

## Chapter 5

Most think only blacks picked cotton in the Delta in those days, but the truth is the poor picked it, no matter the skin color. It was the closest blacks and whites came to shared suffering. And it was how Tucum and I saw each other a year after the accident. It was late in the picking season and having picked the acres they cropped, they were hired to help with the harvest on the Tate Plantation.

Bent over, fixated on cotton bolls while eyeing the ground for the occasional cottonmouth or rattler, I stood to relieve my back and wipe the sweat gathering in my eyebrows. In mid-wipe, I saw him a few rows over. It was only the hair and forehead at first, but it was enough to know it was him. I've never been quick with a thought, but this one escaped too quick to catch it back.

"Be a snake headin yo way."

Tucum jerked up straight and asked what kind, without a hint that he recognized me.

"Black one," I answered.

"Good black or bad black?" He asked, wanting to know, and right now.

"I don't know. He was goin yo way, so I didn't look real hard."

"Shit, boy, that snake bites me and my pa will have your ass."

"My pa gonna beat yo pa bad if he touches me."

Our stares locked tighter than a hunted buck in a thicket. That was bold talk for me. I had never heard a negro talk to any white like that.

Tucum stared me down, his face a mix of anger and disbelief that suddenly melted away. He looked down and kicked the dirt.

"Talk like that will get you killed. Ya know that, don't you?"

That should have been a threatening statement, but there was no danger in it. It was just a statement of fact.

"At least I won't have to pick no damn cotton no mo," I said, looking down at the sack I still needed to fill many times over before this day was done.

We stared at each other for a few seconds, neither of us knowing where our conversation should go.

To break the silence, I asked him his name as if I didn't recognize him, didn't know where he lived, and didn't carry a load of hate no cotton bag could hold.

"Tucum."

A few seconds later, "Yours?"

He was playing the same game of pretending to not know who I was.

"Charlie."

We probably would have gone on if his pa didn't yell, "Get away from that nigger, Tucum, and finish your pickin!"

And just like that, the black boy the white boy had been talking to became a nigger and no longer worthy of his time.

I didn't see a snake, and sometimes I wonder if Tucum knew I made it up. It would be years before I would have the chance to ask him, but under the circumstances, the snake by then was long forgotten.

# Chapter 6

1966

My father died on the day our platoon was slaughtered. I was the only one in our squad not a casualty. Whether skills learned from stalking game in the Delta forests or blind luck kept me unharmed, I can't say. I rediscovered prayer in the worst moments in the jungles of hell, but I felt divine protection had long ago fled from the inferno of hatred and murder that consumed Vietnam.

I cried when I was told of his passing, but only for a moment. Tears didn't come easily anymore; death had stolen that cleansing release. The brothers I lost on deployment had taken all the easy tears: Frankie from Kansas, who should have been destined to take over his father's mechanic shop; Vern from Brooklyn, destined for a dead end likely; Skip (whose real name I never knew) from Utah, destined for a wife, two kids, and a painted house; Davie from Florida, destined for a deeper tan and all the girls he could pick up on Deerfield Beach. Their destinies died before they could even get started on them.

And then there was my father, his destiny found six feet under Delta alluvial dirt. He was a hard and distant man, never to be known any better by me. Rarely happy, carrying bitterness that covered him like a body condom of anger. I always assumed he never got over losing his wife, my mother, when she gave birth to me, but I felt there was something more, something he wouldn't or couldn't speak of. I saw it when he spoke with Mr. Tate; the false veneer of a smile and "Yassuh" replaced by a flash of angry clenched teeth when he turned away. What burned inside him was snuffed out the day he died, but I knew it remained in others like him, others that might reveal the cause of their anguish that forever stole a life of peace from them and those around them.

## Chapter 7

I stepped off the Greyhound bus from Jackson on a Tuesday afternoon. There were no protesters waving signs and yelling insults like there were when we landed in Oakland the week before. There was no uniform on my body either, and never would be again, so help me God.

I picked up my duffle bag and moved a few steps out of the way of the flow of people in the Greenville bus station. The smell of diesel exhaust from idling buses and the body odor of people who had been traveling far too long, myself included, spurred me to walk the two blocks out to highway 61. I slipped the duffel bag off my shoulder and let it plop onto the dusty shoulder of the road. Summer was coming on and the heat from the road and the rustle of short corn stalks rippled by gusts from thunderheads off toward Yazoo City were the first signs telling me I was home. The smell of the Delta dirt confirmed it. It validated my location on earth. It didn't smell like Vietnam, Oakland, Memphis, or even Jackson. Still, something was missing now. Some muscle that gave me a sense of place had broken in Vietnam. With my love of humanity and my father both gone from this earth, I felt aimless. My senses told me I was home, but my heart didn't utter joy or gratitude.

A truck whooshed by, the draft and dust gusting around me. I knew I had to move somewhere. I didn't look north because the highway may as well have dropped off into a canyon around the next curve. There was nothing for me that way and so little the other way to motivate me, but it was all I had. I shouldered my duffel bag and reluctantly began walking south to the only home I had ever known.

Four hours later the late afternoon sun found a crack through building gray clouds heavy with rain and lit up my shack as I stepped off the plantation drive gravel onto the muddy lane that led to all the worker's shacks, mine being the first. I paused to make sense of what I was seeing. Maybe it was from looking at primitive dirt-floor hooches for two years, but my shack looked better than I remembered it. I thought the steps looked new and there was new lumber under the right window where rot had set in. It was then that I noticed new window curtains. I felt grateful that someone had worked on my shack in my absence, but I also felt rising anger from the inside of my shack being messed with.

I climbed the three steps quickly and twisted the door handle. It was locked, and I realized I had no recollection of what happened to my key. Too many memories of Vietnam left little room in my head for something so trivial. I pushed on the door to gauge how strong the door latch was and almost fell into the shack when the door suddenly opened.

"Well, young man, most people knock. Somethin wrong with your knuckles?"

I caught my balance and looked up to see who was in my shack.

"Auntie Luretha?" I asked, confused as ever now.

"Charlie?"

"Yes, ma'am. It's me."

"Well, Charlie Neely, come in. Get that bag in too before it rains. My Lord, you the last person I expected would come to my door. I thought you was dead!"

I set my duffel bag inside the door and gazed around the room that was not at all how I left it.

"What's that? Oh, no ma'am, I ain't dead. Not yet, anyways."

"I's can see that. Come sit down, Charlie, and I'll get you some water. You sweaty as a fish. Where you comin from?"

"Well, Vietnam, Auntie, but I suppose you know that. Spent a few days in Oakland gettin out the Army, then flew to Jackson. Got off the Greyhound in Greenville a few hours ago."

"You walked here? You musta learned to walk quick in Vietnam if you done walked here in a few hours."

"Caught a ride part of the way on the back of a farm truck. Otherwise, it be dark before I got here."

"I hate to think what I'da done if you come rattlin my door after dark, Charlie, but enough bout that. What you doin here?"

"Well, I came back to where I lived before I left for Vietnam. This shack is my home. It was when I left, anyway."

I scanned the room, slowly this time, admiring how Auntie Luretha had made it into a pleasant home, still rough around the edges, but a damn sight better than I had done with it.

"Charlie, I hate to be the one to tell you, but you needs catchin up, and it looks like I be the one to do it."

Auntie Luretha set a glass of water on the rough-topped wooden table and slowly settled into a chair.

"After your dad passed, your shack sat empty for months and everyone expected it to be waitin for you when you got back, but then your Uncle Herbie got sick. Doctors said his lungs weren't workin no mo, maybe from the farm chemicals, maybe from bad genes, or maybe from bad luck. He got to be bedridden and it got to be too much for the rest of the family all together with us in the shack at the end of the lane.

I was comin in from the field after a day of pickin behind the picker machines and Judge Tate was there, probably makin sure our cotton bags were full, and he asked me why Herbie still wasn't working. Huh, that man didn't give a damn about Herbie's health, he was only worried about how much money he'd lose because Herbie wasn't pickin. When I told him what was goin on, he surprised me and said we should move into your shack. He said most boys were comin back in coffins and you probably would too, so there wasn't no sense in keepin this shack empty. But, Charlie, if you want a shack, you can pick from several. A few families done moved off lookin for other work. These pickin machines are gonna take all our jobs before long."

"Where they gettin jobs?"

"Some men are movin to the hills to work in oil drillin, some in pulp wood, others are movin to Vicksburg to work on the river. The women are workin as maids and nannies."

Auntie Luretha exhaled, sat back, and said dejectedly, "I guess I'll be followin right behind them before long."

I let her think about her future for a moment before asking, "Where's Uncle Herbie?"

Auntie Luretha looked down into her lap and ran her hands together.

"He passed. Be two months ago on Thursday."

"I'm so sorry, Auntie. Uncle Herbie was a good man. A good man, and I'm sure he's in Heaven."

Auntie wiped a tear from her eye before raising her head to look at me.

"Thank you, Charlie. That makes me feel good to hear somebody besides me say that. It sure does."

We sat in silence, covered up by thoughts of death.

"How did my father die, Auntie? The telegram didn't give me a reason for his passin."

Auntie gave me a sorrowful look, and I wondered how often that look had visited her face in her lifetime.

"No one knows for sure, Charlie. He was found right out there in front of the shack on a Sunday mornin."

Auntie Luretha stretched out a black finger, shiny smooth skin in between deep, worn out wrinkles.

"As soon as the Tates saw a crowd gatherin they pulled up and put your daddy in the back of a pickup and that was the last time anyone saw him. Monday mornin Judge Tate brought me your daddy's ashes. We buried him next to your mother and brother. You'll see the headstone, nothin fancy, but enough to find him by."

I had so many questions I didn't know which to ask first or which were even the right ones to ask.

"Why did they burn him up so quick?" That was as good a starting point as any.

"Yeah, well, about that. We all thought that was wrong, too. The coroner didn't even get to look at him."

"Could anybody tell if he had been killed…shot, stabbed, or just knocked out dead in the head?"

"The people who found him said they thought the top of his head looked odd-like. One said she thought she saw blood in his hair. We never found a drop on the ground, though."

I thought about that for a moment.

"You think somebody killed him?"

Auntie exhaled and sat back in her chair before giving me a good, long stare.

"Yo daddy was up in the years and wasn't in good health, but he wasn't knockin on death's door either. The day befo, on that Saturday, one of the field hands heard shoutin between your daddy and one of the Tate boys, but he was too far away to make out any words. He said it wasn't a friendly discussion though, that much he could make out fo sho. Next mornin yo daddy's face down in the dirt and befo we know it, he's been burned up. We'll never know what happened but there ain't a soul in any of these shacks who doesn't know somethin terrible wrong was done to your daddy. The only ones who know what that was live up in the big house and they ain't never gonna tell a soul."

We sat in silence for several moments before Auntie spoke.

"What you gonna do, Charlie, for a place to stay?"

I could only stare at the floor, feeling numb and damn hopeless.

"I don't know Auntie. I came here expectin to move back into my shack and work on the plantation like I never left, but I can see I's too late for that."

I swallowed hard as a shiver went down my back.

"Now I wouldn't stay here for all the money in the world. Not while the Tates be livin here."

"You right, Charlie. You know, with the time of hand-pickin cotton comin to an end, it's best you find a different life as far from the Tates as you can get."

I stared at the table, deep in thought. The easy return to my old life had vanished in mere minutes, and now I was full of confusion and hate.

"I see you hurtin, Charlie. The judge said he didn't want you back here if you survived Vietnam; said boys were comin back all squirrelly in the head and he didn't want nobody on the plantation who might snap and kill someone. I don't believe you would have done that, Charlie."

Auntie stretched a hand across the table to wrap my hand in her warm grip, "but now that you know yo daddy might have been killed by one of the Tates, ain't nobody here would blame you if you did."

It was my turn to reach across the table and take Auntie's other hand. I felt a warmth spread through me like an old friend I forgot existed. It was the first time in two years I had connected physically and emotionally with another person. It wasn't enough to chase the demons out of my bitter heart, but it was a welcome start.

"My killin days are over, Auntie Luretha. If I can get justice for my daddy, it's gonna have to be some other way. I don't know what that might be. I got so many thoughts in my head I can't think straight."

"Let me fix you a nice supper, Charlie. I can make a pallet on the floor for you to spend the night on."

I took Auntie up on her kind offer. I had nowhere else to go except the woods, and a clap of thunder ended that option.

## Chapter 8

Me and that duffel bag wandered all the next day. I didn't know where I was walking to, I only knew what I was walking from. Vietnam had stolen my peace, and the Tates had taken my daddy and my future. The only way I knew how to block it all out was to blur and numb the 'now'. After a long day of walking, I found a good place to do it.

Sammy's juke joint had been on the edge of the Delta hamlet of Murphy, which itself was on the edge of nothing, since my grandfather's day. Me and a couple of buddies got up the nerve to walk to Sammy's when we were teenagers. They didn't card us and we each got a beer, but it was an older crowd, of course, and we felt out of place. I never went back and had forgotten about it until I walked up on it, what seemed a lifetime later.

Sitting at one corner of a crossing of dark, rutted farm roads, Sammy's looked as old as the dirt it sat on. Rooms added on over the years were as out of kilter as the cypress siding that sagged from the weariness of hanging onto a structure well past a prime that never was. Rusted beer signs were nailed over holes where siding no longer resided and re-siding had never been attempted. A piece of plywood nailed to the front door, cracked with corners curled up from years of heat, cold, and neglect, once stated boldly, "Any alcahol bring in will be drank up by ownner." A fresh notice, "No dope," was scrawled in white paint that almost leapt off the board, having only been weathered for a decade.

The outside of Sammy's reflected the hard-weathered lives of the patrons. The inside felt safe though, a place where everyone was somebody and appreciated, if only for a few hours. White faces were rare; a lone white musician playing in a black band on Thursday and Saturday nights (Fridays were for hangover recovery on the man's dime and Sundays on the Lord's time).

Sammy's mattered to me because it gave me a job, which then gave me an old, worn-out camper behind the bar to live in. Like Sammy's, the exterior of the camper had seen better days and the shabbiness of the worn interior wasn't helped with me living in it.

I stayed relatively sober while working, at least until the patrons started sliding out into the shroud of darkness unique to moonless Delta nights. A good start at a drunk was followed by a fully successful passing out in the camper. The days only differed with the occasional shower from a hose run from Sammy's through the floor of my camper. The shower doubled as a clothes washer, but those events were sparser than the showers.

Besides bartending and cleaning occasionally (most often brought on by a customer vomiting cheap-ass whiskey), I spent my time asking customers who lit joints inside to take it outside (where I usually joined them in smoking the weed), and breaking up fights, which I did well when sober.

My mind came back from Vietnam squeezed down to a confused pea, but my body was the best it had been. I always wore a tight t-shirt in Sammy's because the muscles on my six foot, two inch frame intimidated most of the men who got out of line. As I helped one such old man out of the club, he and the whiskey he was full of said he would whip my ass if it wasn't for the look.

"What you mean?" I asked, focused on the creaking step boards sagging under our weight.

"You wild. Wild as a pantha, one that's been conered and sees no ways out. You got it, boy. I can see it!

"What you see, old man?" I said, as his words seem to blow wisps of fog from my brain.

"You dead, boy, and some ways deep down you not happy bout it."

I stopped and gave him a hard look, his bloodshot eyes barely visible in the yellow light from a single bulb dangling from a frayed wire over Sammy's front door.

"I knows it and now you knows it."

"Stay outta my business, old man. Now git. Git on home," I let him go and took a few steps toward the bar.

"You knows it, boy. Now do sumthin about it before you really be dead!"

I didn't look back, and anger filled me with every step.

That night I passed out early and when my head hit the camper floor, I imagined I could no longer hear the old man's words, but when I woke, his words were the first stirrings in my mind. Somewhere in my murky brain I knew there was no pretending them away, but it didn't keep me from trying.

## Chapter 9

I stayed busy pretending for the next year; busy, drunk, and high, and I submerged the old man's words in numbed silence. About the same time, Sammy's started attracting better blues musicians who attracted more crowds into an already crowded joint. Over a couple of months on the days we were closed, a few of us added on to the original main room, extending it twenty feet.

With the larger bar, it took some damn fine music to fill the place, and one night when Junior Kimbrough was playing, the whole joint was packed. Church was the only place I'd seen that many blacks together in one place, there and maybe at a barbecue.

1968 in the Delta still felt like the fifties but with a smattering of more tolerance of blacks by whites. Black's tolerance of whites, however, got all used up in the sixties and decades before. We were still polite mostly, up to a point. And that point had been reached in the corner by the front door.

"I'll sit right here, thank you very much," I heard over the noise of so much drunken chatter.

"I suggest you find somewheres else to sit your white ass, preferably outside," a loud voice answered.

The booming voice was from "Gumbo" Lee, a big man with big courage when hitting a big bottle. I couldn't see the person he was arguing with, but the drawl was distinctively Delta white.

"There wasn't no one sittin in this goddamn chair, and my fat ass, which you can kiss by the way, is gonna get real familiar with it until I damn well please to give it up," I heard clearly while pushing through to get to them before they got to each other.

I knew I was too slow when I heard, "I didn't kill gooks for two fuckin years and get shot twice just so you black motherfuckers could give me shit tonight."

"Black motherfuckers" must not have been taken as a compliment as the sound of a punch started a blur of arms swinging, a chair breaking into pieces, and bodies falling on the floor. Whoever that short white boy was, he could fight. I was gonna let the boys, four on him now, have some fun turning that white boy black and blue, until I saw his tattoo.

I grabbed the first fighter I came up on and threw him back into the crowd.

"Hey! Hey! Get off him! Stop this shit! I know this boy! Get the fuck off him!" I yelled as I pulled one more off the cracker who was leaking a pool of blood on my floor.

That pissed me off.

I pulled a snub-nosed .38 from my waistband and fired a shot through the roof. The bar went quiet.

"Leroy, Jake, get off the motherfucker or one of you gonna get shot!" I screamed, not meaning it, but it worked.

Leroy and Jake got up off the white boy and started rubbing their bloody knuckles.

"Go get a drink at the bar. It's on me." That was enough to get them shuffling away.

I bent over and grabbed the boy by the arms and got him to his feet. I leaned in and whispered, "I got you."

I could tell he tried to look at me with the one eye that wasn't completely swollen shut, although I could barely see the eye through the blood oozing from his forehead.

I threw an arm over my shoulders and started staggering to the door.

"Get yo troublin ass out of here and don't even think about comin back!" I yelled loud enough for most customers to hear, especially the brothers who had pummeled him.

We almost stumbled down the steps when one of his legs went out from under him. When we made it to the ground, instead of throwing him out on the road as I had done dozens of times with bar wreckers, I turned left and went around the back of the joint.

# Chapter 10

"I wondered if you was asleep or knocked out for good," I said as the stranger stirred and gave a grunt after being motionless on the camper floor for half an hour. One hand went to his face and the other to his ribs. After a minute of shallow breaths, he spoke in a whisper, "Where the fuck am I?"

"Not far from where you got your ass beat and where you might have met Jesus himself if I hadn't put another bullet hole in Sammy's roof."

He was so still for a minute that I thought he may have passed out again.

"Who are you?" His whisper came from the corner of the floor barely lit by the clock on the camper's stove, the clock being about the last part of the stove to still work.

"The name's Charlie, Charlie Neely, but you can call me your guardian angel."

He went quiet on me again.

"Why…why did you stop them?" he labored to whisper.

"Well, it ain't cause I knows you, because I don't, but it's cause we're brothas. I saw the ink on your arm. I was in the Big Red One '64 to '66. You?"

Whether it was the mention of Vietnam or it was the shock of broken ribs and a concussion, one or both knocked him out again.

I sat in the dark of the camper, throwing beer bottles out the door as I finished one after another. Eventually, the white boy's groans brought me back from thinking about Vietnam, a place I had avoided thinking about for a long time. This trip back did not differ from any before it and it left me feeling like I was dangling from a frayed rope high above the Grand Canyon.

I got up and felt under my mattress until I found the baggie of Quaaludes. Without them, I knew neither of us would escape to any sleep tonight. I opened another beer, downed a pill, and sat back to see if the white boy would come to before I passed out.

My breathing had slowed until exhaling bottomed out in complete peace and breathing in again felt optional, and not entirely preferable. My eyes had closed when the white boy had a coughing spell. I opened my eyes to see his outline on the floor scoot back and rise up to sit against the camper wall.

I fumbled for a beer and opener, pried the top until it fell off and clattered across the floor, and passed it to the stranger. Getting a Quaalude out of the baggie was even more troublesome as the feelin in my fingers was nearly gone. I pulled the baggie up to one eye, closed the other, and finally captured a pill between two fingers.

"Take this," I stretched my hand across to the white boy. Most people would have asked what it is, but he downed it, followed by draining the beer, without a sound other than low grunts from having to move.

My eyes started drooping again, and I knew this time it was for good. I had to concentrate to remember the nagging question I had for the cracker.

"What's yo name?" I asked, slurring the words.

I could see the outline of his head turn slightly toward me, dried blood on his face looking like a mask and his long, oily hair reflecting some faint light from Sammy's.

"Not sure I want to tell you, brotha," he said in a gravelly whisper.

I stared at what I could see of him, the faintness of what I saw becoming darker as my mind closed in on itself. I wanted to speak but couldn't. A minute or more went by, but I could not form a word. I gave up, leaned back in the chair, and closed my eyes. I had one foot into oblivion when I heard, "The name's Tucum."

My mind sparked somewhere deep, but was too far gone to react. "We've met before," was the last thing I heard.

## Chapter 11

Sunlight streamed through curtains that had given up the test of time long ago. Strands hung down in clumps, opening holes that allowed light and bugs to pass through. I had opened the windows to get the smell of alcohol, body sweat, and urine out of the camper. I blamed the rank air on Tucum, still passed out on the floor, but I figured I had a hand in it, too.

Occasional gusts of breeze, a liter of Coke, and sitting upright began to clear some of the shadows from my head. I was doing some hard thinking about why my rifle in the corner had been sitting in my lap when I came to. I couldn't remember getting it from the closet and that sent a shiver through me. A fearful thought caused me to look Tucum over good for blood. Seeing none, I smelled the end of the barrel. No scent of gunpowder was a relief that I never should have had to look for. Living in a shell of reality kept me from being aware of pointing a rifle at a guy. That hurt my soul and almost stopped my heart. I found a sliver of comfort reminding myself he was the man I hated most on this earth, and I would have spent a life sentence in prison telling myself every day that I was justified pulling the trigger.

That thought got my hands shaking; a hangover didn't help. It was the first time since Vietnam I had been so reckless. I was being swept along in a river of drugs, alcohol, horrible memories, and hate, and had almost killed Tucum without knowing it. This had to end, starting with the greasy-haired, nigger-killing, white boy on my floor.

"Get up," I kicked Tucum's foot, but it barely moved.

"Get up!" I screamed, this time causing my head to pound so hard my eyes watered.

Tucum lifted his head and slowly rolled over onto his back. After a few moments, he scooted enough to prop his head against the paneled bulkhead. His eyes opened partially and blinked slowly, revealing a stare into nothing. I knew he was trying to remember where he was and how he got there. I gave him all the time he needed.

"Charlie?" he said in a gravelly whisper.

"I am."

Tucum's stare finally focused on me.

"I wasn't sure I was gonna wake up here or in hell."

I thought about that for a moment.

"Which one you think you in?"

"Too soon to tell. God, my head hurts."

"Take a few of these."

I tossed him a bottle of aspirin, followed by the Coke bottle.

"Take em and as soon as you can walk I want you gone."

Tucum scooted to a sitting position and unscrewed the bottle top with difficulty. He shook aspirins into his hand, but his hangover shakes sent tablets skittering across the floor. He tried to pick them up.

"Leave 'em. Take what's in yo hand and get outta my sight."

It was painful watching Tucum struggle to get three pills into his mouth. Unscrewing the Coke bottle and getting it to his lips put more Coke on him and the floor than in his mouth. By the end of our Vietnam tours we could kill an enemy with hardly a tremor, yet here we were, quivering like jellyfish, trying to kill ourselves instead.

Tucum set the liter back on the floor with both hands, then intertwined his fingers so they couldn't move.

I saw him looking to my side, and I followed his gaze to the rifle.

"You thinkin bout using that?"

I paused before answering. I wanted both of us to feel my answer.

"I did. I don't remember it, but I know I had it pointed at you. Wouldn't doubt my finger was on the trigger."

Tucum sighed and put his chin on his chest.

"I'd a done the same thing, cept I woulda pulled the trigger."

"I think God's feelin good I didn't," I told him.

"How bout you? How you feelin?" Tucum asked.

I had to think long and hard before answering.

"I think I feel good about not shootin you, but not knowin fo sho ain't a good feelin. I gotta lot of hate for you and that makes me a dangerous man to be around. You best get outta here while you can."

Tucum didn't move.

"You hear me?"

"Yes, sir, I hear you. I hear you and I'm gettin."

Tucum grabbed onto the corners of the bulkhead and pulled himself up. I could see piss had soaked into the front of his jeans. He looked down and saw it, too.

"I'm sorry bout the mess. I'll clean it…"

"No. Just git."

Tucum reached for the door handle like a one-year-old, hesitant to let go of the handhold behind before grabbing it. I watched him slowly get his body to respond enough to make it down the two steps. Before closing the door, he looked back in the camper and said, "I'm sorry, Charlie…I'm sorry about everything." His mouth kept moving as if more words would come, but instead he gave up and closed the door.

I was left in the quiet by myself, my own worst enemy. At that moment, I decided that between me and the world, one of us couldn't go on like this.

# Chapter 12

The core of my soul felt it like a stabbing pain. I needed to change, but the thought of it scared me more than death. The fear drove me to chase death instead. That chase lasted several months and finally brought me to my knees in the dark, in a cold rain, my lower legs going numb in inches of frigid mud deep in the national forest. That was the start of the journey back.

The next week was like breaking hardpan ground with a hand plow and an old mule. Each step forward was an effort I doubted I had the strength to make. Giving up and giving in was in my ear every second, begging me to put a bottle or a pill to my lips and fall back into the warm arms of failure. By the grace of God, I didn't, and it gave me the strength and courage to walk into an AA meeting in Greenville, overflowing with fear.

Thanks to the people in that room, the fear was gone before the meeting was halfway over. One by one, they told their stories of the hurt that led them to addiction, some coming within a breath of dying. Before the last person spoke, I knew I was in a home where I belonged, a home that offered life, and a life that offered more than one path. I felt like my eyes were opening after having been closed and staring inward for years. I liked what I saw. I liked what I felt. I thought maybe with the help of these folks I could like myself again.

And I did, and forgetting about the past helped me to focus on being a better man every day. After nearly a year, that night in the camper with Tucum felt like someone else's distant memory. That was until a thunderous storm at three in the morning intruded into my dream. The pounding of thunder sounded as if it was right outside the camper. It became loud enough to finally wake me, and I realized the pounding was at my door. I rubbed my eyes and sat up on the edge of the bed. As I was reaching for the door handle, I thought better of it and got the rifle from the closet. I chambered a round and pushed the door open while lifting the rifle to my waist.

The most pitiful creature lay on my steps, his waist in the mud and his head slumped on the bottom step. One hand was in a fist, the one just able to reach the door and punch it repeatedly.

The rain was coming down in sheets. The lone light bulb behind Sammy's could barely shine through the deluge, the wind gusts moving it away, then close, then away again, casting shadows like dancing spirits.

I put the rifle back in the closet and accepted God was putting my newfound faith to a test. I stepped onto the top step, then over Tucum to land ankle deep in water. Grabbing him by the armpits, I started inching him up the steps.

"Pick yo head up, Tucum, or else you gonna scrape yo face off," I yelled over the roar of the storm.

His head lifted a couple of inches, just enough for me to lift him into the trailer to his shoulders. A few more lifts and I was finally pushing his legs, sliding the rest of him across the cracked linoleum floor.

I climbed into the trailer, slammed the door, and stood there, letting the rain run off me to join the water off Tucum and what the wind blew in.

After toweling off and changing to dry clothes, I stared down at Tucum. I wanted him out of my life. I used to want him dead, but now that my anger had subsided from sobriety, I just wanted him gone. My new heart still struggled with the old one, and probably always would. I did the best to dry him off and two towels later, I at least had his head and arms dry and his shirt less saturated. I propped him up against the bed, covered him with a blanket, and slumped on a dry towel on the floor next to him.

Patting dry his tattoo of the Big Red 1 brought memories of a year ago flooding back. It was like a nightmare I had exorcized was back to torment me. I was free of that person I was that night and, other than a few hardcore customers in Sammy's, I was free from being around alcoholics and addicts like Tucum. Now I felt like my new good life had been broken into and was being shit on.

Tucum began to shake from the chilly rain or nerves shot from abuse. When I had brewed a pot of coffee, I sat down next to him with a steaming cup.

"Tucum. Tucum…wake up," I said, but there was no response.

I slapped him across the face, harder than I intended, but it worked. His eyes popped open, and he quickly looked around, finally settling on my face.

"Take this. You need to warm up. Give me your hands."

One jittery hand came out from under the blanket, followed by another. I wrapped one around the cup, followed by the other, and kept my hand on the bottom of the cup to steady it.

"Drink."

He did and only a small stream wet the blanket. After a few more sips, I let go of the cup and stood up to pour myself one. With a cup in one hand, I eased back down with the other to take my place sitting next to Tucum.

"What you doin here, Tucum?"

A wave of pounding rain on the camper roof swallowed my words, as if I had never spoken them.

"Tucum," I yelled louder, "why you come back here?"

Slowly his head turned and his eyes locked onto mine.

"I got nowhere else to go, Charlie. It was here or hell."

His head slumped, and the coffee cup fell to the floor. Neither of us moved to pick it up.

"I tasted the end of a pistol tonight, Charlie, and it tasted so bad. It was like tastin somethin you've wanted your whole life, just knowin that taste was gonna change your life for good, then findin out the taste was a lie."

Tears welled up as Tucum locked onto my eyes.

"I couldn't pull the trigger, Charlie. After all the bad things I done in my life to other people, bad things that came so easy to me, I couldn't do it to myself."

The sobs came out in a flood, loud enough to overcome the barrage of the rain.

"I've hurt so many people, Charlie. I done you wrong too."

"I done you wrong" was an understatement that revived anger I hoped I had killed and buried deep, but I had been fooling myself. I paused and took a deep breath, followed by a quick prayer for compassion.

"I haven't seen you in a year, Tucum. What you been doin with your life?"

Tucum ran sleeves across his eyes and went still, staring into the camper wall.

"Been runnin…runnin hard. Runnin from the law and memories of Nam. I've been stealin and robbin, hurtin people; hurtin some real bad. I know I've done a lot of awful shit. Some I can remember; some I was too drugged up to remember."

Tucum turned his head and looked at me, his face suddenly like chiseled stone.

"It ain't been a good year, Charlie, and I want it to end."

Tucum started shrinking into the fetal position as his sobs turned into wails. He rolled over, put his head on my shoulder, and swung an arm across my chest. The smell of whiskey was powerful.

"I can't apologize to the people I hurt because they were strangers in the wrong place when I needed money. You're the only one I know I can apologize to. I feel like I killed your brother, Charlie," Tucum got out between gasps for air. "I don't know how I could have stopped it, but I didn't even try, Charlie. I didn't try!"

Wails and sobs lasted minutes. It gave me time to try to make sense of it, of why this was happening. AA had taught me that God has a reason for everything and that a big part of my problem was I never accepted that. I wanted to be my own god and make things happen my way. The 'me' before AA would have never let Tucum into my trailer. I would have left him in the mud to drown and gone back to an alcohol and drug sleep. But here I was, holding onto the boy I instantly hated the moment I saw him staring wide-eyed through the dust at my dead brother; holding onto the man who was racism in the flesh; holding onto the man who needed saving. Tucum's face reflected how I looked a year ago, and his pain was so awful to see it flooded my heart with compassion, no matter how hard I tried to stop it.

I felt tears welling in my eyes and I looked up to the dark ceiling of the camper.

"God, I love you, but you got the humor of the devil," I said to him from somewhere between my heart and my hurting mind.

## Chapter 13

"My name's Charlie, and I'm an alcoholic and drug addict."

"Hello, Charlie. We're glad you're here," the circle chimed as one.

I stretched out my palms to them. "It's through the grace of God and you folks that I been clean and sober for seven and a half months."

The large circle came to life with some clapping, an "alleluia", two "amens", and a "God bless you, brother."

"This is my…friend…my friend, Tucum. He be stayin with me gettin sober. And he be doin a good job, he really is."

I looked around the room at the people, now my friends, before looking down at the source of the last bit of hatred hiding in my heart. Tonight was the first time I had called Tucum 'friend', only by the grace of God. I fought it, though.

"He's here tonight so he can see what God is doin with us. I want him to hear how we all screwed up our lives with booze and drugs and how we fought like hell to get straight again."

I looked at Tucum again and he looked as rigid and uncomfortable as the old metal folding chair he was sitting on.

"I told him he won't have to say a word tonight, unless he wants to, and he promised he would hear y'all out. It's taken a long time to get him here, so I ask you to give him some hope."

One by one, men and women, young and old, blue collar, white collar, unemployed, some with heads still bowed by weariness of the fight, but most with eyes bright for the future, all spilled out details of the dark side of their lives. Even though I heard these stories on my first night in AA, my chest got tighter with every desperate story, and lightened with every encouragement to Tucum that, with God's help, he too could be clean and sober.

I was the last to go. Tucum knew my story, or at least the parts he could remember, as did most people there.

"My name's Charlie and I'm an alcoholic and drug addict."

The group gave the same welcoming response as before.

I looked around at the circle of friends, was about to speak, but had to drop my head and take a long breath before beginning.

"When did it start? I done asked myself that so many times the words are worn out. Was it when I was a boy and I watched my brother get killed, or maybe it was so slow I didn't even know it done started, like breathin in a little anger from my father every day? Workin hard, day after day, and never havin a better life for it; that was a slow fuse always burnin. All that finally done burst in Vietnam. All that crap before Nam was nothin but pilins driven deep in the black dirt. Well, the devil done built his God-awful ugly hooch on them pilins in Nam."

I leaned forward and slumped my head, scenes of dismemberment and death fast-forwarding through my head.

"The veterans here know what I'm talkin bout. The rest of you…don't even try to imagine it."

I choked up and paused before wiping my cheek.

"I came back with a burden I couldn't carry. The only time it would slip off my shoulders was when I was drunk, but when I woke up, it was rooted to me again. I figured stayin drunk as much as I could was how I was gonna live until my dying day. Problem was, those roots didn't want to let go after a while, no matter how drunk I was. So then I looked for somethin else to do the job.

"First it was Valiums, which were like a bottle of whiskey without the stench. Then Quaaludes, on to heroin, hash, and some crack cocaine to stay awake long enough to do mo downers. They work so good those roots didn't have anythin to dig into no mo. But I still didn't feel right. Like I had just won a prize fight, but it turned out to be a dream. There was still a fight to be had and all the booze and all the drugs in the world would never get me in the ring. I couldn't see a way out and I was right scared of findin it.

"Gettin fired and movin to the woods where booze and drugs couldn't find me easily was the first step. It was the night I lay in my sorry-ass army surplus tent, soaked from leaks of icy rain and sweats of withdrawals, that got me to crawl out and sink my knees into the mud and cry to the Lord. For the first time, I became a man and admitted I was no man at all and I never would be on my own. After a while of cryin and I couldn't feel my knees no mo, I climbed back into the tent and slept. I mean like a black bear denned up in an ice storm. The next day, I woke up with a purpose. I told God I was in his hands and asked him to point me where I should go. He sent me back to Sammy's where I told my old boss I was ready for some help and, bein a bar owner, he was quite familiar with AA. He even told me AA had saved his life twenty-some years before. It wasn't until then that I realized I had never seen him take a drink.

"God bless him today and always that he offered me my job back and let me move back into my camper if I came to you folks. He also said my black ass would be back in the woods on my own if I missed a meetin. Like I said, that was over seven months ago and I'm still here."

A round of "amens" and "alleluias" circled the room again.

"Thanks to God and you good people, day by day, I'm gettin rid of the burden I been carryin. AA says one thing we need to do is to forgive people, to tell that load of hate to git, and it will git and some peace will take its place."

I felt a tremor of doubt and fear sweep through me. I asked God to give me strength, and looked around at the group, and finally at Tucum, who I was relieved to see was sittin up straight now with clear eyes giving full attention to me.

"I got a load of hate I been carryin for what seems like two lifetimes and I can't give it a home no mo. I told you I saw my little brother murdered. He was run over by a truck, a truck driven by a plantation owner's son not much older than me, but a boy who saw not a damn lick of value in a nigger. There was somebody else in that truck that I saw, somebody who didn't steer into Isaiah, but damn sure didn't try to steer away from him, either. That boy was Tucum, who sits beside me now. I've done a lot of prayin about this, so much that God finally told me to shut up, but he also told me there's some goodness in Tucum. He had it as a boy and I believe there's still some there. It's why I brung him here, and it's why I ask all of you to help him just like you helped me. Let's do what we can to git that guilt out of him and anger out of me."

Amens and alleluias flowed from every person in the circle.

I scanned the group once more before saying, "This has been a long time and lots of prayers comin."

I sat down and swiveled in my chair, turning to Tucum, our knees touching.

"Tucum, I forgive...," my voice broke and my eyes blurred. "I forgive you for doing nothin to keep Isaiah alive. We was young and dumb...," I wiped my eyes with both sleeves. "I know you would do somethin if you could go back in time."

Looking through my tears made Tucum look like twins and both Tucums had tears running down his cheeks. We stood and hugged for a long time, as hands and arms wrapped around us.

That was when good and strange things began to happen.

## Chapter 14

We drove out of the glow of Greenville into the inkwell of Delta darkness. Cool air infused with the aroma of tilled dirt blew through Tucum's truck. The occasional glow of deer eyes on the field edges was the only interruption to the monotony of darkness.

We didn't speak. His loud rust-bucket of a Chevy made it hard to hold a conversation anyway, but tonight I felt it was best to hold my tongue.

After turning in to Sammy's, Tucum turned his head to look the place over as if he was hoping it was open. I could tell he also glanced toward my trailer tucked into the dark, trying to decide his next move, I guessed.

He returned to staring straight ahead, and I pushed open the rusty door and stepped out. I didn't know what to say, so I didn't.

"I'm goin home, Charlie. Maybe I'll see you tomorrow," Tucum said without emotion.

I nodded and paused if he wanted to say something else.

"Goodnight then," I said to him and slammed the truck door shut. I stood there awhile until the red glow of his one working tail light faded to nothing.

Day One: no Tucum. Day Two: hopeful, but no Tucum. Day Three: lowered expectations and no Tucum. Day Four: a note on my trailer door, "Meet me at Nine Mile Bayou tomorrow at dawn. I know you'll be sober. If I don't show, you'll know I ain't." Then at the bottom, as if an afterthought, "Bring a long gun."

Day Five for me started two hours before dawn. I hadn't been off the booze and drugs long enough to afford a used truck, and no one cared enough about Charlie Neely to give me a ride at that lonesome hour.

It was unnerving walking dirt roads in dark tunnels of high treetop limbs stretching across to socialize with the limbs of trees on the other side. I had to try hard to push memories of nighttime carnage in Vietnam out of my head. Carrying a rifle didn't make it easier.

The eastern sky was beginning to start the show of colors I loved so much when I walked up on Nine Mile Bayou. There wasn't a truck on the side of the road, but it was still dark enough for the forest to hide anything parked off the road. I took in the pastels of the sky and listened for the guttural growl of Tucum's truck. I was too relaxed to be alert, too enthralled with being sober and appreciating the sunrise. A stick, a small one, snapped behind me. I tensed and listened. After consuming the silence for a hint of something or someone there, after breathing in deeply to catch any odor that would identify what was around me, I began to turn.

"I know you were better than that in Nam or else you wouldn't be here."

Tucum's drawl broke the silence, giving me a start. He had the tactical advantage.

He was nearly invisible with the forest darkness behind him and my outline was illuminated more by the second as the sky behind glowed.

"I don't want to have to be that good ever again," I said as my right hand slowly slipped onto the sling. The thought hit me like a falling oak—Tucum could be on acid and he's seeing me as an enemy that hurt him, that somehow shamed him, that needed to be killed.

"You ok, Tucum?" I asked as I tried to peer through the dark to see where his hands were.

He didn't answer for a lot of heartbeats that pounded my chest.

"Not as good as I once was, but better than I've been since I can remember."

I let out the deep breath I had been holding, but I kept my hand on the gun sling.

"What are we doin here, Tucum?" I cut right to the question that my life might depend on.

"Thought we'd do a pig hunt. I need to walk through the woods with a rifle and havin a wing man sounded smart at the time."

"I can live with that," I answered, hoping it didn't come out sounding like a question.

"It's been a long time since I pulled a trigger and I've been thinkin a lot about it lately," Tucum said in a flat tone that tapered off at the end.

The relief I had felt just moments before hightailed it to make room for genuine fear.

"We pig huntin, you say, Tucum?"

"Saw a big black one cross the road here two days ago."

"Ok, as long as you put your sights on a big black one with four legs, I be fine with that."

I tried to pass that off as a joke, but Tucum didn't laugh.

By now I could make out his eyes and they were staring at me, not blinking.

I finally told him, "You got point."

The eyes disappeared and his faint outline started moving slowly into the forest; soft, deliberate footsteps barely able to be heard. Tucum would stop every fifty yards, with me stopping ten yards behind him. His only movement was the slight swivel of his head as his eyes probed every dark blob in the forest, searching for the outline or movement of a pig.

Wild hogs look dumb, act dumb, but are anything but when you hunt them. What they lack in keen vision, they make up for in smell and hearing. Plus, they sometimes just damn sense you. The wind could blow your scent anywhere but to them, the wet leaves could be quiet as stepping on a silk pillow, and everything but half your face can be behind a tree as you slowly stalk up on them and suddenly one will pop his head up out of the dirt, grunt, and they're off to the races. But as I watched Tucum stalk like he was back in

Vietnam, and I mirrored his movement, I knew it was going to be a bad day for at least one hog.

The woods were coming alive. Squirrels scattered high in the trees as they noticed us below, birds called like Muslims to prayer, and it felt great to be alive in the beauty of nature.

"I got to take a shit. I'll catch up to you. This one feels like it's gonna be a fight to see which one of us gives out first," Tucum said with his way of turning words into pictures, and some you didn't want to look at.

"May the best turd win, my friend," I said as I hitched the sling solidly on my shoulder and moved off. I walked at a fast pace until I figured I was safely out of earshot of any grunting happening behind me, and not from a pig. Suddenly, something told me to slow my stalk, maybe a hidden sense of my own, or maybe because if I was a pig, these are the woods I would be in, grunting, rooting, and screwing my brief life away.

I stepped around a fresh pile of pig shit which jacked my senses even more. I froze a moment to confirm the slight movement of air was on my face and not behind me. Movement and sound were the only enemies I had now. I fought my enemies by moving slowly, balancing on one leg as the other extended slowly onto the carpet of leaves ahead. I was getting a sense of two places now. Scanning the ground ahead for sticks that would snap under my foot flickered into a vision of tripwires. I reminded myself I was the dominant animal in this forest and that helped me focus.

After fifteen minutes, I began looking back for Tucum coming up behind me, but I saw only empty woods. I decided I would stalk for another fifteen minutes and then wait for Tucum to catch up.

Only a few minutes later, I saw them. Two fat sows and eight or nine little pigs were under a circle of white oaks. I froze and made sure none had seen my movement. With that many pigs, there was always one or two with its head up. Only one had stopped rooting but was facing away from me. I closed the distance between me and a wide red oak twenty yards ahead, flicking my eyes from the pigs to the ground, back and forth, back and forth. A twig underfoot or a pig sensing me would be game over. I judged the distance at between eighty and a hundred yards, a makeable shot with open sights, if the gun was sighted in.

It was an old Remington 30-.06, and I had never shot it. It was about the only thing of value my old man left me, other than some pots and pans. When I got home from Vietnam, I collected them from Judge Tate's barn, where they had been pushed into a corner. Someone had cleaned out our old shack and must not have thought enough of the nicked up gun to want it. If my father ever had anything of real value in the shack, I'll never know about it.

I decided on the smaller sow. She'd be easier to drag out and would fit real nice on a grill. Still, at somewhere over a hundred pounds, she gave me a good size target. When the whole sounder was head down or away, I raised the rifle and braced it against the oak. It took a while, but the sow finally turned broadside without a little one in front or behind her. I didn't know how much trigger pull it would take to fire the gun. I squeezed it slowly; nothing happened. Squeezed more; nothing. Squeezed some more and the gun immediately fired. My ears screamed with a ringing I hadn't heard since Nam. It took a second to recover from the kick of the rifle and by then the pigs were high-tailing it out of sight, the many hardwoods screening them out completely in seconds. A high shoulder shot where I was aiming should have knocked her down. Now doubts about the shot filled my stomach with the weight of river gravel. Certain the sounder was well out of sight and with no glimpse of a dead sow, I closed the distance to the rooting site.

A tiller couldn't have done a better job of turning the soil over. Upturned black soil embedded with leaves, pieces of roots, and pig shit covered an area 20 yards wide. And there in the middle was a piece of gut and a splotch of blood. Whether my trigger squeeze pulled the rifle off target or the sights were off, what I was looking down at was proof of a fucked up shot. I went over my options: leave and let the sow bleed out—dicey with the temperature rising; track the sow and hope to get a kill shot or get lucky and find her dead; or wait for Tucum before tracking the sow. A warm breeze that suddenly puffed through the canopy of leaves settled the choice. I looked behind for Tucum, half expecting to see him. I moved on, knowing he would want me to recover the pig before she spoiled.

I began stalking again, but this time I was looking for movement or a black blob that didn't move, all the while picking out the quietest route. Maybe ten minutes into it, I caught up to the sounder, but this time they saw me and it was an explosion of fleeing animals. I wasn't certain I had seen both sows, but I had to assume mine had run off. I moved up and found a big splotch of blood and more gut. The blood trail got stronger, drops and then a splash, then more drops and a bigger splash, some with guts, repeated on the trail of upturned leaves. And then there she was, a hundred yards ahead, laid over, her suffering no more.

She was bigger than I first thought. She had run so deep into the forest there was no way I could drag her out alone. I took off my faded plaid shirt and hung it on a limb above the sow, a flag in the forest to look for on our return. I set off to find Tucum to help me drag her out.

Leaves overturned by pigs and me, as well as splotches of blood, marked the trail back. I was almost where I shot the sow when I saw Tucum on the ground, back against a tree, and head on his chest. I ran to him, yelling his name. I dropped to a knee and grabbed his shoulder.

"Tucum!"

No response.

"Tucum! It's Charlie!"

This time, Tucum answered with a head nod. At least he was alive.

"Tucum, what happened? What's goin on? Is you hurt?" Tucum lifted his head, opened his eyes moist with tears and stared straight ahead, whether saying to me or to himself I couldn't tell, "I'm fucked up in a bad way. I need a drink. God damn, I need a drink."

"You don't need a drink, Tucum, you needs me and I be right here."

He finally slowly looked up, and after a few moments my face must have come into focus, in his eyes and in his mind.

"Charlie, that you?"

"It's me Tucum. Everythin alright."

"Tell me I'm home, Charlie. For fuck's sake, tell me I'm home."

"You is, Tucum. You right here with me pig huntin in the woods you been huntin in yo whole life. You home, Tucum. You home."

Tucum blinked, the first time since I found him slumped against the tree, looking lifeless. He looked around and his chest heaved.

"I can't take this place no more, Charlie. I want to go."

"Damn right. I'm gonna help you out of here. You can tell me later what the fuck happened to you, but right now we gonna get up and get out of these woods."

Tucum looked up at me with a pleading, sorrowful look.

"It ain't just the woods. It's the whole damn place. I can't take no more."

Tucum's voice had changed, his words riding on resignation. They made me pause.

I reached beyond him and picked up his rifle, leaning against the oak, making sure the safety was on. Then a feeling made me unload it completely, putting his bullets deep into my pants pocket. I then helped him put a boot back on. I wondered why it was off, but let it go for the moment.

It was a slow walk back to his truck, his arm slung across my shoulder. He was wobbly and seemed to forget he was walking. When he slowed, I spurred him on with the promise of food and hot coffee at my trailer. He kept mumbling he wanted whiskey until I told him to shut up or I'd leave him in the woods where no one would ever find him. Afterwards, I wondered if he took that as a threat or an opportunity.

Back at my camper, I rummaged through clothes in a drawer and untangled a flannel shirt with a few stains and holes along the bottom that didn't matter. They said we were getting the first real cold front of the fall today and it felt like the whole thing was coming into the trailer just as a trial run first.

Tucum was on the bench nursing a cup of coffee, steam rising into his greasy bangs that trembled along with his shaking hands. Neither of us had spoken a word since getting back. I had stayed busy turning on the propane, lighting a flaky burner, and making coffee. Tucum sat and stared at something not of this world until I couldn't take the silence.

"What happened out there, Tucum?"

A full minute ticked by, slow as a near-frozen turtle clawing across an icy road.

He blinked and set the cup down.

"I came to where I heard you shoot. I was hopin to find you guttin a nice hog. I was happy for you, Charlie. I really was. My thoughts, my body, my mind, at least what's left, was right there in the woods. I felt good, real good. The best in a while. Almost happy…," his voice trailed off.

"And then what?"

"I saw the guts in a puddle of blood on the forest floor and it was like the devil flung me back in time. Charlie, it wasn't like I thought I was back in Vietnam, I was in Nam. I was standin over my buddy Eddie and his screams mixed with God-awful gunfire that seemed like Hell itself. He was tryin to hold his guts in but they had mostly spilled out onto the leaves, turning everythin blood red."

I could tell Tucum was re-seeing that hallucination and I didn't dare speak.

"I pointed my rifle everywhere, Charlie, spinnin like a top, but I couldn't pull the trigger. I couldn't pull the trigger, Charlie, because I didn't want to kill again. I stopped, dropped the rifle, closed my eyes, and waited. I just waited to be killed, hopin it would come fast, but the gunfire slowly faded away. When I opened my eyes, the forest was empty and still. It was so damn still, Charlie. I thought maybe I had died and gone to a place where no one else was. It was a place even God was afraid to go. I got weak, Charlie, so damn weak. I had to sit and try to force all of it out of my head. Everythin went dark. When I came to, the cold steel of my rifle barrel was numbin a circle on my forehead, and a boot was off and thrown to the side. My big toe wasn't on the trigger yet, but I knew I had come so close to it. If I hadn't snapped back when I did, you would have found a fuckin bloody mess, Charlie."

I didn't know what to say. I had to let it all sink in before I could even sit down across from Tucum.

"I need a drink, Charlie," Tucum pleaded.

"Fuck a drink, Tucum. That's the last thing you need."

Aggravation quickly replaced my sympathy for Tucum's struggle in the woods.

"It be nice though, wouldn't it? Nice and easy. All yo problems swept away and the only work you gots to do is lift a bottle to your face. Only takes one arm too, it's so easy, unless yo shakes be so bad you gots to use both hands. You want that? Say so and I'll get a bottle from the bar right now. It's just right over there, Tucum. So close you can taste it from here."

I pointed out the window, but his eyes didn't follow. He was looking at me like he was trying to figure out who the hell I was.

"Everythin be alright for another night, huh Tucum? Then what about tomorrow? Everythin gonna be alright then? Huh? How bout the day after that? How bout next month? 1970? Is that gonna be a good year, Tucum?"

Tucum's eyes cleared the louder I yelled.

"They say 1976 is gonna be somethin else, be it the big ass birthday of America and all. You gonna see the celebration, Tucum?"

I meant it as a question for him to answer, but his face looked like it was full up with rigor mortis.

"I wouldn't be bettin my worn-out trailer on it, Tucum, or your sorry-ass truck. I got one question you gots to answer; no, I gots two questions. One, is you gonna be walking this earth much longer? It only matters to you, Tucum. Save for me, this world and everybody on it don't know or care whether you be here or not. And if you don't care, then you may as well be somewhere else."

I let that sink in for a moment.

Tucum blinked.

"The second question is whether you gonna walk alone or with God; whether you gonna be walkin the black dirt of the Delta or the white clouds of heaven? Cause if you want to walk with God while you still here, all you got to do is ask him. He ain't afraid of comin here, Tucum. Not afraid of comin to this earth, to the Delta, this trailer, hell, he'll even go to Sammy's on a Thursday night if he's wanted there. And if he'll go anywhere he's asked, he'll come to you too. But ask him when you be sober and then get drunk again and you won't hear him when he's at your front door. You gots to be sober when he comes so you hear him knockin,"

I took a long breath while waiting for a reaction. None came.

"I think God has a lot of patience, but I can't say fo sho. I can say fo sho he will answer your call because he answered me. I felt it when he answered, Tucum, felt it in my body and my soul. You feel it too, Tucum, if you sober enough to feel."

I was drained, and I think Tucum saw it on my face.

"I'll be here for you, Tucum. It still don't feel right, but I told God I would do what I can for you. We're still brothas in arms, we're just on a different battleground now. And you got to decide if this one be worth the fight. I'll help you with what I can, brotha, but you got point on this, not me."

I stood up and took several deep breaths. Tucum didn't speak. I didn't know if that was good or bad, but I couldn't think about it. I had no more to say.

"I got to get the bar ready to open," I said and reached for the door, but stopped.

"You free to go if you want, Tucum, but you best stay here."

With that, I closed the door behind me and left him to feel the agonizing firefight between his will and God's.

## Chapter 15

It ate at me all night, wondering if Tucum was still in the camper. If he was, I figured by now he'd be trying to sort out whether he was fighting with God or Beelzebub himself. As hard as it was to resist, I didn't check on him until I was done working.

The camper door gave out a squeak as I slowly opened it to peer into the darkness of the trailer.

"I'm over here," a voice came from the other side of the trailer.

I closed the door and walked around the trailer to find, once my eyes adjusted to the side blocked from Sammy's light, Tucum sitting against the flattened camper tire. It was hard to say which was more deflated.

I sat down next to Tucum.

"I'm glad to see you didn't run off."

"Thought about it. A thousand times. Still thinkin bout it," Tucum said.

His voice was better, clearer, and a tad stronger.

"You went back to drinkin, didn't you?" I asked, but knew the answer.

It took a few moments for Tucum to answer.

"Sure the fuck did," Tucum said, staring into the darkness.

"Why, Tucum? You was doin good."

"Cause I ain't as strong as you, Charlie."

He turned to look at me, saying, "I ain't got your determination."

That really pissed me off.

"What a load of bullshit, Tucum, and you knows it. I ain't Superman and you would tell that same shit to anybody just to give you an excuse to drink. You got to see me as I am; see me for real. I'm not strong, I ain't got no superpowers, and I sure as hell ain't perfect, so don't make me out that way. In fact, I probably be the last person on earth to have enough willpower to stand on my own with no help from a bottle—booze or pill. I'll help you, Tucum, but you gots to show me you gonna try, and try like it's the only thing you gonna do before you die."

I had blown off my steam and was ready to be civil again.

"If you can do that, you welcome to stay here as long as you like. You know it ain't the Peabody but it ain't sleepin in a foxhole neither. I can move things around and make you a place to sleep that will be comfortable enough for tonight. In fact, I'll go fix your bed right now and then hit mine. I'm pretty tired, Tucum, and I'm guessin you are too."

I stood up, brushed the dirt off my pants, and said, "Goodnight, Tucum Tutweiller. I hope you get some sleep."

"I ain't got no say in that. It's all up to the thoughts in my head."

"Well, tell them to take the night off and come back tomorrow."

I turned to walk around the trailer when Tucum spoke again.

"Charlie, you gonna get your pig in the mornin?"

I had forgotten all about the pig and had to think for a moment before answering.

"There's no sense in it. By the mornin the hogs, coyotes and bobcats will have eaten it down to the bone."

Tucum paused a moment before asking, "How about your shirt you said you left hangin?"

"It ain't worth the hike. I'll leave it to be somethin curious for someone to ponder. They won't know it marks the spot where the woods disappeared another creature and didn't leave a trace."

## Chapter 16

I stayed with Tucum the next day through shakes as bad as I've seen them. I got him to drink a couple of glasses of water, but food made him gag after a few bites. The next couple of days were make or break.

I couldn't lie to Sammy and tell him I couldn't work because I was sick. I told him everything; the entire story. He listened, shaking his head. He said no white man was worth the trouble, but it was my trailer to put in it whoever I wanted as long as he didn't come into the bar. If Sammy had thought back and connected Tucum to the white man who had his ass kicked on that Thursday night, he might have felt differently.

"You gots to eat these crackas and drink this water. I ain't gonna quit ridin yo ass until you do," I said as sternly as I could.

Tucum only gave me a look that said this would not be easy.

"I done took off work over there just so I can make this my job over here. Now one of us is gonna eat and drink what's in front of you and it sure as shit ain't me."

With that, I sat down and began to stare. After a few minutes, he cracked.

"Well, hell, if you want puke in your mansion, here it goes."

He took a while, but the crackers and water went down and didn't come back up. And day after day, less shaking, more sleeping, and a hell of a lot more appetite.

"Today's bath day," I announced one morning over steaming grits and butter.

"What the fuck for?"

"For one, you smell like the sow I shot, that's what the fuck for," I said, meaning it.

"And…?"

“And you’re drivin us to our AA meeting tonight. We missed last week because…well, you know why…so we ain’t gonna miss tonight. Now finish your breakfast and get your ass in that tub or I’ll spray you down outside like a dog,” I said, serious-like.

## Chapter 17

Tucum did well that night. He introduced himself and the group responded with the standard greeting and a couple of God bless you's thrown in. He didn't say much, but it was a start.

He was his old self on the ride back to Sammy's, talking and cursing. He asked questions about the AA meetings.

"How long do I have to go to graduate?" He asked, serious as an ass-whooping.

I was glad he couldn't see me smirk in the dark.

"For the rest of your life, maybe. Until you can live without it, fo sho."

"Say what?" He swerved the wheel while jerking his head around to look at me. Like most of the Delta, the road was empty and crossing a center line was not a worry.

"There's no graduation, Tucum. No one says, "You did it. You kicked alcohol and here's your diploma." You go as long as you need. Some are good after a few months and some aren't good until the dirt hits their coffin by the shovelful. It's up to you."

He got real quiet and still. I did too, waiting for him to say something. The drone of the loud exhaust and the cool wind flickering into the window open an inch or two were soothing distractions.

"You can come and go, too," I finally said, thinking it best I soften up the future for him. "You do whatever it takes to keep yoself sober, Tucum."

We rode the rest of the way in silence. When the engine thankfully went quiet, I went in the trailer and went to bed. Tucum went around back to sit on the ground and go somewhere else.

A week later, the day after our next AA meeting, Tucum moved back home. He said he was good, that if he was heading to a bad place, he'd come back. He also said he'd be by every Tuesday evening to drive us to the AA meeting in Greenville. I stood in the dirt parking lot of Sammy's seeing him off. As the dust kicked up by his truck settled back to the ground, the truck also seemed to shrink into the road and finally disappear. I stood there long after he was gone, staring and wondering at the road he was on.

## Chapter 18

"…and while we're proud of all the recipients of these chips marking their sobriety, this one is a milestone I won't ever forget and I know he won't either. Tucum, congratulations on one year of sobriety. Come on up and get your chip."

Applause and hoots broke out and I can't lie and tell you I didn't get teary-eyed. It was a hell of a year. Being a mentor to Tucum was like riding a roller coaster. You never knew how far down you'd fall on the other side of the high. It wasn't because he fell off the wagon. Some people just never get over the struggle of justifying the killing of combat and Tucum is in that number. In Vietnam, life was precious on the one hand, so precious you'd give your life to save the man next to you. But the enemy's life meant nothing, at least nothing while alive. Dead meant something. It meant it was one less fucker shooting at the good guys. And for some, the deader the better. Split open and dismembered felt like more of an accomplishment to some than just a single bullet hole in the head. It didn't make sense unless you were living it, unless you were where nothing made sense.

Tucum was reliving those days every so often, and the journey could last nearly a week. No amount of knocking and calling out would open the door until one day he would appear, looking and sounding tired, but ready to be alive again. The first time he checked out, I feared the worst-that he had hitched a ride on whiskey and pills, a long ride to nowhere, but I quickly realized he was committed to the long haul with a strength I didn't know he had. And now, standing and clapping for the man I hated as a boy and now called my friend, I knew he had been saved.

Thank God.

## Chapter 19

The past year was good for me, too. I had saved enough working at Sammy's and doing farm work planting and harvesting to buy a truck. It was a junker, but it was mine. It meant I no longer had to bum rides. I didn't have to wait for Tucum to come; now I had the means to go to him, unexpected, most times welcome but sometimes not.

I even upgraded to a bigger crappy camper thanks to an acquaintance of Sammy's, a white man who asked if he knew a poor nigger who could haul it off his property.

I was feeling some solid ground under my feet. Sobriety became me so much I rarely thought of it. Financially, I still had little, but I had enough. Socially, I had fun now and again with women customers who took a liking to me. Liquored-up eyes took my rough edges off, I guess. But the biggest difference in life was my friendship with Tucum. I never would have guessed he was the reader like no one else I knew. Not only did he read a lot, but he kept a lot of it locked in his head, unlike my memory that was tight as a colander. He was a fine storyteller too, so much so I learned a lot about history and I enjoyed it. Our visits were like trips back in time and around the world. It didn't feel like school, but I was definitely getting schooled.

I missed the stories and the learning between our visits. I finally asked Tucum if he could get me an easy book with small words so I could learn to read like him. He wasn't surprised when I told him my father pulled me out of school after third grade. Tucum's did the same to him, but at least he made it through the seventh grade. A lot of fathers didn't want to invest in a future payout, preferring a payout in more labor earning money in the fields right then.

"I tell you what. We're goin to the library in Greenville Tuesday afternoon before our meetin and we're gonna get you started on readin," Tucum said excitedly one day.

And that's what we did. It was my first time in a library and all I could do was look every which way.

"All these books tell stories?" I asked Tucum, staring in disbelief.

"Yes, they do, every one of them. Some are true, too. The rest of them are made up. Some are easy to read and some are hard. We're startin with the easy and we'll work up to the hard," Tucum said as we walked to the section with books with lots of colors on them. I later realized it was where children got their books.

I went home with two books that day, *Where the Wild Things Are*, and *Charlie and the Chocolate Factory*. That night I went through both books three times. I looked at every detail of every picture and imagined I was in them somewhere. I looked at the words too, once. The shortest ones I recognized, but the rest were hopeless.

# Chapter 20

"It's damn early, Charlie. What the hell's goin on? You in some kinda trouble?"

Tucum was squinting in the early morning light, holding his door halfway open,standing in underwear that looked more like underwear-ed out.

"Tucum, it's these books you got me. I can't stop lookin at them, but I'm having trouble readin them. Can you help me so I know what the stories be about?"

"Well, other than sleepin, I guess I got nothin better to do. Come on in and I'll put some coffee on."

After two cups and some chitchat, Tucum asked me to show him the words I didn't know. I had to admit to him it would be a lot quicker if I showed him the few I knew. I was thankful Tucum didn't look at me funny, ask me if I was kidding, or plain make me feel stupid as an armadillo. Instead, he picked up a book, saying with a smile, "Let's start with the book about you and the chocolate factory."

I liked that.

There wasn't a day I didn't practice reading that book alone or with Tucum. I was improving a little every day; I could hear it; I could feel it. It's all I wanted to do. I wanted to get so good at reading I could stand on Sammy's bar on a Thursday night and read the book aloud without hardly taking a breath, like I was talking like a man and not reading like a child.

My heart sank when Tucum said the books would be due back at the library on Tuesday.

"My time is over with them?" I said, not understanding why I couldn't keep them.

"You get to check them out for two weeks and then you have to give them back or you can check them out for another two weeks if nobody else wants them."

"So, what happens if somebody wants them?"

"You have to give them back to the library and wait until the next person is done with them."

I spent the ride to Greenville praying there wasn't nobody wanting these books.

I was hooked.

Within half a year, I was reading young adult novels as fast as a jackrabbit, at least one with a broken leg. I came across words I didn't know, but I could skip them and still know what the story was about. I circled those words in pencil so I could ask Tucum to explain them. He said I shouldn't mark in library books, but he didn't let it stop him from teaching me. If the white ladies in the library didn't like my circles, I figured they could erase them.

Pretend stories, or what they call fiction, took me for rides, a lot feel-good, some not-so-good, but the rides were always worth the time. And who's to say those stories didn't happen, before or after the book?

While working a field on a tractor, breaking ground in a line two miles long, I'd pretend that in a wall of trees on the horizon there was once a secret garden, or maybe unmarked graves known only by a serial killer, or maybe real fairies whose light gave them away on the darkest nights. The long, tedious, mind-numbing tractor lines became time to escape into the pretend world. If I knew there were bodies buried in the woods, what would I do? I couldn't pretend they weren't there. No, I'd have to dig them up and look for clues. Looking at their bones protruding from stringy broken-down clothing covered in dirt, I'd imagine the pain of their last moments. I'd feel their terror and see death through their eyes. I would also see the killer plunging the knife into them over and over, or strangling the life out of them, or simply putting a bullet through their head. My mind would race deeper and deeper into the darkness of the story and then I would suddenly plop back onto the seat of the tractor, heart racing, with a straight line of broken ground I couldn't remember behind me.

When a story like that one took me, where someone suffered at the hands of a despicable soulless person, my mind would rejoin my body on the tractor with a burning need to bring the victims justice, to solve the crimes, to expose the evil-doers for the whole world to see so they could feel shame and punishment. It exhausted me and I would vow to imagine, and step into, only happy stories. But the feeling of doing something the victims couldn't do, something that wouldn't happen if I didn't do it, had taken root in my mind like weeds on a shallow grave. I welcomed that feeling and vowed to hang onto it.

# Chapter 21

Otis was his real name, but for a reason lost to time he was called Mr. Larry. He turned one hundred on a Thursday and that night he was at Sammy's, surrounded by family, friends, and moochers who wanted free food and booze. I put up some decorations, stapled streamers to the ceiling, tied balloons here and there; just enough stuff to stand out from the permanent wall coverings of faded posters, license plates, beer signs, and a black, lacy, and dusty bra hanging by the lady's bathroom that was a mystery of history.

June Bug and the Swamp Frog had played their last song and were packing up what little there was of their equipment: electric guitar, amp, two speakers, microphone, and a sparse drum set that did the job just enough.

The moochers were leaving with full bellies and blurry eyes. Family talked to themselves, having quickly run out of things to say to the birthday boy who sat in the corner, hands on top of his cane, looking dapper in a somewhat baggy suit and hat, and a mouth that seemed to always be in motion searching for teeth it had a long memory of.

Mr. Larry waved me over.

"I want to thank you, Charlie, for a right nice birthday party. It was right nice, it was. One I'll remember when I get old."

He looked at me with a devious smile, a gold tooth catching a glint that matched the one in his eyes.

"Well, I'm glad you enjoyed your birthday party, Mr. Larry. You did somethin most people don't."

"Oh, hell, I didn't 'do' somethin, I just didn't die is all. But my time here is gonna be over real soon. You can bet on that to happen like the sun is gonna rise in the mornin and the cotton's gonna grow next season."

I never have figured out what to say when someone says they're gonna die soon.

"You've seen a lot, Mr. Larry. You sho have seen a lot of changes."

Mr. Larry looked away; far away.

"Yes, sir, I suppose I have. I have at that. But you gonna see changes in yo life I can't imagine Charlie. Just do what you can to make them good."

We both went quiet for a moment, the gumbo of talking and laughter wrapping around us until one of us cut through it.

"What you wanna do with your life, Charlie? You got plans beyond puttin on birthday parties for half-dead old men?"

"Well, Mr. Larry… seems like all I been doin is plannin on how to deal with the past and I ain't had much time to think about the future. I'm learnin to read real good…"

"Good for you, Charlie. I never did and I guess I'll never know what that's like, but you keep it up, Charlie. Keep that readin up."

"Yessa, yessa, I will. They no stoppin me now!" It felt good to say that.

"What else you wants to do?"

"Well, I's pretty good at farmin and I thought from time to time what it would be like if I could buy some land and work my own farm. I'd be my own man, makin my own money, and I'd have somethin to be proud about."

"You right about that, Charlie, you sure right about that. You needs to do that, son." He looked at me so seriously, as if it was more than a suggestion.

"It'd be hard to do, Mr. Larry. I don't know if I could ever make enough money to afford the acres to make it work. I damn sure know no bank's gonna loan a poor nigger a pot of money when he's barely scratchin by. That's all my family's ever done, Mr. Larry. We scratched by and then died. Never had a patch of dirt to call our own. I doubt I'm gonna be the first either."

I hung my head and the words I had never admitted to myself lingered in the cigarette smoke.

"You wrong about that."

I looked over at Mr. Larry. He had hitched up a bit, lookin taller in the booth, the suit not as baggy.

"Thank you, Mr. Larry, for believin I could do it, but I just don't see how."

"You may not be wrong about that, time will sho tell, but that's not what I'm talkin bout. You wrong yo family never had land."

I spun on the split leather to look straight at him; making sure he wasn't drunk or having a stroke.

"I knew yo father, at least in passin. He stood out is the reason I noticed him. He couldn't have been more than eight or nine when he started workin full-time in the fields on the Tate Plantation, just another nigga boy gettin dirt in his blood. What set him apart was he would never stop workin. If that boy slept a wink then I be the mayor of Greenville. Did you know much about your father, Charlie?"

"No, sir, not much at all. My dad never wanted to talk about anythin that happened before I came along. I don't know why."

"I might be a help with that, if you wants to hear it."

I stared at Mr. Larry and the sense that this opportunity was one that might never come again made me blurt, "Oh, yessuh, I do. Please, Mr. Larry."

Before he could speak, I broke in asking if I could get him a drink, partly to make sure he stayed long enough for me to hear his stories, true ones for a change.

"I don't need a drink. I done drank enough in my life to float a boat. Plus, I better finish what I'm saying before I croak."

He chuckled at himself and then got real serious-like.

"Joshua, or Josh as most called him, your father, was actin like he be the foreman by the time he was twenty. He was as big as you, maybe bigger. He knew more about farmin than any white man on the plantation. Now, Old Man Tate was a stern man, and he complied with the ways of man. He also listened to God now an then, I suppose, because he treated niggas better than most. He sho caused a ruckus when he made Josh the assistant foreman, but he figured business was mo impotant than skin. And he was right. Yo father made Mr. Tate a lot of money. That farm was the top producin farm nearly every year."

"Did my father see any of that money?"

"Not at first. He stayed as poor as the rest of the niggas on the farm and he lived in a shack like the rest of them. Mr. Tate would throw him a bone every once in a while, but it wasn't until he was on his deathbed that he threw Joshua the whole cow."

I was being pulled into the story, was starting to see the plantation, even my father.

"Joshua was called by Mr. Tate to come to him quick before he passed. In fact, the last person he touched in this life was your father. As I heard it, he was holdin Josh's hand when he took his last breath. Before he died, though, in front of his wife, grown children, and a couple of the house help, he told Joshua how much he had meant to him. He thanked him for workin so hard to give him and his family a comfortable life. Then he told his wife to write out a bill of sale of a hundred acres to your father. He died a few minutes after he signed it."

I went numb. The true story I had been drawn into had suddenly become a hundred percent pretend. Mr. Larry, who seemed clear-headed a moment ago, suddenly was just another confused old man living in pretend memories.

"Well, that's a good story, Mr. Larry, but I best get back to work. Looks like there's some clean up needed after your party."

I started getting up, but Mr. Larry grabbed my arm with surprising strength.

"Don't take me for a fool, boy. This all happened true as the gospels, and you dare not think otherwise."

His stern stare of suddenly clear eyes and strong voice made me shift back into the seat I had tried to leave, and his grip relaxed.

"This story don't make no matter to me, but somethin tells me it might to you, so I's gonna tell it to you, and you gonna hear it."

Again, not a suggestion.

"Yessuh," I said as his eyes bored into mine.

"So, Tate's sons, especially Lamar, didn't take kindly to their dad sellin off a piece of their plantation to a nigga. It just wasn't hardly done in them days. Problem was, there were too many witnesses, black and white.

"The county clerk was a spineless little man who be scared of his own shadow. After hearin stories from Josh, and Mrs. Tate, a fair woman, that confirmed Mr. Tate's wish, and the bill of sale to boot, he put the acres in your father's name. The sons, though, threatened the clerk with who knows what harm and he took it back. It took Mrs. Tate threatenin to go to court to get the clerk to put it back in Joshua's name. That was the end of that family. The good Mrs. Tate's children turned on her and before long she had moved to Memphis and never saw the plantation or her children again. There are rumors that after she died, the children paid her lawyer to destroy her will. Of course, she was not about to leave the plantation to those leaches but who knows what's true."

"But my father kept a hold of the hundred acres?"

"Yea, he did…for a while. Did real well too. His little farm did mighty fine while the plantation did poorly. With Joshua gone, and several others who moved on - Lamar and his brothers was nasty to work for, you know - there wasn't one with a lick of sense workin that farm. They already hated your father, and him doing good and them doing bad, really made them madder than a rattlesnake in April. They was wantin to screw your father and was sho nuff hungry for his land."

Mr. Larry quit talking, his mouth suddenly busy moving around, looking for those missing teeth.

"How did the Tates get the land from him?" No matter the answer, I knew I wouldn't like it.

"Oh, like land was stolen all through the Delta, hell, through the state. It was somethin to do with taxes. The white landowners and the white tax people in guv'ment got together and did whatever the hell they wanted. Went on for years."

"Nobody went to jail for doing that?"

"Jail? Hell no. The sheriffs were in on it too, threatenin the blacks to either move off the land or get arrested. They moved off, they sho 'nuff did."

"Can't nothin be done?"

"Oh, Lord no. Time's done washed away them sins. Most of the ones needin punishin are deep in the ground. I be tellin you this only cause it be good to know what you wants is somethin that was done befo in your family. It be almost as hard now to get the money to buy land but nowadays you mo likely to hold on to it, as long as you steer clear of Lamar Tate. What little bad was in his father ended up in his genes and he's done growed that a hundred times over. He's a snake and can bite you all over this county. You just stay low and don't let his eyes set on you and you be alright."

"I hear you, Mr. Larry, and thank you for tellin me all this about my father. I gots to think all that through. I'm feelin some anger comin up in me and I gots to figure it all out."

"Don't let it eat you, boy. Best to not think about it at all. Pretend it never happened and put it out yo mind."

That was good advice for someone else. Me, I had a scar burned on my heart that night. I didn't know what to do, but I knew it would hurt until I scratched it. My thoughts while driving the tractor now were not about pretend stories.

Pretend, my ass; this was real, and I wasn't letting go.

## Chapter 22

The next day I stopped by Tucum's to see if he wanted to ride with me to the library, but he didn't open the door. His mind was likely on another extended wrestling match with itself, so I went on down the road to Greenville.

I probably could have found the books by myself, but I asked the librarian to save time.

"Mississippi history? What kind of history?" She asked, annoyed that I wasn't specific.

"Well, the kind that's already happened, I suppose." I didn't know what else to say.

She shook her head and made a face like she had smelled something rotten.

"No. Do you want ancient history, how the river formed the Delta, and such? There's Indian history, Spanish and French explorer history, Civil War history, Reconstruction ..."

I stopped her there. "I suppose I want history after the civil war up to, well ma'am, maybe now."

"That's a start. Now what subjects are you looking for in that time period?"

"How farms started and got bigger, ma'am. That and civil rights."

She gave me a quick looking-down at. I could hear her thinking, "Another uppity nigger…"

"Follow me," she said instead.

And off I went on a learning trip I didn't see coming and couldn't have imagined.

Growing up, I thought whites and blacks got along ok. We knew our place, the whites expected us to stay in it, and we did. I heard grumblings about the Klan still doing nasty shit to blacks, not outright lynchings, but some young buck would up and disappear sometimes. Maybe he ran off with a married woman or something like that; something worth leaving for. Or maybe he didn't. I didn't get involved in all that.

I was a regular at those library shelves for the next few months, dropping a book off in the return bin and handing another one to Miss Judgy White Woman to check out. She gave me the same look every time, like I had no business reading that much. I always left her with a "Thank you, ma'am, and have a blessed day." I didn't have to look back and see her scowl; I could feel it. After a while, I looked forward to it.

I learned things from those books that made my soul cry. Things I had never heard of but should be required learning for all children everywhere.

Didn't know about Springfield, Illinois, summer of 1908. A mob of 5,000 white men destroyed dozens of black businesses and an entire neighborhood known as the Badlands. 16 blacks were killed. The NAACP was started because of it.

Didn't know about the East Saint Louis massacre of 1917. One hundred or more blacks killed, hundreds injured, 6,000 run out of their homes.

Didn't know about the race riots and lynchings in the summer of 1919, from California to Florida to New York, to Nebraska. So much blood flowed it was called the Red Summer.

And somehow I had never heard of Elaine, Arkansas, where in 1919 a suit filed by sharecroppers against plantation owners resulted in 856 blacks murdered.

But now I knew. My heart ached thinking about all the innocent, hard-working people killed and maimed who otherwise might be best buds with the killers if only their skin was white.

I couldn't read any more books about the killings. They were keeping me from what I needed to learn—how the Tates stole land from my family. I couldn't find anything in the library about black farms disappearing and Miss Judgy seemed less and less helpful the more I asked for help.

"We don't have any information on that," she spoke, like Moses saying it was God's word.

"What about in any books from the guv'ment?"

"If we did, I would know about it." She gave me a stare down her long nose.

"So, if it ain't here, where is it?"

"I suppose you could try the library in Yazoo City, but your best chance of finding something, if there's something to be found, would be in Jackson."

She may as well have said New York City. The thought of even finding the library in the big city, figuring my way around a new and bigger library, and dealing with even more women like Miss Judgy was too much to imagine.

"Good luck with that." She made it sound like a challenge as she walked off.

## Chapter 23

"I ain't been here in a coon's age, but if these walls could talk, this nigga be shamed of the fun he had in here back in the day!" Mr. Robbie said with a long laugh, joined by Mr. Sandy and Mr. Larry.

"Here's your coffee, gentlemen." I placed the cups down carefully on the corner table in Sammy's.

"You take anything in it?"

"I like my coffee black, like most of my women."

Mr. Sandy got laughs around the table that slowly tapered off. I love how old people like to hold on to something funny, like it might be the last thing they hear.

Mr. Larry took a sip of coffee, using both hands and moving slowly.

"This must be somethin impo-tant, Charlie, getting us out here durin Sammy's closin hours. I gots to admit I might prefer the quiet more these days."

Mr. Larry paused, and the bar went silent as if in answer to him.

"You asked me to bring some fellas who lived here almost as long as me. Well here we are, me and these two young bucks." The two gentlemen in their 90's chuckled.

I had made introductions when they arrived at the bar and we had exchanged some chitchat while I helped each of them up the stairs.

"Mr. Larry, Mr. Sandy, Mr. Robbie, thank you again for comin."

I looked at each of them and was struck by the thought I was looking at decades of history I'd never find in a library.

"My daddy never talked about his daddy, or his grandpa, or none of the family back then. All I knew was we always been dirt farmers workin on plantations for wages or croppin some white man's land. Mr. Larry, though, on his birthday right here, as a matter of fact, told me my daddy actually owned a hundred acres sold to him by old man Tate."

All three men gave slight nods.

"He also told me my daddy's land was stolen from him by the sons of old man Tate."

Again, nods around the table.

"And I figure if those sons of bitches figured out how to steal my daddy's land, there were other white landowners figured it out too."

"Yessah, yessah, you right about that," Mr. Sandy muttered as he stared down at the table.

"Damn right they did. Yessah, they done figured that out," Mr. Robbie said as his hands unwrapped from the coffee cup and rolled up into wrinkly fists.

"So, how did they do it? That's what I wants to know."

I settled my elbows on the table and glanced at the three, holding my breath, waiting for one of them to speak. Finally, Mr. Robbie tilted his head in my direction.

"How much coffee you got?"

## Chapter 24

"First off, what you see of how niggas live and farm in the Delta today ain't how it used to be. When I was a young man, befo the turn of the cen'try, there were more of us farmers than them. Course they owned a lot mo land, but we owned enough to make a decent livin. Problem was, back then, the bankers, the local gov'ment men, the feds, the sheriff; all dem was white. When they finally figured out how to get in cahoots with each other, it was all over fo us," Mr. Larry said matter-of-factly.

"Wasn't nothin we could do about it, neither," Mr. Sandy said, with more anger than Mr. Larry. "Wasn't nobody who mattered lookin out for us. Way the whites saw us was we was gettin to be too much like them; ownin land, makin a livin farmin like them, startin to live in decent houses. They didn't like us gettin out of the place they put us in. They was losin control of us and they finally done figured ways to put things back right."

"You all owned land?" I asked.

"Hell, yes," Mr. Sandy answered.

That came as a shock.

"Me, I had over a hundred acres on two parcels near Anguilla. Farmed that ground for close to five years, gettin a loan from the USD and A every year to buy seed, and paid it back after harvest along with my land note, until one year my paperwork was held up. Why they couldn't say. Spring came, and they told me they lost the paperwork and I had to put new papers in. By then, it was too late to plant. We grew what we could to eat, and we held on, payin our note from the last of our savins, until the next season. Then the same thing happened again, and I had to sell. The guv'ment man told me there was buyers and others might not come around, so I better sell or they'd take my land for nothin. Turns out the white farmer next to me got my land for pennies on the dollar. After fees was took out, and penalties for what, I don't know, wasn't much left and I had to go back to the only thing I knew - croppin. You know what the worst part was? I eventually had to crop the ground I used to own."

Mr. Sandy paused, taking a deep breath.

"Been a long time since I told anybody that. Sho didn't know I was gonna today."

Mr. Sandy pulled out a white handkerchief, folded just right, wiped his eyes and gave a loud blow of his nose, the way only old men can do.

I had to take moments to let that all sink in and I could tell the other two gentlemen weren't trying to rush away from Mr. Sandy's story, either.

I finally asked, "Same thing happened to you, Mr. Robbie?"

"Well, same thing in the end, but I done took a different route to get there. I had company, though. Kind of the same happened to Larry here, too, if my memories be clear, Larry?"

Mr. Larry's mouth stopped running circles looking for teeth. He looked up and shifted his gaze to Mr. Robbie. "Best I remember, we both got screwed by the guv'ment."

"Yessa, we did." Mr. Robbie looked back at me and continued his story.

"You see, the first couple of years everythin be fine. I grew some good crops, yes I did. Made enough money to pay my land note and taxes and buy supplies. I must have been doin too good, the way the whites in power saw it. Now, I heard of black farmers bein threatened with lynchin, them and their whole family, if they didn't quit farmin and move. White farmers would snatch up their land when they did."

"You were threatened, Mr. Robbie?" I asked as anger built in me.

"No. The white folk in Washington County must have been smarter than most. One day the county tax man came out and told me my farm was turnin out to be more valuable than he had figured and my land was worth a lot more now. That sounded good to me until he gave me a tax bill I couldn't pay. You know the only people complainin bout their taxes going way up were black farmers? Never heard a peep out of white farmers and we all know why. Hell, I wouldn't be surprised if their tax bills went down! Anyway, my land was bought up at a tax sale by the white farmer next to me and he got it dirt cheap. It was a damn shame, but what ya gonna do?" Mr. Robbie's voice trailed off, and he looked as if the memories hurt him like a hot skewer.

"I had no idea," I said, barely above a whisper.

"Most folks don't," Mr. Larry said, looking my way.

"In my case, I was a few years behind Robbie and Sandy, losin my farm. We had a god-awful drought, and the heat burned up most of the crops. Those same USDA fellas took paperwork to get crop disaster payments. Everybody should have gotten some money but when I went to Greenville to get mine, the man told me they was out of money. Said it was just as well cause I would just drink and gamble it away, and I did neither of those. The white farmers around me got their payments even though they had plenty of money, they drank like white perch, and some lost more money gamblin than I would ever earn. The hatred that drove white men to ruin black farmers ain't as bad now, but back then it was boilin over."

I was overwhelmed and felt I had been pummeled.

"Didn't anybody take the white men to court?" I asked and was answered with laughter from all three.

Mr. Sandy looked at me like he was schoolin an innocent boy.

"Back then, a black couldn't be on a jury or even testify in court against somebody. There wasn't no legal system for niggas back then."

I paused before realizing I was mired so deep in their stories I had forgotten my goal.

"Tell me how the Tates got a hold of my daddy's land."

The three looked at each other, and Mr. Robbie spoke up.

"We all know the story. Your daddy, like most of us, didn't know the things you had to do when you owned land. Most of us were told we had to pay a land tax to the county every year and most of us got a piece of paper notice in the mail. We couldn't read it but we knew it was somethin important. Your daddy never got the word. Tax man said he never got on the mailin list - some kind of "paperwork error." Well, after a couple of years, Lamar Tate and his brothers showed up with the deed to his farm they bought at a tax sale. They gave him one day to get off their land."

"That ain't right!" I blurted the obvious truth.

"No, it ain't," Mr. Robbie said, "but somehow it didn't seem wrong to the Tates, the county tax man, and the sheriff. And with them against you, who you got left to go to?"

# Chapter 25

I couldn't get back to the library fast enough. The next day, I was waiting for Miss Judgy to open up. She looked at me standing at the front door like I was a cat turd dumped there overnight.

I smiled and gave her a bright, "Good mornin', ma'am."

After a couple of hours, my eyes were about to give out. I lifted my head and gave them a good rub. That quick, I was aware of voices coming from the table behind me and other voices on the other side of the bookshelf. I had been so deep in searching through book after book I hadn't seen or heard the good number of folks come in. I stared out the skinny window next to my table, trying to focus far away to relieve my eyes. I wasn't there to listen to conversations, but the young men behind me were loud enough to be annoying. I started reading again, frustrated at not finding something, anything, related to the stories the old men told me.

The loud talk from the boys finally made me stop reading. I was aggravated and would have moved right then, but maybe my mind wanted the distraction, maybe I needed the break, but whatever the reason, I sat back and listened.

"I think you should be the lead attorney, David. You scored the highest in corporate law."

"You guys aren't slouches either, but I'll do it unless someone else wants it."

Another boy said, "We'll back you up, but you're definitely the man."

"Frank, what do you think?"

"Uh, yeah, sure, whatever you guys say."

"Are you hungover?"

"No, I mean just a bit. Sorry, I'll get focused. I just had a picture of us in Florida on spring break with all the undergrad babes. Instead, we're in a library."

"Those days have been over, buddy. You knew what you were signing up for in law school. Not much fun in the sun and a whole lotta fun in the dim light of libraries."

"I know, I know. I'll focus. This time next year, the classes, the exams, and moot court will all be behind us."

I heard the slap of high-fives behind me. When the college pep rally wound down, the talk behind me quieted to where I could concentrate on reading with some effort, so I thought, but my aggravation with the chatter grew. After another ten minutes of law talk, I left, but I had to clear my head of a nagging question first. On the way out, I stopped at the dictionary sitting on a table of reference books. What I found, I read and reread to make sure I understood it.

That nagging question gave way to pounding curiosity. I went back to where those young men were sitting.

A half hour later, I approached Miss Judgy. I gave her not a smile, no cheerful greeting, nor proper manners. I didn't have time for bullshit.

"You got a Jackson phone book in here?"

# Chapter 26

Two weeks later, at 5:00 on a Friday afternoon, I pulled into a public parking lot in Jackson across from the Davis Building. Parking spaces were opening from a steady exit of cars at the end of the work week. Men, and some women, all white, were walking to their nice cars. It was like watching a parade of fine clothes. The women looked elegant even. There were professionals in Greenville, but the number in Jackson was making me self-conscious.

I turned off the truck and sat for a minute, wondering if I had shown my ignorance by even asking for a meeting with Mr. Cleve McDowell. I thought my chances were slim to none before I called his office two weeks ago, and I felt them dropping when Mr. McDowell's secretary couldn't coax a reason for the meeting from me.

"Ma'am, it's not that I don't want to tell you what it's about, it's just that I don't know exactly how to say it. I'm just thinkin Mr. McDowell might understand what's rattlin around in my head."

I clearly heard a sigh of frustration on the line. Finally, the secretary spoke in a less annoyed tone.

"How do you spell your last name, Mr. Neely?"

"With e's ma'am…I mean with two e's…and a y."

"The earliest Mr. McDowell could possibly see you is on Friday the 19th, just before he goes home. He's a busy man, you know, Mr. Neely."

"Oh, I know, ma'am. I heard about him in the Greenville library."

She had never booked a client who only knew Mr. McDowell from what he heard in the library. She wasn't sure if she should be impressed or insulted.

"Well, ok then. Be here at 5:30, and Mr. Neely, he may not have much time for you, so you need to be able to talk fast."

"Yes ma'am, I be ready. Thank you, ma'am. Thank you very much. You have a blessed day."

And now I sat, hands clenching the steering wheel, staring at the building where I was about to meet an up and coming civil rights lawyer in Mississippi. What those law school students told me was Cleve McDowell was the first black law student at Ole Miss. The feds who protected James Meredith in 1962 were gone when Cleve enrolled in 1963, but the death threats didn't leave with them. The school administration denied Cleve's request to carry a gun for protection, but he did anyway. On his way up the steps of the law school building on the third day of classes, he bent over to pick up his sunglasses that had fallen and a .22 pistol fell out of his pocket. Ole Miss wasted no time acting; they expelled Cleve the next day.

Most would have left the state and never looked back. Cleve, however, returned with a law degree from Texas Southern University, known as the "Negro" college, in Houston. In only a few years, he had made a name for himself filing and winning civil rights cases. One thing hadn't changed since his days at Ole Miss, though. The death threats were still the cost of being a smart black man trying to change an unjust white world.

"Mr. McDowell, Mr. Charlie Neely here to see you."

I stood behind the secretary, trying to peer around her and the office door she had opened halfway.

"He's the gentleman I told you couldn't describe his problem."

"Ah, yes, just a moment."

I heard the shuffling of paper and a desk drawer opening and closing.

"I'm leaving now, sir. Have a great weekend."

"You too, Miss Cahill," the voice said from the office.

Miss Cahill picked up her purse from her desk and looked at me as she stepped to the outer door.

"Good luck, Mr. Neely."

"Yes…yes, ma'am. Thank you."

The outer door closed quietly and the only sound I could hear was the beating in my chest. I didn't know what to do without her telling me if I should go into the office or stand there. I looked down to make sure I looked ok. A clean work shirt and clean jeans, only starting to fray, looked as good as my wardrobe could manage. Suddenly, I heard the scrape of a chair, followed by, "Come in, Mr. Neely."

I hurried in and was surprised to see the giant of a man in my mind was simply of average height and build. Distinguished in his suit, glasses, and close-cropped hair, but nothing like I had imagined.

"I'm sorry to keep you waiting. Please, have a seat."

Mr. McDowell stood behind his desk with an arm outstretched to indicate a chair immediately in front. He remained standing until I sat, and that unusual welcoming gesture put me at ease.

"I'm sorry I couldn't see you earlier in the day and I really should be getting home to the family, so if we can get right to it I would appreciate it. What can I do for you, Mr. Neely?"

I had prepared; prepared sitting in the camper, in bed, in the fields, on the drive to Jackson. I had my lines memorized like an actor, but one a world away from Broadway. I stammered without forming a word, then stopped and took a deep breath.

"You a man who rights wrong, Mr. McDowell. I knows that much about you and I knows there are some wrongs so far in the past, educated men, white men, don't want us to even try to wrestle with. "Let sleepin dogs lie," they say. "Well, I got an idea to tell you and I want you to tell me if it would have a chance of wakin those dogs up and gettin em barkin."

I was encouraged to see Cleve's right eyebrow arch up; encouraged enough to follow up.

"And barkin loud enough to be heard fifty years ago, Mr. McDowell."

Cleve set the pen down he had been fiddling with and leaned forward to put his forearms on the desk.

"I'm all ears, Mr. Neely. After the week I've had something out of the ordinary would be a welcome way to end it."

The short meeting I expected went nearly an hour and only ended when Mr. McDowell glanced at the wall clock for the first time since I had begun talking.

"Mr. Neely, I have to say I've never heard a proposal like this and you've given me a lot to think about. Let me talk to a friend of mine who works in that field and I'll give you a call at Sammy's. I wish we had more time, but I can't keep my family waiting any longer."

We both stood at the same time, and I extended my hand across the desk.

"Not a problem, Mr. McDowell. Ain't nothin more important than family. Thank you for seein me, sir. I be lookin forward to your call."

I had entered the Davis building weighed down with doubt that Mr. McDowell would take me seriously. I left it with a calm assurance that his interest was as genuine and deep as the Mississippi.

## Chapter 27

Five months later

Greenville's 25,000 residents can support enough businesses to feel like a small city. The population is growing ever so slowly; enough for people to think they can open competing businesses. Some make it, most don't. River Theater was one of those that folded within a year. Folks had grown up going to Labo's Theater downtown and habits are hard to change. Sitting in a new theater on the outskirts just didn't feel right except for teenagers, and they caused more trouble than they were worth.

River Theater had been dark for almost two years with interest from only a couple of out of town business people. Their interest fizzled quickly, which is why Robert Morse was overjoyed to sign a monthly rental agreement with a clean, middle-aged, well-dressed, and well-spoken black fellow from New York City, who had grand plans for a supper club with entertainment. Robert didn't care to hear any details as he took the check and passed over the keys.

The buzz that the River Theater would be something, anything, went around town quickly, but just as quickly died down as weeks went by without more details coming out. People were focused on something more serious. Greenville's first 'mass killing', as some called it—even though a husband and his girlfriend hardly made a 'mass'—was still the talk. The investigation had dragged on for months without an arrest and people were edgy, thinking the killer was nearby. Support of the law was fraying, snide comments about the police chief, the county sheriff, the city judge, and even the chancery court judge (who officially had nothing to do with the case, but unofficially, to many citizens, seemed to carry 'wrongdoing' as his middle name) were being heard quietly, but often, around town.

The chief and sheriff were only mildly concerned. They'd seen it before. As soon as an arrest was made, they would be golden again. The chancery court judge, Lamar Tate, wasn't concerned in the least. He was far enough removed from both law enforcement chiefs that any tarnish from them would only stick to him in the feeblest minds in Greenville. Besides, Judge Tate had his own portent to deal with.

Aaron Doucet was a long-time friend of Lamar's and county supervisor for 22 years. Aaron had represented his district well, with emphasis on those who could contribute to his next campaign, and not a second thought to those who couldn't. The Mississippi Bureau of Investigation, with help from the FBI, had arrested Aaron on charges of embezzlement and public corruption for allegedly taking bribes to redirect public money to benefactors, himself being the biggest. The state presented a solid case, the evidence showed Aaron spent county funds on white areas exclusively when he was bound by statute to support all citizens in his district. An open and shut case until the judge declared a mistrial when one juror dug in as the lone holdout. That lone juror happened to be the foreman on the Tate Plantation. Black folks were outraged that even with the FBI involved, state justice had lost to local Delta justice, where a juror could be pressured to derail due process, with the most detestable fact being the pressure came from another judge sworn to uphold the law, Lamar Tate.

That was half a year ago and the talk among the blacks had not backed down a bit, which was a concern to Judge Tate with the election four months away. His campaign plan to get the blacks on his side was unchanged from his last three, though – put up a tent in the poorest areas of the county, give away fried fish, hush puppies, and potato salad, deliver a sympathetic speech and make vague promises no one would remember, and the votes would roll in. Even though he was running unopposed, it was important to Tate to have black votes he could point to as proof of him being the noble defender of equal rights for all.

## Chapter 28

There were several lunch spots to choose from in Greenville, but Ruth's Diner had been attracting locals for sixty-five years like flies to a grease pot. If you wanted home cooking, wanted the best red beans and rice around, or wanted to see and be seen at lunch, you went to Ruth's.

The clerk at the front desk of the Harvest Inn had recommended Ruth's to LJ.

"Mr. Marshall, their chicken fried steak and greens are some fine eatin. And the mashed potatoes will put you down for a knockout nap, that's fo sho."

Driving down Main Street, LJ thought a stretch of businesses looked untouched for decades; old America still thriving. Other stretches reflected a changing America, with cheap imports putting stores that relied on American-made products out of business. As he parked across from Ruth's, he was delighted to see the diner could have come from a 1930s movie. The plate-glass windows were bordered with faded hand-painted red, white, and blue stripes and the staples they were known for were painted on with thick, lumpy strokes. "Burgers, Meat Loaf, Fried Catfish" painted on with pride decades ago were now dingy. LJ hoped the food inside was so good that the outside didn't matter.

He pushed the front door open, his palm pressing on a concave depression worn down over the years. Bells barely audible in the din of the lunchtime crowd jingled overhead as the door brushed under them. He scanned the room to see if there was an open table. A plump waitress brushed past, carrying a platter of fried catfish, hush puppies, and coleslaw. LJ almost followed, the smell was so good.

"Sit wherever you can, honey. I'll find you in a minute," she hollered over her shoulder.

Every table was full around him, and every table was full of white faces. LJ moved toward the far side of the restaurant, heading for an extension that formed an L.

"Mr. Marshall." A voice came from a table behind him. LJ turned to see Robert Morse and another gentleman at a table for four, empty plates piled in the middle and toothpicks twirling in their mouths.

"Mr. Morse."

"For someone new in town, you sure found the best spot for lunch real quick."

"Yes, sir, it smells like I did." LJ felt awkward as he looked down at the other gentleman, who looked to be sizing him up. It only took a second for LJ to do the same. He was looking down at an obese man who would break a sweat getting to his feet in a snowstorm. His wrinkled blue shirt that wouldn't button at the top around the fat neck it had the misfortune of touching, his undone tie with a food stain in the center, and droopy eyes too lazy to fully open all repulsed LJ.

LJ smiled broadly and gave a nod that the gentleman didn't return.

"Mr. Mayor, this is LJ Marshall, the fella who rented the River Theater."

The mayor's demeanor suddenly changed.

"Ah, so it is. I'm so happy that old building is gonna be brought back from the past, LG." The mayor offered his hand, but didn't stand up.

"LJ, sir. The name's LJ," LJ said as he shook the mayor's light and brief handshake.

"Ok, well, LJ, what are you gonna do with the old building?"

"I'm going to open a dinner theater, Mr. Mayor."

The mayor's eyes squinted, and his forehead furrowed.

"I hope the guy doesn't play poker. His face says he thinks it's a stupid idea," LJ thought.

"Well, that's good. We don't have one of them in town. We probably should, don't you think, Robert?"

Robert quickly swallowed his tea in mid-drink. "Oh, yes sir, absolutely. Every town should have one. It's going to be a big hit, mayor."

"I'm sure it will, I'm sure it will. Well, son, let me know if I can help." And with a quick nod, the mayor stuck the toothpick back in his mouth and went to twirling.

"Actually, Mr. Mayor, there might be."

The mayor looked up, not bothering to remove the toothpick this time.

"How's that?"

"Well, I'm looking for some actors and you may know some outgoing citizens who would enjoy being in a play."

The mayor looked at LJ, expression frozen.

"No acting experience required," LJ added.

The mayor glanced around the diner and then back to LJ.

"Well, I've never thought of such a thing, but I'll get back to you if anyone comes to mind."

"I'll bring you a list of characters I need actors for."

"That will be fine. Come by City Hall and give it to my secretary and I'll see what I can do. Have a good day."

Knowing a dismissal when he heard one, LJ moved on around the corner to the only open table; a table for two next to the swinging kitchen doors.

LJ sat with his back to the kitchen so he could see at least a part of the main dining room.

"Found yo'self the best seat in the house, I see."

LJ looked up to see the large waitress standing there, both doors still swinging from her passage.

"Only because the tables in the men's room were taken," LJ gave her a wink.

“Now, honey, don’t you feel bad. I’ve had lots of important people sit here.”

“Oh, yeah, like who?”

“Well, umm, for one, I see you was talking with the mayor, he’s sat…oh, hell, I can’t lie. He’s never sat anywhere but front and center. That man’s so full of himself…but I’m gettin out of line, honey, and I ain’t even told you the special.”

“Don’t bother,” LJ interrupted, “I have to try that fried catfish plate you walked under my nose when I came in.”

“You as smart as you look. You’ll be lookin for the coroner cause you’ll think you died and gone to heaven. Ice tea to go with that?”

“Unsweet, please.”

“No such thing here. Sweet tea or nothin.” She swirled her hips to go, her red and white checkerboard dress and lavender apron doing their best to keep up.

LJ ate slowly to keep pace with the patrons leaving Ruth’s. From his table at the back of the L, he could see a few tables in the main room and he passed the time watching the interaction of people as they ate over checkered plastic tablecloths that matched the waitress’s dress. He imagined who they were and what they did, as if they were all in a play. He also ate slowly to savor every bite. A handful of customers were all that remained when he took the last bite.

“Piece of pie go real good after that,” The waitress said as she picked up LJ’s empty plate.

He gave a sigh and said, “No, Ma’am, I’m hurting enough. That could be the best catfish plate I’ve ever had.”

“Could be? Round here we take that as an insult.”

“My apologies. I stand corrected. That was absolutely, without a doubt, the very best catfish plate I’ve ever had.”

“That’s what I thought you said the first time. With flattery like that, you can come back anytime.”

"I didn't catch your name."

"That's cause I was too busy to throw it. I'm Ruth."

LJ thought for a moment.

"You're much too young to be the original owner."

"That be my mother, God rest her soul."

Ruth was interrupted by the yell of "Order up".

"Excuse me. Be right back," Ruth said, already making her way to the kitchen window.

After delivering a meatloaf plate to one of only a few tables still occupied, Ruth came back to LJ.

"Coffee?"

"No, thank you. But if you have a minute, tell me about your mother starting the restaurant. That couldn't have been easy back then."

Ruth fanned her face with a menu for a moment before answering. "She started with five tables and nothin but colored customers. At first it was just a hole-in-the-wall, but it didn't take long for that to change, her cookin was so good. She became so popular the Klan took notice and they made the fire chief come in and shut her down for havin a gas leak in the stove. Momma Ruth told him her stove worked just fine and to prove it, she sat him down with a plate of fresh fried chicken and greens. After a second order of chicken, on the house, of course, he decided he couldn't smell any gas but would be back to make sure a gas line didn't bust while he was gone. That man got fat eatin free fried chicken and everythin else on the menu, and one white face in the diner, the face of a city official at that, gave nerve to other whites to step inside."

"Looks like it's flipped over the years. I felt out of place."

"Colored know they can come in but they stay away because of that feelin. The whites love me, though, because they sees me different. I's just a dumb black woman who was born to serve them. You be a different animal. Whitewash yo face and hands and they'd look at you as one of their own, what with your fancy clothes and shiny shoes. You even sound like one of em. How'd that happen?"

"Hanging around the wrong people, I suppose. My name's LJ, Miss Ruth." LJ stood and extended his hand, which Ruth eagerly shook.

"It's nice to meet you, Mr. LJ. Come on up to the front and I'll ring you up. I gots to get back to work, but I hope you come back."

"Oh, I will, Miss Ruth, if you promise to tell me more about your town."

"The meal won't take long, but you got lots to learn about this town, Mr. LJ, and I'd be happy to teach you, especially if you try my apple pie."

"Save this table for me, Miss Ruth, and I'll certainly do that."

"That won't be a problem, Mr. LJ. Won't be a problem at all."

# Chapter 29

The line of towering red oaks appeared on the horizon like a wall rising from the barren fields; fields waiting patiently for the retreating cold to cue planting time. LJ cracked the window and fresh air tinged with earthy tones wafted in. He breathed in deeply while mentally adding scent to the sights, tastes, and feeling of the Delta senses that were foreign to someone who grew up in a city.

Unlike the city, the 'blocks' made by the roads that cut the landscape at right angles were sometimes miles long. What he saw told him he was looking at emptiness, but what he was feeling was a fullness rooted in the history of the soil. This history was supposedly gone, buried in the past, but he felt the presence of past strife always waiting to sprout from the soil, watered by memories of unsettled scores.

As he turned off the farm road onto the long oak-lined road with the plantation house at the far end, LJ had to stop and stare. He felt those bygone days suddenly come to life. He was seeing today, but as he began to move slowly down the drive, it felt like today was a translucent wrapper on the past.

LJ laughed at himself. "You're just a paranoid city boy. This isn't *Gone with the Wind*, Mr. Tate's not going to be wearing a white suit and bow tie, and the help won't be slaves."

He sounded more hopeful than convincing.

He parked in the circular drive, a fountain surrounded by rose plants in the center, and a wide brick walkway leading to the front steps of the home. No longer shielded by trees, LJ saw the immensity of the home. Six massive white pillars stretched across a raised brick porch on the ground floor, the porch adorned with wicker furniture, potted ferns, and several ceiling fans that had remained motionless since November. A smaller porch above was attached to the columns that continued upward, tapering inward, to support a massive roof of gray slate tiles.

As he strode up the last step to the porch, LJ paused, looked down both lengths of the porch and thought, "If this house could talk…I don't think I could listen."

His eyes widened when his knock was answered by a young black girl in a full length black and white dress, topped off with a white scarf; a sudden and vivid reminder of the Gone with the Wind scenes he had been seeing.

"Hello, suh." Her voice was sweet and subtle, sounding much younger than a girl LJ estimated to be twenty should sound.

"Hello…ma'am," LJ stammered a bit. "LJ Marshall to see Mr. Tate."

"Yessa. Come in. Mr. Tate will see you in the library. Right this way."

LJ felt like he was stepping onto the stage of one of his plays and stepping back in time. He followed the girl between double curved staircases underneath a ceiling over thirty feet above that supported a massive crystal chandelier. Portraits of gentlemen in suits, coiffed with perfect gray beards or goatees and close-cropped hair, lined the staircases as if handholds to the past ascending to the second floor. A twenty foot wide central hallway opened up beyond the staircases, also adorned with legacy Tates, presumably of somewhat lower stature than the staircase Tates.

The servant girl led LJ to the last door on the right, knocked softly and after hearing a reply, entered and announced the guest.

"Mr. LJ Marshall to see you, Mr. Tate."

Lamar Tate's only acknowledgement of the girl was to say, "Bring us some ice."

"Mr. Marshall, come in," Lamar said, louder than necessary.

As LJ stepped into the room, Lamar put both hands on the desk and rose slowly from the wing-backed chair behind his massive dark oak desk. LJ thought if he were casting an elderly white plantation owner for a play, he would look no further than Lamar. White hair, short at the front with a slight curl on the neck; white mustache and goatee; turtle-shell wire-rim glasses, with white shirt and slacks, and white shoes to boot, shocked LJ as being over the top stereotypical. They shook hands as Lamar rounded the corner of the desk and Lamar motioned to two high-backed leather chairs in front of a fireplace. Embers were still glowing from a morning fire to take the dampness out of the air; air infused with the smell of a morning cigar.

"Thank you for seeing me, Mr. Tate."

"Call me Lamar, and I'm happy to oblige someone who's bringing some commerce to Greenville. So, what brings you all the way out here on this fine Sunday afternoon?"

LJ heard a soft clicking and glanced over to see the servant girl setting a silver ice tub on the marble bar behind them. He hadn't heard her come in, treading so lightly and so unnaturally, he thought.

"Pour us a couple of whiskeys," again, not calling the girl by name, LJ noted.

"That's assuming you're a drinking man, Mr. Marshall?"

"Yes, sir, I am, and please call me LJ."

In short order, two hefty crystal glasses perfectly encased in napkins, nearly full with dark bourbon and ice, were placed on the small table between them. The girl's exit was marked with only the slightest click of the door latch.

As they lifted their drinks from the table, with a tip of glasses to each other, LJ said,"Well sir, as you know, I'm opening a dinner theater in the old River Theater."

Lamar gave a nod after a long swig.

"It's about time, too. That old building used to shine."

"And I hope to have it shining again. The kitchen installation is going to take some time though, but I don't want to wait to give the people of Greenville a taste of what to look forward to."

"What do you have in mind?"

"I want to put on a play. Now the inside of the building is still going to be rough, and the seats may just be folding chairs, but I think it will generate a lot of interest and excitement in the community."

"What's the play about?"

"Well, sir, that's where it's different from a typical play. It has the barest of scripts."

"How the hell can you call it a play, then?"

"It's a new kind of play. It's been produced in New York with wonderful success," LJ lied with a straight face. "It's an impromptu play where even the actors don't know everything it will be about. Each will be told what character they will be playing, the basics of the scene will be described, and enough information given to get the play started. From there, it's up to the actors to take the play in any direction. Trust me, actors, especially amateur actors, love it since they don't have to memorize lines and they can use their imagination."

Lamar set his glass down after another long sip.

"Sounds hokey to me, but what do I have to do with any of this?"

LJ took his first sip, a long one, set his glass down, and looked Lamar in the eyes.

"I want you to play the lead character."

Lamar laughed so suddenly it brought on a coughing fit he had to douse with a pull of whiskey.

"You want me to be in your play?" Lamar bellowed. "Hell, boy, I've never acted a day in my life. You're scraping the bottom of the barrel, coming way out here looking for an actor."

LJ took another long sip and cradled his glass, rubbing it between his palms, the ice gently ticking.

"Oh, but I think you'd be a natural."

LJ leaned in closer to Lamar, as if to share a secret.

"Now I told myself I wouldn't give any of the actors a hint of the character they'd be playing, but let me just say it might be related to the office you're trying to get re-elected to," LJ said with a wink.

Lamar's left eyebrow suddenly raised up.

"And I think it would be good for the voters to see you in that role to remind them what kind of man you are."

LJ gave Lamar the biggest smile he could muster.

"Let's have another drink." Lamar said with a smirk. He pushed a buzzer and the door to the library opened so quietly, as if the servant wasn't even there.

"Before that, Judge, if you don't mind I would like to use your bathroom."

"Certainly."

"Show Mr. Marshall to the bathroom." LJ looked at the young girl, who gave a half wave toward the door. He followed her out and down the hall, she with her head down and him intrigued.

"I didn't catch your name, Miss. The Judge talks like he doesn't know it either."

She stopped in front of a closed door and turned to face LJ, but made eye contact only for a second.

"It's April, Mr. Marshall. And no, he don't call me by my name unless he's real angry."

"Does that happen often?"

April's hands suddenly clasped together, and she stammered, "I…I don't…Mr. Marshall, I got to fix your drinks. This be the bathroom right here." And with that, she hurried down the hall as quietly as a pin oak leaf blowing across the forest floor.

After the second bourbon, which helped to get Lamar to commit to being in the play, Lamar was happy to call the mayor and tell him LJ was coming over to see him in the morning and that he needed to make the time.

LJ decided to press his luck while the bourbon was working on Tate.

“If I could ask one more thing of your kind generosity, Judge, I would be most appreciative.”

“You caught me in a good mood. What do you need?”

“I also want the Sheriff to be in the play. Would you be so kind and arrange for me to meet with him?”

“No, I won’t waste my time, or yours for that matter.”

“Excuse me?” LJ wondered if he had crossed a line.

“No need for a meeting. I’ll call Sheriff Black and tell him he’s in the play. You see, that boy owes me from now until the sun burns out. I’ve got big pockets, LJ, and a lot of people in them. You want something to happen in Washington County? Well, you’ve come to the right man.”

LJ could not have imagined a more ironic statement.

## Chapter 30

"That's about the craziest thing I ever heard. A play without a script and people who have never acted?" The mayor squinted at LJ, and not from the morning sun streaming through the blinds of the mayor's office on the second floor of City Hall. LJ figured the mayor's puzzlement was real, since it caused him to set a half-eaten donut back on his desk.

"That's a pretty good description, yes."

"Well, I'll be. And why should I say yes?"

"Well, for one, you'll be in good company. Your good friend, Lamar Tate, is going to be in it."

"You're shitting me. He really said that?"

"Yes, sir. Excited about it too."

The mayor thought for a moment.

"You called us good friends. What makes you think that? You just got here."

"I listen and I'm a quick learner, that's all."

"Hmm, well, what character do you have in mind? I'm not dressing up in anything that makes me look sissy-fied or anything like that. I have my image to maintain, you know."

LJ glanced at the portly figure and stifled a laugh.

"Oh, I'm well aware, mayor, and that's why I've cast you as a model citizen doing his civic duty. It's an honorable role, mayor."

"And you say Lamar is gonna be in this play, or whatever you call it?"

"Yes, sir. I think both of you will play important roles and I have the feeling you're both naturals."

The mayor chuckled. "Naturals, huh? You think if I do it, Hollywood will come calling?"

"You never know, mayor. This could be the start of something big."

## Chapter 31

It was late on a Thursday night that had started slowly and never picked up. The one-man band had packed up and left and I had delivered two cold beers to the older gentlemen at the bar, telling them they were the last beers of the night. They were giving me good-natured shit when a black man walked into Sammy's, a place I could tell with one glance he didn't belong in. Fortyish, short-cropped hair speckled with gray, pressed button-down shirt and slacks, and the shiniest brown loafers I had ever seen.

I met him at the end of the bar to turn him away.

"We're closing, sir."

"Well, that's fine with me. I'm not here to drink. I'm looking for Charlie and I suspect that might be you."

I straightened up and looked at him distrustfully.

"I might be, or maybe not. Depends on who you are."

LJ glanced at the old men at the end of the bar, who were deep in an argument they wouldn't remember tomorrow.

"LJ. I'm a friend of Cleve's."

I stared at him, still not connecting the dots.

"I'm here to turn your idea into reality, Charlie."

My eyes went wide and my spirit came alive.

"Oh, Lord, Mr…LJ? I'm sorry…I mean, I'm so glad to meet you. I had no idea…I ain't heard from Cleve for a while."

"Cleve thought it might be better that way. He also recommended I not be seen in public with you." LJ glanced back at the drunk old men. "Looks like we're safe here."

"Please, Mr. LJ, let's sit over here." I motioned to a corner booth, and I was already jabbering as we sat down.

"How long you been here, Mr. LJ?"

"Please, Charlie, just LJ will do. I've been driving around in the dark long enough to know I should have come looking for Sammy's in the daylight."

I laughed. "That beaten path we're off of? It's in the next county. This your first time to the Delta?"

"It is and I have to say, it's unlike any place I've been in the States. Honestly, I know nothing about the Delta and I can tell there's a lot to learn, some good."

"Sounds like there are other parts you don't like."

"It's nothing like New York, Charlie. At home, it seems like most everything is on the surface. Who you see and what you see are who and what they are. What you see is what you get, as they say. But here...," LJ let out a sigh and stared out the plate-glass window into the dark, "...here I get the feeling that sometimes there's more out of sight than what you can see. I mean, day-to-day life goes on like anywhere else, but it all seems to be riding on some undercurrent, some shadow world an outsider like me can't see. I'm probably not making any sense, Charlie, and maybe it's just my imagination, but it's why I came to see you, one of the reasons, actually. I first want to tell you my meeting with Lamar Tate was a little shaky at first, but by the end he bought into it and he signed up the sheriff, too. And, thanks to a referral from the judge, Mayor Campbell's in, as well."

"Well, that's great news, LJ! You done good."

"Yes, but something else has been bothering me about my visit to the Tate Plantation and I can't shake it."

He paused, looking at me. I looked at him expectantly.

"Do you know the girl, April, who works for Lamar?"

"April Legare? I do remember her. Remember her father better. We was all livin on the plantation together. Her father was a hard worker."

The memory of him caused me to look down at my rough, calloused hands on the worn table top.

"He was on the woods-clearin crew when there wasn't work in the fields. He got careless one day and didn't see a tree that snapped and rolled where it wasn't supposed to go. At least the poor man didn't suffer but for a second or two."

The memory of the news spreading through the plantation brought back pain gone dormant. I took a deep breath before continuing.

"Anyway, I was never close to April's family, but I remember April's mother died of somethin they never could figure out. After that, April moved into the big house to be the Tate's maid. I remember that much, but I figured she had moved on by now. Now you tellin me she never left the Plantation? What's her job?"

"Well, a kind of maid and butler job as far as I saw. She answered the door and brought me to Tate. She came when he summoned her and brought us drinks."

"Well, nothin wrong with that job. At least it's indoors, out of the heat and cold."

"True, but there's something not right there. She looked like a dog that had been beaten into submission. She looked to be on the verge of tears when she answered the door and she almost cowered when she entered the room Tate was in. He never acknowledged her. I mean, he didn't treat her badly, he just didn't treat her at all, if you know what I mean."

"I ain't surprised to hear that. Mr. Tate is not a friendly man by nature, at least to blacks, that is, blacks who work for him. I imagine he was kindly toward you since you got some white standin up north."

White standing?"

"That means you pretty much equal to the white Yankees, or at least they let you believe that. Tate probably believes it's best to go along with it, not agree with it, mind you, but just go along with it. Hell, we all do, if you don't mind me bein honest with you. You dress nice, talk nice, got you a professional white job and probably live in a nice house in a white neighborhood. We shake our heads at that though, Mr. LJ, and I don't mean to piss you off, but I think they got you fooled into thinkin you one of them. Down here we ain't got any of them, what they call optimal illusions."

"Optical illusions?"

"Those too. We knows who's what and where in this life. Maybe the next life we all be flipped or we all be the same. Only God knows and we will too shortly, but for now, things are just the way they are. If you can't live with that, then you can work yoself up into a lather and get yoself killed or you can leave. If you stay though, you best decide you ain't changin a thing."

LJ sighed and thought about that.

"So, Miss April. What's yo business with her?" I asked.

"No business. I'm just worried about her. She looked so scared and now you tell me she's got no family. I just think she needs a friend, and I was hoping you could go talk with her, maybe find out if there's anything I could do for her?"

I wondered for a moment. "Like what?"

"I don't know, Charlie. I mean, I'm not going to be here very long and I'm too busy to do anything in person, but I could give her some money if she's in a bind, if that would help her."

"Money and the po go together like bologna and bread. I'll drop in on her and see how she's doin. I'll let you know."

"And Charlie, don't mention to anyone we talked about April. It wouldn't do good for it to get back to Lamar that I'm meddling in his help."

"You right about that. Wouldn't do good for you or April," I answered, stopping short of putting myself on that list.

There was a seed of fear planted in my gut at that moment. I hadn't been smart enough to think this all through, so I didn't see it coming. And worse, it never left.

# Chapter 32

The Fourth Circuit District covers Leflore, Sunflower, and Washington Counties with Judge Judy Benton presiding in her offices in Greenville. LJ hit a brick wall trying to get an appointment when he called, so the next day he walked into the county building and through the frosted glass door with Judge Benton's name in gold letters. A middle-aged woman wearing horn-rimmed glasses and purple lipstick looked up from her typewriter when LJ gently and respectfully closed the door behind him.

"Can I help you?" The woman asked, somewhat suspiciously, LJ thought.

"Yes, ma'am, I need to make an appointment for a very brief meeting with Judge Benton. Any day this week would be fine."

The woman looked over her glasses at him as if he had asked for the moon.

"And what is the subject?"

"I am putting on a play in town and would very much like for her to be in it."

"A play," she said as if it was the silliest thing she'd heard.

"Yes, ma'am. I'm sure she would be interested if I could just get ten minutes with her."

"Well, I'll put it on her list of priorities just under prosecuting bloodthirsty criminals, hooligans, jaywalkers, and people who are late on library fines."

She stopped short, realizing she bumped up against the line of rudeness.

I'm sorry, Mr....."

"LJ Marshall, ma'am."

"...Mr. Marshall, but the judge is busy and doesn't have time for anything other than criminal matters. If your matter is urgent, you'd get to see her quick-like if you rob the Planter's Bank down the street, but otherwise I can't tell you when she might have time to see you."

At least she said it with a thin smile.

LJ had struck out again and he couldn't help but wonder if it was because Miss Purple Lipstick didn't respect his northern 'white standing'.

# Chapter 33

LJ hadn't been to this part of Greenville, not intentionally, it's just that he had no reason to go until now. It was early afternoon and the brilliant blue sky and soothing sunshine contrasted with the neighborhoods where 'soothing' was seldom spoken of. Block after block felt as oppressive as the cumulative years of neglect. The homes, businesses, and people wore it like a permanent stain. So many homes were beyond repair that bulldozing was probably the fate when the elderly residents passed away. Young men were gathered in front yards, under carports or on street corners; far too many on a workday. He drove slowly by Sacred Heart Catholic Church, a square city block of old live oaks that broke the monotony of blight.

LJ stopped in front of a plain, one-story brick building. A large plate-glass window dominated the street frontage, faded and stained green curtains pulled tight inside. A metal door stood to the left of the window, no name on it, only the street number. LJ stood on the sidewalk and checked the number on a scrap of paper he pulled from his shirt pocket before turning the handle and pushing the door open.

The reception area of the Miller & Associates Law Firm, or what would be a reception area in a proper law firm, was occupied by one metal desk, most likely government surplus from the 1940's. Nothing was on the desk but a noticeable layer of dust. When a guy sees it, it's noticeable.

The sound of a rolling chair came from the one out of three offices that was lit. The Associates must like to work in the dark, LJ thought sarcastically. He was wondering if Charlie's recommendation was ill-placed.

A black man in his late 20s came through the office doorway. LJ was pleased with the first impression. The trim young man wore a suit, sans jacket, a pressed white button down with gold cufflinks, and a muted red tie that messaged restrained intensity. His immediate smile seemed genuine.

"Hello. I'm Lon Miller. Can I help you?"

LJ caught almost a hint of pleading in the question.

"LJ Marshall, Mr. Miller," LJ extended his hand. "Do you have a few minutes to talk?"

"I'd ask my secretary, but as you can probably tell, she went out to lunch a couple of years ago and never came back. That's ok, though. I was going to fire her over her cluttered desk." Lon smiled and let go of LJ's hand. LJ returned the smile, appreciating someone keeping a sense of humor through less than prosperous times.

Lon took his place behind his desk and motioned for LJ to take a seat in one of the two modern and dust-free leather chairs on the other side. LJ scanned the office and was surprised. If the reception area was a desert, Lon's office was an oasis. Tasteful art hung on the light colored tongue-and-groove wood walls. A framed Ole Miss Law degree hung behind the desk, straddled by oil paintings of a giant magnolia and an early 19th century steamboat on the Mississippi River. Lon's desk was clean and orderly. A law book lay open next to a yellow legal pad. A burnt orange Parker fountain pen rested on the pad of notes. A proper law office, LJ thought; maybe apologies to Charlie for doubting him.

"What can I help you with, Mr. Marshall?"

"Well, it's more how we can help each other, Mr. Miller."

And so began LJ's recruitment of the next to last major actor. Lon became increasingly interested as LJ talked, and by the end was perched on the edge of his chair, elbows spread wide on his desk. Not only would he be in the play, but he would also find the ten bit players LJ needed.

"When do we start rehearsing?" Lon asked.

"Well, we don't. There's no need to rehearse as this is an impromptu play, so to speak. Opening night is next Friday at 7:00.

We'll have an informational run-through at 6:30 for the entire cast. Before then, though, I'll give you more information so you can prepare a strategy."

"What about a wardrobe?"

"You're wearing it. That suit is your wardrobe," LJ stood before adding, "Oh, and having that Parker pen in your shirt pocket would be a nice touch. Thank you, Mr. Miller, for your time and I'll be calling you soon to meet again."

Lon grabbed a card out of his center drawer and extended it to LJ.

"My home phone number is on this just in case my secretary doesn't answer the office phone."

LJ smiled and said, "I'm not holding out any hope of talking with her."

As LJ turned to leave, Lon said, "Oh, I forgot to ask. How many nights will the play last?"

LJ looked back at Lon and stated with emphasis, "That depends on how good of a lawyer you are, Mr. Miller."

## Chapter 34

To say it was hard for a black professional with no connection to Greenville to prosper in the city would underestimate the disdain many professional whites had for educated outsider blacks moving in and acting like they were equals. A black native of Greenville, who left to get a college education and returned with a graduate degree, fared better, but not by much.

Lon had felt the frustration growing in his wife over the last year over his career not taking off as they both had hoped. He tried to stay upbeat and positive for both of them, which was why he was excited to tell Kim he had been recruited to be in a play.

Instead of a smile, a laugh, or any interest at all, Lon was looking at the longest stare his wife had ever given him.

"A play? That's the big news you said you had for me?" Kim slumped back into the soft sofa cushions that felt like a cocoon. She looked back up to Lon, "Honey, I'm sorry. That's good news, I guess…out of the ordinary, anyway. I was just hoping for more. You know I've supported you every way I can, but I don't see living in your hometown paying off for either of us. After three years still all you get are divorces and car accidents, and most are cases the white lawyers don't want. 'Nigger work' is what they call it and you know it."

Things had been unsaid since they moved to Greenville, but the words finally spoken hung in the house like a stink no ceiling fan could clear. Lon sat on the couch close enough to touch Kim, but instead he turned away to stare at the floor.

"You know it and I know it. I hoped it was going to change, but tell me how that's going to happen? They like having you around to have a black face at their lawyer get-togethers, but only some of them. Just so happens the ones you get invited to have a photographer from the Greenville Current there." Kim paused, feeling relief from finally saying what had been building in her head.

"Are you happy here at all?" Lon asked.

"You know I'm not. I mean, I love the kids, the administration is screwed up, but no worse than anywhere else," she said and took a breath.

"It's not the job, Lon. It's the feeling, no, it's knowing that nothing will ever change if we stay here. You'll always have your small street corner office away from downtown and the bigshot white lawyers will be on the fifth floor of the Cotton Exchange. And I will always be an elementary school teacher unless we move to a city where I can work as a journalist or a copy editor and you'd have opportunities to practice whatever law you want. We don't have those options here, babe, and I feel like we're both locked in cages."

The room went quiet, neither knowing where the conversation should go from there.

Lon finally broke the silence. "Give me two more years. If I'm not doing better, then we'll move."

Kim took a long look at Lon, then looked down to where she was squeezing a gold tassel on the pillow she held close. She shook her head slowly and said, "Hon, I don't know if I can wait that long. I really don't."

She got up and stepped out to the front porch, softly closing the door behind her.

Lon sat in the quiet with his thoughts that were anything but. His mind felt like it was getting whipped by a January cold front.

## Chapter 35

Ruth's was again bustling and the jingle of the door bells quickly faded into the medley of conversations mixed with kitchen aromas. LJ stood at the door for a moment, but not seeing Ruth out front, he made his way around the corner and, as he expected, his table next to the kitchen doors was empty.

A few minutes later, Ruth came bustling up, smoothing her hair back and blowing on her upper lip.

"Whew, Lord, I'm running my tail off today. How ya doin, Mr. LJ?"

"I'm doing just fine, Miss Ruth. You go on and take care of some other tables if you need to. I can wait."

"I'd think of no such thing. All them yahoos out front can wait. I got a very important New York City producer sittin back here who right now is my number one customer."

The kitchen doors swung open wide, almost hitting LJ's shoulder. Ruth swung her ample hips to make room for another waitress carrying a tray for a party of four.

"I apologize, again, for you havin to sit here. It ain't exactly the VIP table."

"Not at all, Miss Ruth. I kind of like it. I get to talk to you a little longer back here, and that's even better than the food."

"Oh, shush, flattery like that is wasted on me. I've heard it all in here, but I tell you, that was pretty good. If you got any more like it, I won't stop you from sayin it." She winked and slapped her order book down lightly on his shoulder.

"Now, what you want?"

"Red beans and rice, cornbread, and a side of fried okra."

"Hah! You new here and you already becomin a southern boy. There's hope for you yet."

She gave another wink and headed into the kitchen.

While he waited, LJ watched customers' mannerisms, noticed their dress, and enjoyed the accents in clips of conversations he overheard. “This is a southern play in real time,” he thought.

When she brought LJ his food, he said, “I would like to talk to you when it dies down. Unless you have a line of customers demanding this table, I’ll have a cup of coffee when I’m done and I’ll wait until you’re free for a few minutes.”

“That sounds fine. Coffee and me for dessert. You got it.”

LJ sprinkled Tabasco on his red beans, said a prayer of thanks, and dug into flavors from heaven.

An hour later, his plate cleared and his coffee cup empty, Ruth came around the corner untying her apron. She pulled out the other chair and slowly plopped down.

“How were those beans?”

“The best I’ve had. Those are your beans?”

“Cooked them yesterday. They’re better the second day. Glad you liked them. Now, what did you want to talk to me about?”

“Well, Miss Ruth, I’ve gotten people to volunteer to be in my play, but…”

“Who you got?” Ruth interrupted.

“Well, the main ones are Lamar Tate, Mayor Campbell, Sheriff Black, and Lon Miller.”

“Well, that’s a bag full of cat shit right there, except for Lon. He’s a good man, but those others you best not tangle with, especially the so-called judge. Huh, I can’t wait for him to be judged by the Lord God Almighty.”

LJ had a good idea of who he was dealing with, but Ruth’s abrupt honesty took him by surprise.

“You’ve had run-ins with those three?”

“Who hasn’t? At least what black, and a few whites, haven't?”

“Are they racist men?” LJ asked the rhetorical question to get a rise out of Ruth.

"Are they racist? Does an alligator have teeth? They be racist devils in preacher suits. None of em worth spittin on if they was on fire. You be careful, being a black man and all."

"And all…?"

"A Yankee. That's twice the reason not to like you, the way they sees it. But you're a smart fella. I suppose I'm not telling you somethin you don't already know."

"I suspected that about them, yes. Now, I want to ask you about Judge Benton."

Ruth's face didn't change in reaction to her name, which LJ took as a good thing.

"I can't get an appointment to see her and I was wondering if you knew where I might run into her after hours. Have you ever seen her at the grocery after work, out walking, anywhere?"

"Well, it be easier than that. She eats lunch here most Fridays at the corner table by the window up front. Usually brings a couple of her people. I keep that table open until noon. If she ain't here by then, I give it up. You wants to talk with her you be here by 11:30 Friday and I'll see if I can work some of my magic to get you two together."

Ruth pushed up from the table, her backside tilting the chair back until the chair behind stopped it from toppling.

"I'm indebted to you, Miss Ruth, and if you don't mind, I'll have another cup of coffee and sit here until you're done with the lunch customers. If you can spare the time, I'd like to hear more about those three devils, as you call them."

An hour after the last lunch customer left and Ruth had flipped the closed sign over, LJ walked out of what had become in his mind the town center of tactical intelligence and Miss Ruth, undoubtedly, was the town spymaster.

## Chapter 36

LJ took his spot at his table at 11:15, his back to the kitchen as usual, giving him a clear view of Judge Benton's table.

"Got here early so you can pounce on da judge when she walks in?" Ruth said as she placed extra napkins on LJ's table.

"Actually, Ruth, I have a big favor to ask of you."

"Hmm, little favors I don't mind, but the sound of big favors scares me."

"Okay, then, consider it a little favor. After you take the judge's order, tell her there's a Broadway producer in the restaurant who wants to give her something."

Ruth dropped her head toward LJ and raised her eyebrows, "A Broadway producer? And who might that be?"

LJ laughed at Ruth's feign of disbelief.

"Ok, maybe I'm a few blocks away from Broadway, but I'm inching toward it. Just try to say it with a straight face…please."

Ruth's face relaxed. "Whatever you say."

At 11:40 a tall woman, mid-50's, with slender hips, stern face, and unremarkable hair, took a seat at the corner table. Ruth approached the table and began talking with the judge, Ruth's wide hips leaving just enough of a view of the judge's face for LJ to tell that niceties and smiles were rarely associated with Ms. Benton. Ruth took the menu from the judge, and before walking away, leaned in closer. A pair of furrows appeared on her forehead as she scanned the room. She said a few words to Ruth and Ruth turned and made a plodding beeline to the kitchen.

"You got three minutes before her lawyer servants join her. Good luck, Broadway," she said as she passed and pushed through the kitchen door, without a glance in LJ's direction.

LJ got up and was halfway to the judge's table when her eyes locked on him. He felt as if he was being given a psychological assessment from a distance. LJ began speaking as he took the seat across from the judge.

"Judge Benton, thank you for seeing me, and I know you have others about to join you, so I'll be quick."

"I would appreciate that, Mr.....?"

"LJ Marshall, ma'am. I'm pleased to meet you."

LJ thought the judge hesitated a moment before taking his hand, and the lack of any grip by her said she was not enthusiastic about this intrusion.

"You may have heard the old Ford Theater is being reopened as a dinner playhouse."

"I did and I take it you came all the way down here from Broadway fame to make your fortune in Greenville?"

LJ smiled. "Not exactly. More of a sabbatical, if you will. Anyway, we're putting on a pre-opening play to give a surprise taste of what's coming.  All I can tell you about it is we have Mayor Campbell, Judge Tate, Sheriff Black, and Lon Miller starring in the play and I want to invite you to star in it as well."

A truncated sales pitch usually brought back a quick no, but the stone face only stared back at LJ.

"Did you know that in the public's perception of the legal profession, district attorneys are in the negative territory?" LJ said quickly. He would congratulate himself later for making that up on the fly.

"Skipping the reasons why, for time's sake, it would do your office good for the public to see you, or an Assistant DA at least, engaged in their profession and showing the public a professional and personal side they don't see."

LJ suddenly became aware of the door jingles. The judge glanced beyond him and the stone face finally cracked.

"My associates are here for lunch, Mr. Marshall. I will consider your proposal and will let you know my decision. How can I reach you?"

“I’m staying at the Harvest Inn or I can come to your office, tomorrow or the next?”

“That won’t be necessary. I’ll leave you a message if you’re not in. Have a nice day, Mr. Marshall.”

LJ felt bodies standing close by. That, and the curt ‘have a nice day’ dismissal, spurred him up and away from the good judge’s lunch chambers.

That evening after dinner, LJ strode through the small lobby of the Harvest Inn and was stopped by the call of the desk clerk.

“Yes?” he asked and approached the desk.

“You have a message,” the clerk said and handed over a sheet folded in half.

LJ opened it and was surprised it was from the judge this soon after their meeting. It was concise, as he would expect.

“Mr. Calder Ambrose has volunteered to be in your play. He is young, smart, and outgoing; ideal for public performances. He’ll be in touch.”

The good news was followed by several blank lines, and then, “Bring no harm to my office.”

LJ knew the good judge had not written that line with a smile on her face. She was serious and smart, but unaware how appropriate her warning was.

## Chapter 37

I picked up Tucum as the sun was setting, the sky letting go of the last colors of the day a little later every day. Winter was slipping out the back while spring was gently tapping at the front door.

Tucum got in and we headed down the gravel road, headlights cutting into the deep shadows creeping across the farmland.

“Well, this is a rare treat nowadays, Charlie. Been wonderin if you left town to find your fame and fortune, as they say, whoever the fuck ‘they’ is.”

“Been spendin time helpin out a friend,” I said. That much was true.

“That sick friend in Jackson?” Tucum asked. A jolt of guilt went through my heart from lying to Tucum when I met with Cleve.

“No, but this is a friend of his. In fact, I want you to meet him and I got a big favor to ask of you.”

“Well, Charlie, you know I’d do anything to help my brotha in Christ, though I’d rather not kill another person unless the mother fucker really needs takin off this earth.”

I looked over at Tucum to see his expression. His face was barely illuminated by twilight’s pastels, but I couldn’t see a hint of the smile I hoped for.

“Tucum, I would never ask you to kill anyone, but I would ask you to put some stink on somebody who deserves it.”

“I’m in. Who is it and what can I do?”

“We’ll talk all about it when you meet my friend. Until then, I would appreciate it if this conversation stays between us.”

After a few moments, Tucum said, “Sounds like a conversation we’d have over a bottle of whiskey.”

We drove the rest of the way to our AA meeting in silence, Tucum occasionally stroking his gray goatee, deep in thought.

## Chapter 38

We met the next night at Tucum's, the only witnesses of comings and goings being coons and possums.

He greeted us at the door, polite as his usual self, but I could sense his suspicion.

"Tucum, this is LJ. LJ, Tucum."

"Good to meet you, LJ. Y'all come in. Excuse the mess. I'm gonna clean when the Saints win the Super Bowl. Until then, just move shit around and make yourself at home."

I could tell LJ didn't know what to make of Tucum being shirtless or his living room. Rolled linoleum was buckled in places and missing by the front door, jagged cuts in an approximation of a semi-circle suggested it was easier than trimming off the bottom of the dragging door. A shotgun stood at the ready in the corner by the door, a rifle in the corner by Tucum's worn leather chair, and a pistol sat among papers and cups on a TV tray. Dog hair adorned most everything, with the heaviest being on the couch we were motioned to sit on. After moving newspapers and a chew bone, LJ and I sat with resigned glances at each other.

Tucum sat in his chair that had a permanent lean conveniently toward us. He reached over and turned off the AM radio behind him on the bookshelf, the last words before fading out being, "Corn down eighteen a bushel…".

"Well, LJ, you're somewhat of a mystery guest. I ain't seen Charlie so tight-lipped since he bit into one of my habanero peppers. Shit, pardon my manners. Can I get y'all some ice tea?"

LJ looked at me.

"It's some of the best tea this side of Jackson," I told him.

Tucum didn't wait for answers, but jumped up and disappeared into the kitchen.

"Is unsweet alright or do y'all want some sugar? I apologize for not having sweet tea. Doc says if I drink any more of it, he'd be losing a paying customer in no time."

"Bring it like it is, Tucum. That will be just fine," I answered.

Once Tucum settled back in and we all had a long sip, he asked, "Well, what do you gentlemen want with a short, fat, country boy like Tucum Tutweiller?"

LJ cleared his throat and scooted an inch more away from the dog's hair on the back of the couch.

"Charlie tells me you're pretty good at building things…," LJ stated as I fought the urge to glance at the repairs needed in this worn room alone, "…and I, we, need help with some light construction."

Tucum listened attentively as LJ told him what he needed built for the set of his play.

"As long as you just need somethin built quick, cheap, and good enough, then I believe I can help you, but if you're needin stuff built you'd brag about to your momma then I'm afraid I'm not your man."

"If you're willing to do the work then I'm willing to keep my bragging mouth shut." LJ said with a smile.

"Well, good. When do we start?"

LJ handed over drawings he sketched out with dimensions of what he needed.

Tucum looked over the drawings, nodded, and said, "I'll get started tomorrow. Charlie, nine o'clock good for you?"

LJ and I exchanged glances.

"Tell him," LJ said.

I finally looked over at Tucum, and said, "I can help you here tomorrow, Tucum, if you needs it, but I can't help you with the theater. I can't explain now, so you gonna have to trust me. I can't be seen as bein a part of all this until the time's right."

Tucum looked at me as if his dog had spoken.

"A part of all what? A fuckin play?"

I didn't know what to say, so we sat in silence for a moment.

"Charlie, I don't know what the fuck is going on or what you got yourself into, but as long as I'm gonna be left out of any bad shit, I'll help you - you and your friend here. I done had enough trouble to spread around a small country and have some left over. You know that, Charlie. You know I don't want no more," Tucum said sternly, his icy stare leaving no doubt he was dead serious.

"I knows that, Tucum. If anyone's gonna find trouble it be me. You gonna be alright, I promise."

That calmed Tucum and led us to small talk about fishing and some politics that got cut short when it became clear LJ and Tucum had little in common on that subject. I took that as the opportunity to get up and bring our visit to an end.

"It was nice meeting you, Tucum. I thank you for your help. It's much appreciated." LJ extended his hand and Tucum returned the gesture, shaking firmly.

"I'm happy to help."

I turned to the door, only to hear behind me, "I'm glad you feel that way. Actually, there's one other thing I'd like to ask you to do."

"What's that?"

"Be in my play."

That request wasn't answered nearly as enthusiastically so we left it as something we'd talk about in a couple of days.

## Chapter 39

From downtown Greenville, traveling south on highway 61, the town dwindled quickly over a few miles. Where the town ended and cropland took over stood The Gin Inn, as it had for over sixty years. Its heyday, if it ever had one, was a faded memory in a handful of people. New paint had been spared from it for too many years, and landscaping with rose bushes and azaleas years before had quickly succumbed to neglect and weeds. It was the perfect place for someone who wanted to go unnoticed.

There were twenty-five rooms but only three cars in the parking lot when Abaddon Thomas parked by the office door. A bare sixty-watt bulb, moths orbiting it ferociously, cast a dim yellow light. The glass door resisted opening from hinge spindles worn down back when customers were plentiful. An elderly Indian man, bald with black and gray hair thinning on the sides but valiantly hanging on, looked up from his newspaper.

"Good evening. How may I help you?" A blend of Indian and British accents greeted Abaddon.

"I have a reservation under Abaddon Thomas."

"Ah, yes, sir. I clearly remember your name. It's unique, yes?"

"Yes, my parents liked biblical names."

"Very good, sir. If you would sign, please."

The clerk motioned toward an oversized ledger.

"Just like in an old movie," Abaddon thought. He skipped the line for an address and wrote Chicago on the line for city and state.

The clerk gave a quizzical look saying, "And your address, sir?"

"I don't have one at the moment," Abaddon said firmly. His look told the clerk not to press the question.

“Very well, sir. And how will you be paying?”

“Cash, four nights for now, maybe more. I’ll let you know.”

Abaddon pulled a $100 bill from his worn leather wallet and dropped it on the counter.

“The bill is $80, sir. I’ll get your change,” The clerk made a motion toward a room behind the desk area but only got a step away.

“Consider the extra $20 as a tip for giving me a room furthest from the road. I like the quiet. I also like my privacy, so there’ll be no need for anyone to clean my room. If I need anything, I’ll let you know, otherwise it can be cleaned when I leave.”

“Very well, then…,” the clerk moved his hand over the board of keys on the paneled wall, “room twenty-one will afford you peace and quiet.”

Abaddon took the key and started for the door as the clerk wrote the room number in the ledger.

“Enjoy your stay, sir. If there’s anything…,” the manager looked up to see the door had already closed with an annoying squeak.

The last member of the play had arrived in Greenville.

# Chapter 40

This day had been a long time coming. I felt like I was standing at the end of a long trail on a cliff with black clouds swirling at my feet. I had finally reached the destination, but I still didn't know what it looked like.

It was Friday and the day I thought was so far out of reach was now slapping my emotions into tatters. I had the windows down and was heading to Greenville just fast enough for the gusts to send fast food wrappers chasing each other around the passenger floorboard. I already couldn't eat breakfast and the frantic chaos of the wrappers only made my stomach tighten further. Peering out the window attempting to follow the intermittent center line through the fog only added to my anxiousness.

I pulled off highway 61 a few minutes before 9:00 and slowly navigated the obstacle course of potholes in the motel parking lot. As instructed, I parked behind the motel, out of sight of the highway. I parked far enough away from an overflowing dumpster that a truck could empty it, any week or month now.

After knocking, the door of room twenty-one was opened just wide enough for a right eye and sliver of cheek to peer out. I immediately recognized LJ and, after a glance to either side of me, he opened the door and shut it quickly behind me. A tall gentleman in crisp khakis and a blue button-down shirt, sleeves rolled up, stood behind LJ in front of a wall that looked like a wallpaper job by five-year-olds had gone as well as could be expected. My eyes adjusted to the poorly lit room, with an overall color of yellow abused by time and nicotine. The drapes were pulled tight and I could feel the dank, musky smell of years of sex, pets, and body sweat burrowing into the fibers of my clothes. It was a step up from my camper but had to be insulting to the well-dressed black gentleman.

"Charlie Neely, this is Abaddon Thomas. Abaddon, Charlie."

The gentleman, Abaddon, closed the gap between us and extended his hand before I could take a step.

"Charlie, I can't tell you how honored it is to finally meet you. I want you to know you have my utmost respect for what you have done."

I stammered, off balance by his formality and sincerity. "Well…well thank you, Mr. Abbe dun?"

"Abaddon."

"Yessuh, Abaddon. See, I ain't really done much of anythin. LJ here took a crazy idea and is makin it into somethin. I'm still not sure what, but somethin."

Abaddon laughed, "It is something, Charlie. It certainly is. I'm going to make sure of that."

I looked at LJ to calm my confusion.

"Sit down, Charlie, and we'll explain it all to you, beginning with why Abaddon's here." LJ saw me glance at the posters covered with handwriting and arrows. "We're going to cover all that, too."

The only break we took was for LJ to run and pick up burgers for lunch. I was swimming upstream in a torrent of information, some I understood and some was too confusing. I was in awe of the smarts of LJ and Abaddon, although at this point I was getting suspicious those weren't their real names.

LJ called an end to our discussions at 3:00 to get to the Ford Theater and ensure everything was in place.

"Now, Charlie, I want you to stay unnoticed in the background. For the time being, you're just an interested citizen who has come to see a play. That means no talking to any press if they ask you how you like the play, why you came to see it, nothing. You understand?" Abaddon said as he walked me to the door, his hand on my shoulder.

"Newspaper people gonna be there?"

"Radio and TV too. At least they've been invited. Anyway, your time will come, but until then, sit in the back and leave as soon as it's over."

Abaddon held the door open after scanning the parking lot.

"I will, Mr. Abaddon. I got no problem doing that. And thank you. I can't say I figured it all out, but I know you and Mr. LJ have, so I'm good with it."

"Good, Charlie. It was nice meeting you."

The door shut quickly behind me.

I blinked in the harsh afternoon sun after spending all day in the depressing motel room. My head was swimming as I walked to my truck next to the still-overflowing dumpster that now sported a bumper crop of flies and aromas hard to forget. I wasn't sure what I had started, what was real, and how it had suddenly turned frightening. I was a black man born and raised in the Delta, so I knew fear; the kind I could see and hear and didn't surprise me anymore. But this was a fear of the blindness of what lay ahead, and I was scared of what it was going to look like when it came to pass.

I was so fixated on getting home to tame the whirlwinds in my head that I almost pulled out of the motel parking lot onto highway 61 in front of a speeding propane tanker. It thundered by, horn blaring, feet from my front bumper.

That was twice in one day I had the shit scared out of me.

## Part II

"Fathers shall not be put to death for their children, nor children for their fathers; only for his own guilt shall a man be put to death."

Deuteronomy 24:16

## Chapter 41

The closer the sun raced to the horizon, the better the front of the Ford Theater looked. LJ had paid two part-time painters / full-time dope heads to scrape and paint the wood trim and wash the white, hard plastic marquee. New black letters hung in the now less dingy slots of the marquee, "A Play like No Other in ? Acts" on top, and below, "Opening Night April 1st, 7 pm". New bulbs in the floodlights beckoned one and all to the island in a sea of blight. I parked down the street where it was darker. Abaddon's directive to go unnoticed had taken root.

As I walked under the marquee, I thought it didn't bode well that there were more open parking spots than taken in front of the theater.

The old ticket booth was unusable, with buckled paneling and missing ceiling tiles. Instead, a card table was set up at the door with a cash box and attended by a young, attractive black woman. I nodded, said hello, and paid her the minimal fee. As she looked down to make change, I couldn't help but admire the gloss of her straight hair with the slightest of curls resting on her shoulders. Her skin was light colored, almost matched by the soft brown blouse on her thin frame. When she looked up quickly, my eyes gave me away, and I looked down, feeling awkward. She smiled, handed me a ticket and a program and I sought relief through two black curtains. It wasn't what I expected.

Tucum's work surprised me. I guess I never noticed the carpentry work around his house because I wasn't looking past the years of wear that made it look like most farm houses. I looked for Tucum to compliment him, but he wasn't in sight.

I took a seat in the back row of a dozen folding chairs, nine or ten rows back from the stage. It was far from perfect, but there was no mistaking the courtroom softly illuminated by dim overhead lights.

The judge's bench was in the center, raised in the typical prominent position. It was sheathed in plywood but had been painted a dark brown and, from a distance, was a close-enough approximation of dignified courtroom wood. Attached to the right side of the bench, a foot lower and protruding out beyond the bench, was the witness stand, waist-high railing of 2x4's across the front, and behind it a simple wooden chair. To the left, along the wall, was the jury box, the back row of folding chairs higher than the front row. In front of the bench were two large tables covered in black cloth, probably to cover whatever marks and scratches eventually put them in a discount store. Two gray metal folding chairs were behind each table. On the wall to the right, on the edge of the illuminated courtroom, was a small desk and chair. The walls, likely canvasses for graffiti, were covered by more black curtains. Black also was stretched behind the bench from wall to wall, all meant to give focus and intensity to the stage.

I was impressed with what they had done, but as I looked at my watch and saw it was a few minutes from 7:00, I was disappointed by how few people sat in the courtroom gallery. I recognized a couple of faces in the dozen and a half people in the audience. There was an older man sitting in the front row who had walked around the stage looking through the viewfinder of a camera. The notepad and pen in his front pocket told me he was a reporter from the Greenville Current, obliged to write a story because of the money spent on advertisements of the play in their paper for the last week. Looking over the empty seats, I wondered if the money and effort spent on the newspaper ads and flyers around town were worth it.

With no other patrons having come in after me and no sign of late-comers out front, promptly at 7:00, the overhead lights went off, dousing the room in darkness.

Soft, random noises came from the stage and a moment later, a single flood light shone down on Abaddon, the intensity causing those few in the front row to squint and blink.

I thought Abaddon was overdressed in the motel room, but now I understood he considered those to be casual dress-down clothes. He wore a dark three-piece suit, the occasional glint showing from the sheen of the suit's quality fabric. I couldn't see much below his waist, but I expected his shoes would be a name I wouldn't recognize or ever afford. A red kerchief extended from his coat pocket, matching the solid red tie which contrasted and highlighted the gray speckled throughout his closely cropped hair. I'd never have the means to wear good style, but I knew it when I saw it. During our time in the motel, he didn't wear glasses, so I was surprised to see him wearing gold wire-rimmed glasses. They added to his air of sophistication, and I wondered if that was their sole purpose.

The room went silent.

"Ladies and gentlemen, welcome to a play unlike any you've seen. My name is Abaddon Thomas and I am the play's director. All the actors are amateurs and only a few actors have been given profile sheets of their characters and the pertinent facts of life and business in the year the play takes place.

"When the actors are in place, I will introduce the overall landscape of the play, if you will, and set the scene of the first act. No script means the time it will take for the play to reach a logical and natural conclusion is unknown, therefore, the ticket you purchased tonight will get you admittance every night the play continues. Tonight's first act will be the shortest; long enough, though, to set the scene of the trial and let the actors get their footing and become familiar with their roles."

Abaddon paused, slowly scanning the sparse audience.

"We will now dim the lights and allow the actors, some of whom have just been told their roles, to take their places. And as the play itself is now being revealed, so is the play's name." Abaddon gave another pause before spreading his hands wide.

"Ladies and gentlemen, I hope you enjoy...Delayed Justice."

The spotlight went dark and there was a smattering of short-lived clapping. Low lighting slowly brightened, allowing enough light for the audience to see bodies moving around the set, accompanied by shuffling feet and metal chairs scraping the concrete floor. As silence enveloped the room again, as if it were holding its breath, another lone spotlight shone on Abaddon, now standing next to the small desk and chair along the right-hand wall.

"The year is 1923. The place is Greenville. Our actors represent the people of that time; a time of growth and prosperity for a few, but also a time of stagnation and poverty for many. It was a time, in some ways unchanged for generations, in some ways a time that would–had to–inevitably change. But that was the future, unseen and incomprehensible in 1923. The past, though, was seen every day, felt every day, endured, perpetuated, and suffered.

"Ladies and gentlemen, imagine that among all the injustices occurring in 1923, one grievous yet common act, the stealing of land from one weaker by one stronger, would have been put on trial. In 1923 and all the previous years since the first acre of land was cleared and planted in the Delta, and for many years after, land was life, land was freedom, and land was independence. Without ownership of land, there was only servitude, there was hope abandoned, there was human potential vanquished. But, ladies and gentlemen, what if life was given a chance? What if life had its day in court in 1923?"

The spotlight faded and a moment later, bright light flooded the entire set, causing actors and audience alike to squint for several moments.

Abaddon had moved to the center of the courtroom and again addressed the audience.

"Each cast member will rise as I introduce them, beginning with the honorable Judge Lamar Tate. Judge Tate was elected to the bench in 1912 and is also a successful planter."

Lamar stood quickly, smiled broadly, and waved to the sparse audience he undoubtedly plainly saw as voters. Before sitting down, he adjusted the corners of his black gown as if to ensure the voters saw him in the garb he rightfully deserved.

"What an arrogant, self-centered asshole," I thought.

"Next, our jury members. First Mayor Campbell…"

The jurors rose as their names were called. Most were unrecognizable, but I hoped they would be well known when this was over. A glance over all the empty seats in the audience, and the lone reporter, tempered my hope.

"The defense attorney, Mr. Calder Ambrose. Mr. Ambrose graduated from Ole Miss Law School in 1920, but is already making a name for himself in Greenville."

Calder swiveled and gave a smile to the room.

"The prosecuting attorney is Mr. Lon Miller, an esteemed Greenville attorney."

Lon turned to the scattered audience and gave a half-wave before re-taking his seat.

"The defendant is Mr. Tucum Tutweiller…"

I was dumbfounded to see Tucum stand and turn toward the audience and I realized why I hadn't recognized him in the dim light. He looked more than well-groomed, he looked dignified, not quite on par with Abaddon, but darn good for the man I knew who preferred to go shirtless on all but the coldest days. His suit fit well and hid his ample belly. His goatee was trimmed, his blonde hair brushed back and free to glide around his back collar, now that oil that had looked permanently ingrained had been shampooed out. He looked Old South and for a moment I pictured a young Colonel Sanders on a chicken bucket.

"…Mr. Tutweiller is a wealthy planter, with over 1200 acres farmed with hands from 27 families who live in former slave quarters near the stately Tutweiller mansion. Some of the families, in fact, are descendants of slaves who were owned by Mr. Tutweiller's father."

"The plaintiff in the case is Mr. Elron Porter."

A light-skinned black man in his forties stood up, raised his hand, and retook his seat. Other than hearing his name in the motel earlier, I didn't recognize him.

"Mr. Porter grew up on the Tutweiller Plantation, toiling in those fields until he became the owner of his own land. Land that was allegedly stolen from him by the defendant.

"My role here is to act as a director of sorts, a moderator as needed, and to intercede to keep the trial moving along. As much as possible, I will only interrupt to keep the play following actual courtroom procedures. In deference to the experience of Judge Tate, I will only overrule him if an order will unduly affect a timely and satisfying conclusion of the play."

Abaddon had chosen his words carefully, but delivered them with little emphasis.

"Previously, I gave the attorneys a summary of the charges against Mr. Tutweiller, as well as a list of documents they can present as evidence and witnesses they may call as they wish. While the attorneys have had a short time to prepare their strategies, the judge and especially the jury, as in an actual trial, have little to no knowledge of what is to be presented. And neither do you, the audience, so consider yourselves a second jury, so to speak. At the conclusion of the trial, whenever that occurs, you will have made up your mind as to the guilt or innocence of the defendant, and all like him in 1923, and will be able to justify your decision to the world. We also hope you will have learned something new about history, good or bad, and something of human nature."

Abaddon paused and scanned the court.

"Let us begin our journey on delayed justice. Judge Tate, the courtroom is yours."

The spotlight over Abaddon faded to dark, and he took his place at the small table in the shadows against the wall.

'Crack', the sound of the gavel reverberated off the cinder blocks.

"This court is now in session with the case of Mr. Elron Porter vs. Mr. Tucum Tutweiller. The plaintiff's attorney, Mr. Lon Miller, will now present his opening statement," Judge Tate said, almost giddy from being in the spotlight of a play.

Mr. Miller rose and strode slowly by the defense table, stopping in front of the jury box railing. Twelve white faces stared back. He made eye contact with each juror, clasped his hands together, and boomed his words so loudly it made some jump in their chairs.

"A travesty! That's what this is. A travesty!"

As he began to pivot away from the jury, Lon continued, "A man...," he quickly swung back to the jury, leaning in, "...oh, and his wife...and his children...his parents, grandparents...his whole family who's dependent on him for shelter and food, can be given less, much less than what a chosen few have, can work so much harder than those few, can suffer a life those few can look at every day but never see, can finally achieve his...and his family's...dream of owning land, only to have it stolen by the few whose hearts have turned black with greed; dark hearts that pump blood infused with ego, arrogance, and a lust for power over others."

I realized I was holding my breath, so powerful were those words that echoed off the black walls. I exhaled and thought it was the loudest sound in the room. The jury was motionless, all eyes upon Mr. Miller.

"I will present to each and every one of you the evidence that shows the defendant, Mr. Tutweiller," Lon turned quickly and pointed, "initiated a conspiracy to steal land rightfully owned by my client, Mr. Elron Porter, to return that land to his ownership, and Mr. Porter back under his control and subservience. With the knowledge from witness accounts, you will have the opportunity, no, you will have the duty as objective jurors and the obligation as compassionate and God-fearing people, to find Mr. Tutweiller guilty of charges of criminal conspiracy and theft."

Mr. Miller looked at each juror with the faintest hint of a smile before returning to his seat.

Lamar Tate stared intently at Lon as he strode by the bench. The smile Lamar sported a minute ago was gone. He finally looked at Calder Ambrose and said, "The attorney for the defense, Mr. Calder Ambrose, will now give his opening statement."

Calder stood and buttoned his suit jacket, looking apprehensive, not unusual for a late-twenties junior lawyer. His youthful look was accentuated by a too-closely cropped haircut and large eyeglasses that made his head look the size of a twelve-year-old's. He closed the short distance over to the jury box, wringing his hands nervously on the way.

Young Calder stopped in front of the jurors, adjusted his glasses, and cleared his throat.

"Ladies and gentlemen of the jury, thank you for doing your civic duty and serving as jurists. You do it freely and willfully, but you also do it with a commitment to the rule of law that says you must respond to a jury summons and, if selected, serve for the duration of the trial. Abiding by the law is not a gray area. It's not a decision based on whether you like or dislike the law. For you, me, and most in the courtroom, it's an obligation to respect and abide by the law and to respect those who, like us, do the same."

I could see Calder shaking off his nervousness with every sentence.

"The charges against my client, Mr. Tutweiller, would never have been brought if the plaintiff and his attorney believed the same as you and me that the law is the law, the law cannot be described, construed, or imagined to be anything other than what it is.

"This will be a short trial, ladies and gentlemen. As you will see, my client followed the law in legally taking possession of the land he is unjustly charged with stealing. The plaintiff obviously didn't like the result, but he has no basis for charging my client with any crime when, as I will show, it was the plaintiff himself who did not follow the law, either through ignorance or willful negligence."

Calder smiled at the jury. In a lower, kindly voice, he said, "Thank you again for serving, and I assure you that you'll be back home and back to work soon."

Calder unbuttoned his suit jacket and sat, a satisfied smirk hanging on his face.

Judge Tate shuffled papers, most, if not all, blank, I assumed.

"Mr. Miller, would you like to call a witness?"

"Yes, Your Honor, I would like to call the defendant, Mr. Tucum Tutweiller, to the stand."

Tucum stood, buttoned his jacket, and walked to the stand. I was surprised that Tucum knew it was proper etiquette to button the jacket when standing. He must have been coached more than he let on, I thought.

There was no swearing on the Bible, so Tucum took his seat.

Lon Miller approached Tucum and stood a foot away for several long moments, looking him over. Tucum was not intimidated; in fact, I thought he already looked to be on the verge of losing his patience.

"Mr. Tutweiller, would you tell the court how long you have lived at the Tutweiller Plantation?" Lon asked.

"Well, I suppose…," Tucum glanced over at Abaddon, who remained expressionless in the shadows, "… that would be all my life."

"And at what point did you buy the plantation?"

"Buy?"

"Yes, sir. Buy."

Tucum shifted in his seat. "Well, I never paid any money in order to become the owner, if that's what you mean."

"Oh, so you became the owner of 1200 acres of prime farmland, a palatial plantation home, and many servants and farmhands, as well as their living quarters, and you didn't pay a dime for it?"

"That's right." Tucum's teeth were clenching. Not only could he dress up, but he could act too.

"So, would you please tell the Court how someone acquires such expensive property for free? We'd all like to know so we can do it too."

Tucum squinted hard at Lon and looked as if he was taking this questioning personally. He squared his shoulders before answering.

"My daddy left it to me."

"So there you go. You did it the old-fashioned way, Mr. Tutweiller. Congratulations and count your blessings. All but a very few have a much different path to land ownership. First, we have to work hard to make enough money, not only to survive on but to save a little. Once years of savings have built up, we have to find a banker who will loan us money, which is as rare as snow in July for a black farmer in 1923, or get money from the USDA if the agent is inclined to treat black farmers fairly."

Lon had been slowly making his way to the jury box as he spoke. He now turned back to Tucum.

"Mr. Tutweiller, are you aware of the process I just described?"

"Sure. You threw in some bullshit, or rather…," Tucum paused to look up to the judge, saying, "...sorry, Your Honor," before continuing, "it's straightforward without trying to confuse it like you did."

"And how is it straightforward, Mr. Tutweiller?"

"You get a bank loan or you go to the USDA if you need to. It ain't magic."

"For some, it is quite mystical," Lon said as he saw Calder begin to rise from his chair.

"But we'll come back to that later," Lon said as he glanced up and locked eyes with Judge Tate's stare.

"And are you aware of any farmers who bought farmland by the straightforward process you described?"

"Oh, sure. Most of them."

"And how many are black farmers, Mr. Tutweiller?"

"Today?" Tucum looked genuinely confused, real or acting, I couldn't tell.

"Today, as in 1923 today."

"Well, I don't personally know any, but I'm sure there are some."

"So, you've heard about more blacks who were unsuccessful than successful, is that right?"

Calder Ambrose had been inching closer to the front of his seat, but looked apprehensive about objecting. It wasn't until Judge Tate gave him the eye that Calder rose and said sternly, "Objection, Your Honor, the plaintiff's counsel is leading the defendant with conjecture."

"Sustained." Judge Tate looked at Lon and said, "Mr. Miller, let's move along, and I strongly recommend going in a different direction."

Lon looked at the floor for several seconds before answering, "Yes, Your Honor."

After pacing in front of Tucum, Lon turned and asked, "How many white farmers do you know of who have lost their land through foreclosure?"

Tucum seemed to think intently for a moment.

"None that I can rightly recall."

"And how many black farmers do you know who lost their land through foreclosure?"

"Well, it's none of my business who pays their bills and who don't. It don't matter a rat's ass whether they're white, black, or plaid; it ain't none of my business."

Tucum was getting intense, and it was the first time I wondered how much of this act was coming from his heart instead of his head.

Lon turned away from Tucum, as if to discount his answer. He then pivoted to face the jury.

"Mr. Tutweiller, tell me about your dealings with the USDA."

Tucum looked over in Abaddon's direction for a second, gathering his thoughts.

"Well, I've done some business with them in the past, but if we've had good years, I usually don't have to get help from them."

"And if farmers such as yourself have, say, a couple of bad years, would you lose your farm to a bank or the USDA?"

Tucum looked at the floor as he stroked his goatee before answering.

"No sir, it would take a lot of bad years for me to lose my farm."

"And why is that?"

"My farm's worth a lot of money and I own it free and clear. The bank and USDA respect that. They know I'm good for the money, eventually."

"Would they have the same respect, as you call it, if you had an outstanding loan on the farm?"

"Hell, I don't know. You gotta ask them." Tucum looked at Lon like he had asked the most absurd question.

"Do you think small farms should receive the same generous accommodations large farms like yours have been given?"

Calder wasn't fast enough to object before the gavel hit the judge's desk with a loud crack, causing the audience and jurors to jump once again.

"Counselors, approach the bench," Lamar said loudly, his face turning red.

Lon and Calder, followed by Abaddon, lined up against, and chest high, to the edge of the bench, looking up at Judge Tate, who was visibly irritated. Judge Tate leaned over and yelled in a whisper.

"What the hell is this, Mr. Thomas? I didn't know what to expect, but it sure as hell wasn't this. It seems you intend to hold a public, make-believe lynching of plantation owners, and I'm not going to be a part of it. My ass is going to make-believe right out of your so-called play, if that's what this is all about."

Tate glared at Abaddon, who remained composed.

"Judge Tate, I'm sorry you're upset. Please accept my apologies. I can assure you my intent is to also show the good side of Mr. Tutweiller and I expect Calder here will do just that. Please have patience, Judge. You've seen how quickly attitudes toward defendants change in real trials."

Judge Tate was silent for a moment and visibly took a deep breath, his hunched stature relaxing a fraction.

"Well, it better happen damn quick."

Abaddon nodded.

"Let's get back to it, then," Judge Tate said as he set the gavel down.

The three left the bench and returned to their positions.

Abaddon quickly sat at the desk in the shadows and began writing.

Lon Miller resumed his questioning, standing close enough to Tucum he could smell his aftershave.

"Mr. Tutweiller, you've had business dealings with Mr. Faron Church, the USDA representative?"

"Didn't I already tell you that?" Tucum said with obvious aggravation.

Lon pivoted toward the jury, ignoring Tucum's question.

"Do you associate with him socially?"

Tucum's chest came out as his right hand clenched the armrest.

"Socially? Yeah, I mean we frequent the same restaurants and run across each other at events. It's a small town, Mr. Miller."

"Yes, it is, Mr. Tutweiller…in so many ways," Lon said as he looked at each individual on the jury.

Lon turned and took two steps back toward Tucum again.

"Has Mr. Church been to your home, Mr. Tutweiller?"

"Objection, Your Honor!" Calder stood so quickly his chair slid back, making a short screech against the concrete floor.

"This line of questioning pertains to Mr. Tutweiller's private life and is not related to the charges against him."

Judge Tate gave a slight nod and glanced at Lon.

"Your Honor, I intend to show the extent of relationships between Mr. Tutweiller and those he has business dealings with in order to show it was in his power to do what he is accused of. I will also point out that without establishing the facts, Mr. Tutweiller's defense will rest on conjecture and opinion."

Judge Tate's irritation spread across his face in a grimace.

"Mr. Miller, and Mr. Thomas…," Judge Tate glanced back to the darkened wall, "…I will allow this line of questioning to continue, but…," the Judge paused as he regained his composure, "...overruled. You may continue, Mr. Miller, carefully," Judge Tate said irritably.

Lon took a deep breath, shoulders rising, back straightening.

I realized my eyes were dry and wondered if I had stopped blinking. I scanned the audience and stopped on the newspaper reporter staring ahead intently, his writing hand clenching his pencil poised for action.

"Mr. Tutweiller, as I was saying, has Mr. Church been to your home, socially or professionally?"

"Yes, he and his wife have come to Christmas parties and I guess they've been invited to a dinner party or two," Tucum answered.

"Over how many years would you say?"

Tucum stroked his goatee slowly.

"Twenty years or so."

"It's my understanding your father passed away and willed the land to you seven years ago. Is that right?"

"That's about right."

"So, what you're saying is that since the first day you inherited the land, you've continued the custom of inviting the USDA representative to your house for parties many times each year."

"Objection. Counsel is leading the defendant!" Calder shouted.

Judge Tate shrunk in stature as he exhaled. "Overruled. It's a harmless question, counselor," Judge Tate said. "Let's get on with it."

"Yes, Your Honor," Calder answered and sat down.

Suddenly, Abaddon emerged from the shadows.

"Ladies and gentlemen, please allow for a director's pause for just a moment."

Abaddon motioned Calder and Lon over. I looked at Judge Tate and found his look reminded me of confusion, aggravation, and helplessness, all thrown in a blender.

Abaddon leaned close to Calder and Lon, saying, "Gentlemen, you are doing exceptionally well, but let's not spin up the Judge any more for the time being. Calder, do your best to show your client in the best light."

Calder and Lon nodded, and the three returned to their positions.

Lon looked up at the judge, “No further questions for now, Your Honor.”

Judge Tate stared into the gloom that nearly shrouded Abaddon as he said, “Mr. Ambrose, are you going to cross-exam your client?”

Calder rose quickly, buttoning his coat as he stepped around the desk.

“I am, Your Honor.” Calder wasted no time; talking as he stepped toward the witness box.

“Mr. Tutweiller, you own approximately 1200 acres, is that correct?”

“Yes, sir.”

“And in the year of our Lord, 1923, that’s a sizable farm, would you say?”

“Not the biggest, but big enough.”

Calder paused, considering Tucum’s response.

“Big enough, you say. Big enough for what, exactly?”

“Well, big enough to generate enough income to keep the farm a viable business.”

“Oh, but Mr. Tutweiller, we all know planters like you with land stretching to the horizon, even seen from the second-floor balcony of your mansions, have no concern about money. You’re all rich beyond what the common man can even imagine, isn’t that right?”

“Well, I don’t know where you got that idea, but you don’t become a farmer if you want to get rich. You start a railroad, or lumber mills, or steel factories, but you don’t become a farmer.”

“And why is that Mr. Tutweiller?”

“Too many risks that can wipe you out.”

Calder looked at Tucum with raised eyebrows.

“There’s the weather, too little or too much rain, plant disease, insect infestations, low prices at harvest time. There’s a lot that can cost you a lot, but it takes a lot to go right to make a little money."

Calder turned toward the jury. "Interesting clarification, Mr. Tutweiller. It seems relying on a large farm isn't a sure thing."

"The only sure thing is that it's sure going to be hard and risky every damn year." Tucum glanced up at the judge, "Excuse me, Your Honor, I meant every year."

"Mr. Tutweiller, how many people do you employ on your farm?" Calder continued without a pause.

"Well, there are twenty-seven families living on my place. The men work the farm year-round and the women and older children help out at harvest time. Plus, if we've had a good growin year, I hire more help to get the crops in."

"You say families live on your place. Do they live outdoors or in tents?"

"Of course not. I wouldn't abide by that. I provide each family with a house to live in."

"Well, that is mighty fine and I imagine you charge your employees a reasonable rent?"

"Not at all."

"You mean the rent's unreasonable?"

"No. I mean I don't charge them anything."

"Well, Mr. Tutweiller, that doesn't sound like a good business practice. Why in the world would you ignore a good source of income?"

"I treat my employees like I would want to be treated. I want them to be happy and stay on the farm. Most have lived right alongside me all my life, so much that they're like family to me."

Motion from the bench averted my eyes from Tucum. Judge Tate had reclined in his chair and folded his hands across his belly, a satisfied look settling on his face.

"Well Mr. Tutweiller, clearly you are a magnanimous employer who…"

"Objection, Your Honor," Lon stated loudly as he rose. "Defense counsel is concluding the defendant's character based solely on the slimmest of testimony from the defendant himself." Judge Tate unclasped his hands and sat up. The satisfied look vacated as quickly as it had arrived.

"Overruled. The testimony is quite convincing, Mr. Miller."

Lon looked at Judge Tate for a moment before answering, "Yes, Your Honor."

Calder put his hand to his chin, regrouping as he stared at chips in the concrete floor.

"Mr. Tutweiller, is it safe to say some of the families have lived on your farm for generations?"

"Yes, sir, some go back to my grandfather's time."

"And, here, almost sixty years after the end of slavery, they're still on the farm. Nothing's changed for them then?"

Tucum paused for a moment, giving his goatee a slow stroke.

"Maybe from a distance it looks like it did back then, but everything's changed. Back then, those people had no freedoms at all. Today my people are free to stay or leave anytime they want. They're free to work for me, another planter, or move to a city and work in a factory. They can do whatever they want to, just like you and me."

"So, they could even leave your employ and start their own farm. You'd be ok with that?"

"Absolutely. I'd even help them get started if they needed it."

"But the fact is that very few do that. You clearly provide such a good life for them they have no reason to leave."

"Objection. Defense has not clearly demonstrated the employees have a 'good life'," Lon interjected.

Judge Tate hunched forward and stared at Lon for a moment. Again, glancing in Abaddon's direction, he said, "Overruled. Continue, Mr. Ambrose."

Movement from the front row caught my eye. The Current reporter's pencil was scrambling across the notepad.

"Do they, Mr. Tutweiller? Do your employees have reason to leave your plantation?"

"None at all. I provide them a good home, honest work, and I treat them like family. It's a good life for those people."

Calder turned toward the judge, "No further questions, Your Honor."

Before the judge could speak, Abaddon emerged from the shadows and took his place in the center of the courtroom.

"Ladies and gentlemen. As I stated in the introduction, this first act will be the shortest and therefore this concludes the first night of Delayed Justice. Living outside the confines of a script enables us all to be a part of an emerging creation, minute by minute. I hope you've enjoyed the beginning of this journey, one we'll continue tomorrow night. Again, your ticket is good for the length of the play, so we hope to see you tomorrow night. Thank you for coming."

The lights dimmed and through the scraping of chairs and the start of conversations among the few audience members came Judge Tate's voice from the bench.

"Abaddon, Abaddon. Come here!"

Abaddon was expecting the summons.

"Yes, Judge?"

"We need to talk. You have some serious explaining to do!"

Abaddon turned to scan who remained in the room.

"Follow me, Judge."

Abaddon walked around the bench to the black curtain stretching the width of the room. After grabbing and pulling, he found the seam between two sections and held it open for the Judge to step through. A few feet beyond was a wooden door that had given up trying to hold paint that was applied decades before. Abaddon held the door open for the Judge, then switched on an overhead bulb and closed the storage room door. Mainly empty rusty shelves surrounded them, an old mop bucket with fetid water occupied a corner, and rat droppings were scattered across the rest of the room.

"Now what do you want to…" Abaddon was cut off.

"I will not be lied to, do you understand me? Not by a farmhand, a sheriff, or some out-of-town play director! Do you hear me?"

Abaddon felt spit land on his chin, but remained expressionless.

"And what have I lied to you about?"

"No fucking script, that's what. A blind armadillo can see you've given everyone a script except me. And I want to know why!"

Judge Tate's face was the color of a ripe Ponchatoula strawberry.

"Judge, if you remember, I did mention in the introduction tonight that I gave a few actors a brief advance notice of the architecture of the case so they could prepare their roles. They are the catalyst that moves the play along and if they did not have a tactical plan ahead of time, the play would sputter out, I'm afraid."

Lamar glared at Abaddon, absorbing his explanation, but finding no faults.

"Well, how do you explain Tucum Tutweiller? He has an answer ready for every question. You're telling me you didn't give him a script?"

"No, sir, I did not. I will admit that I described the character he is playing, the plantation he owns, the employees he has, and life in 1923, but I did not give him a script. He has surprised me with his acting. You're right, he clearly prepared himself for the role."

"Huh, he seems like a dumb country boy who probably didn't make it to high school…."

"He didn't."

"What? Make it to high school?"

"I certainly don't know the gentleman, but that's what I've been told. He's supposedly very well-read, though. Intelligence takes many forms, Judge, and my experience has taught me it sometimes takes the right situation to see it. I think this play is showing us Tucum's and I'm thankful for it."

The judge looked away and ran his stubby fingers through his sparse gray hair.

"I don't like where this is going. It seems this is just a fucking public bashing of white planters. You can say it's 1923 but folks may forget that and then I'll have racist stink on me. I've got an election in a few months and I will not jeopardize losing votes, black ones especially, over this shit."

"Judge, I hear your concerns, and let's talk after the performance tomorrow night. Give it another night and I trust you'll be more comfortable."

"You better hope so, or you'll be looking for another judge."

Lamar brushed past Abaddon, flinging the old door open hard enough to knock off a flurry of paint chips.

Abaddon watched him go and thought, "We're already way beyond that, Judge."

# Chapter 42

As I got out of my car parked in the shadows at the back of the Gin Inn, an 18 wheeler rolled by on highway 61, seen for a moment before being absorbed into the heavy darkness that covered the farmland. My knock on room 21 was answered with a crack of the door, a glimpse of one eye peering out before the door opened wide. I quickly stepped in, and LJ closed the door behind me.

"Well, Charlie, what did you think of Act One of your play?" Abaddon asked. He sat in what passed as a lounge chair, looking comfortable in slacks and a polo shirt, a glass of brown water in hand I assumed was whiskey.

"I didn't know what to expect of y'all's play, but I tell you, if I could snap my fingers and it would be 7:00 tomorrow night, I sho nuff would. I can't wait to see where this goes." I smiled and shook my head at the faces around the room.

"We can't either, Charlie, so let's figure out where we want it to go."

Past midnight, a line of vehicles weaved around the potholes of The Gin Inn and onto 61, most turning north, a couple turning south; all heading toward Act Two.

## Chapter 43

Kim retrieved the Saturday paper from the walk, wearing a robe and slippers. The morning was cool and the first of spring pollen cast a faint dusting of yellow on the cars and concrete. Light green buds shimmered from hardwoods up and down their quiet street of modest homes.

"Another quiet day, in a quiet town, living a quiet life. Yee-haw." Kim muttered, but then shook resentment out of her mind as she stepped into the house, part of a late and frequently forgotten New Year's resolution to improve her positivity.

She settled into the small living room that looked out to the oaks in the front yard and nearly identical houses across the street, a scene that hadn't changed in fifty years. She scanned the front page of the Current while taking the first sips of a steaming cup of coffee, inhaling the soothing fragrance, and burrowing into the couch. Politics, crime, and a women's shelter fundraiser were noteworthy enough to fill page one. Setting her cup down, she opened the paper to pages two and three. As expected, ads dominated and the few articles were of no interest to her. She breathed a sigh of frustration, wondering again why they even bothered to buy the paper. Page four continued the prevalence of ads but one skinny column snatched her attention.

**It May Be "A Play like No Other"**

by Andrew Falstaff

Last night, the scantily renovated Ford Theater was the site of an unusual but surprisingly stimulating experiment in impromptu play production. As absurd as the premise is of Justice Delayed, a 1920s courtroom cast with amateur actors without a script, the subject—the stealing of small black-owned farms by wealthy white planters— provides the potential for raw, emotional debates on local history seldom discussed.

This reviewer began with low expectations, but when the lights dimmed at the end of the night, I had the feeling I had been in an actual courtroom watching the start of a saga I'm now eager to see play out.

While I am recommending this play, I do so with the caveat that with no script, the trial could quickly turn from engaging to tedious at the drop of a gavel. But if tonight builds on the intrigue introduced last night, you'll be sorry if you're not in the front row.

Kim settled the paper on her lap, retrieved her cup, and took sips while savoring the warmth on her palms. She had been skeptical about the idea and didn't hold back when Lon first told her about it. But now, she had to admit she felt the same as the writer. While the stage was not what one would expect in the high culture of a major city, Kim found the play interesting. Lon's performance was pleasantly impressive. His acting came across as natural, almost instinctive, just as she had seen him in actual courtrooms. She knew his demeanor came from a mental detachment from himself and an immersion in the case, the right and wrong of it, the perpetrator and the aggrieved party. It's that ability to focus on objectivity and not emotion that made him an excellent lawyer, and she was thankful to be reminded of that.

The sound of the bedroom door opening and the rapid click-click-click of Holly's nails on the hardwood floor snapped her out of daydream thoughts. Slurping from a water bowl and a clank of a coffee cup sliding by another in the cabinet came from the kitchen. The slurping stopped and the rat terrier came tearing around the corner to leap up on Kim's lap, scrunching the paper and causing her to lift her cup high.

"Holly! Easy girl. Momma's not ready for all that excitement."

Lon followed Holly around the corner, eyed the scene on the couch, and decided the love seat was the safer option.

"You were out late last night," Kim said without looking at Lon. Her tone was beyond merely conversational.

"Yea, later than I thought I'd be," Lon replied as he took a long sip of coffee, followed by a deep exhale and rubbing of eyes.

"You know, for an impromptu play, y'all sure do a lot of talking about it ahead of time. Some might even call that 'scripting'."

Lon's bloodshot eyes stared at her over his cup. He lowered his cup, and she waited for his explanation. Instead, he deflected as a good lawyer does.

"You still like it as much this morning as you did last night?"

Kim's shoulders dropped in disappointment at being manipulated.

"Way to dodge my comment, Mr. Prosecutor. Even after the exhausting job I did for you selling tickets at the door?" She said facetiously. "Yes, I did. The jury's still out though…or is it? Well, I don't know, but I have to admit it became interesting enough that I'm looking forward to tonight. Someone else liked it too."

Kim stretched to hand the paper over to Lon.

"Page four. He doesn't praise you by name, and I think that's grounds for a lawsuit."

Lon set his coffee down, smiled at Kim, and opened the paper. Kim watched his face for any reaction as he read the article twice, but he showed none.

"Well, I think that would be called a good review in any theater circles."

"I'll go ahead and make a spot on the bookshelf for your Tony award," Kim said playfully.

Lon threw a pillow at Kim, causing her to spill her coffee and Holly to scamper for safety.

They spent the rest of the morning back in bed, enjoying each other and the quiet of a small town Saturday. Kim felt like she was reconnecting with an old friend, actually two old friends - her husband and a feeling from memories of contentment.

## Chapter 44

The gentle spring breeze drifted through the French doors, wafting the aroma of hot filet mignon steaks throughout the dining room, into the expansive living room, and out the far doors to mingle with the smells of sun-warmed dirt and emerging cotton plants. Judge Tate and Mayor Campbell savored their first bites in silence, letting the hill country beef nearly melt in their mouths.

"Damn, that's better than a penny whore at a dollar store convention," Judge Tate said as his steak knife sliced through another ample piece.

The mayor grunted.

And so the conversation, or lack of, went until the two declared victory and retreated to wing-back chairs and heavy whiskey glasses.

"That was a damn fine meal, Judge. Damn fine."

"Yes, it was, Mayor, but I wasn't sure I was going to have much of an appetite. My stomach's been twisted around a skinning pole since last night, trying to figure out what these niggers are up to."

"I wish I could say I got it figured out, but I can't decide if we're doing our part to support the so-called arts in town or we're setting ourselves up to be skewered from asshole to eyeball," Mayor Campbell answered.

Lamar pondered that mental image and took a long swig of whiskey, the ice cubes tinkling the bottom of the glass. He then picked up a brass bell by the long wooden handle and swung it vigorously.

The mayor winced at the loud clanging.

A moment later, a side door opened behind them and Lamar hollered, "Two more whiskeys." The door shut softly with a faint click. The mayor noted Lamar didn't acknowledge the help any more than he would have if the wind had blown the door open.

Lamar set the bell down and said, "It feels like this could be one of those *Revenge of the Swamp Monster* movies, except it's *Revenge of the Niggers*. And if it is, why the hell are they going after me, and probably you too, before it's all over? We need to dig into this before we're covered up in shit. We can start by finding out who Abaddon and LJ are. Put the sheriff on finding out everything he can about these characters."

"I'll drop by his house this afternoon," the mayor answered dutifully.

"And have his deputies find out where they're staying and keep an eye on them. I want to know everything they do when they're not putting on an impromptu screwing of the white man."

# Chapter 45

I pulled up to Tucum's around dinner time, or lunch as folks up north call it, two deer sausage sandwiches and cokes in a bag. His old mutt didn't bother getting up from his depression in the front yard among the tires and car parts. A gust of wind picked up scraps of paper and displaced them a few feet. Otherwise, everything looked the same as it had for years. Change in this part of the Delta rarely visited and never stayed long when it did.

"I wanted to see what it was like sharing a meal with a famous actor," I said as I handed over a sandwich to Tucum. He had laid down paper towels as plates and unrolled the last few inches of a potato chip bag, about as fancy a table setting as seen at Tucum's.

"Well, your ass stopped at the wrong house. You best get back in your truck and head down the dusty road cause you ain't gonna find one here, that's for damn sure."

We both chuckled. We then clasped hands and bowed our heads so Tucum could say grace.

"Dear Lord, we thank you for your love and forgiveness. You've seen fit to rescue us from wasted lives and we thank you every day. Please help us stay strong and work our way a little closer to you every day, Lord. And we pray we justify our lives to you today, that we may do somethin to help others. Please bless this food and bless my friend Charlie here. In your name, Jesus Christ, we pray. Amen."

"Amen." I answered. We unclasped our hands, and I looked at Tucum.

He broke the momentary silence, saying, "Well, what you waiting for? This sandwich ain't gonna jump to your mouth on its own."

"Tucum, I've always thought it, but now I'm seeing there's more than meets the eye with you. Your love for Christ really inspires me; always has. You know, and don't take this wrong, but I figure if Jesus can forgive you for doing worse things than me, then he shouldn't have to think twice about forgivin me."

Tucum set his sandwich down and gave a belly-shaking laugh.

"Charlie, no offense taken, my friend." His laugh trailed off, and he stared down deep into the table."Here's what I think, and I've never spoken these words to nobody. The way me and Christ get along is he promised to save my soul if I truly believe in him, and I do with all my heart. My part is to follow his commandments and treat everyone as my brother or sister. And I do, for the most part. The part of me that will never change, and I've told him he's just got to accept it, is I will tolerate sins against me up to a point. If I am threatened or someone steals from me, I will beat their ass to within their last breath. Difference is now, other than not killin them, I will drop to my knees afterwards and ask God's forgiveness if I have offended him. You've read the Old Testament, Charlie. God had a temper and so do I. I figure he made me in his image in that respect."

"I can see God in you, Tucum, I surely can. I didn't at first, but I sure do now," I said, sincere as hell.

We each took substantial bites of sandwich and chewed for a few moments. I took a swig of Coke before saying, "I also see a hint of Marlon Brando, maybe Cary Grant, and a few other stars in you. You old fox, you been keeping yo actin talent a secret!"

"Shit, Charlie, thank you for the flattery, but I'm playin the only character I know. I just try to imagine how old Tucum Tutweiller would behave if he was a plantation owner back in the day. Let me tell you, I don't think me or you would want to hang around him for long."

"Well, I can't wait to see him again tonight. Does he have any surprises for us?"

"I don't know, Charlie. You know there's no script…," Tucum winked at me, "…but I have thought about what he would likely say if given the opportunity. Now, that's enough talk. Let's get busy with this fine deer sausage."

## Chapter 46

I felt a pang in my heart when I turned onto the long Tate Plantation drive and saw the mansion at the end of the oak alley illuminated by the late afternoon sun. Suppressed memories of my old life living here tried to escape the dark box I kept them in. It's how I had decided to live, one life dead and best forgotten; a new life off the plantation as alive as I could make it. I felt the two starting to mingle the closer I got. I vowed not to stay long.

Down the rutted shack road a quarter mile past my old shack stood what I remembered was the Legare's. I turned the truck off and gave the door a loud slam so as not to surprise April with an unexpected knock on the door. While I was circling around a large mud puddle in front of the door, the squeak of a hinge stopped me. Looking up, I saw the side of a face peering out.

"Miss April, is that you? It's Charlie, Charlie Neely. Not sure if you remember me. You was a little girl last I saw you. I used to work here. I knew your parents."

The door opened wider.

"Yessa, Mr. Neely, I remember you a little."

"Could we talk, Miss April, if it's not too much trouble?"

April looked me over, thinking, and then she opened the door wide and smoothed out her dress.

"Come in, Mr. Neely. Be careful on those bricks. They'll move on you."

I hopped to the bricks that were nearly submerged in the puddle and grabbed the doorframe when the bricks wobbled underfoot.

I stepped into a memory with things rearranged over time. Each shack was altered by successive residents, but the bones of the structures showed through every one of them. April's decorating, though, made the shack feel welcoming. A light colored rug covered the center of the room and most of the well-worn wood flooring that long ago lost any luster it once had. Framed pictures of family hung on the walls, distracting attention from the yellowed newspaper tacked to the wood walls for insulation. Pots, pans, and dishes were stacked orderly on shelves above the sink and her bed was neatly made, covered by a white quilt with randomly embroidered rose buds and stems.

"Would you like a cup of coffee, Mr. Neely? It will take a few minutes to make, but it ain't no bother."

"No thank you, Miss April. It be late for me to drink coffee. I'll take a glass of water, though."

April filled a glass from a faded white pitcher, crossed over to a small table for two, and set my glass down. She motioned to the other chair, and we both sat. An awkward hush settled over us. I was suddenly unsure of myself, feeling like a stranger in an all too familiar setting. The young girl I knew was now a grown young woman sitting across from me, waiting for me to speak.

"That's good water," I said, wiping my lips with my shirtsleeve, then feeling self-conscious about my lack of manners.

"I don't suppose you came out here after all these years to check on my water, Mr. Neely."

Her words snapped my eyes to hers and I was looking into eyes much older than her years. They had a depth and darkness deepened by sorrow I recognized from my mother and grandmother when I was a child. The difference was I now understood some of what caused it.

I smiled at her, appreciative of her honest talk.

"No, Miss April, yo water wasn't even on my mind. Not at all." I paused and could see a hint of aggravation forming at the corner of her eyes.

"Do you remember a man named LJ visitin Mr. Tate a few days ago?"

"I do. Mr. Marshall."

"Yes, well, he's from up north, I'm sure you could tell, and probably not used to readin people down here, but he asked me to check on you."

April's gaze quickly dropped to her hands.

"Why would he think I need checkin on? We hardly spoke."

"It's because he read you to be sad, beyond sad is what he said, with a big dose of scared mixed in."

April turned her head to the wall. I felt like I was trespassing on something so private even she stayed away from it.

"Anyway, Miss April, it might have complicated things if he came back out here, so he asked me to come see you."

April turned back to the table and took a deep breath before raising her eyes.

"I don't know what you want, Mr. Neely. If you came to see if I's fine, then yes, I's fine."

I had to think for a moment. I had the urge to thank her and be on my way and off the plantation I never wanted to return to, but something made it pass.

"You bein treated alright, Miss April? Is somebody not treatin you right?"

She stared at me so intensely I thought she might explode with anger. Instead, her bottom lip began to tremble, and a tear spilled out of her left eye. Many more followed before I left.

I drove in slow gear down the plantation drive, so slow I could count the rows in the cotton fields on either side of the road and every piece of gravel that crunched under the tires. Confused anger and fear boiled inside me. I wanted to be back in my life bartending, living in my trailer, being dirt poor, with not a care in the world. Now I was suddenly filled with the heaviness of caring for others, some passed and some wishing for their turn. I felt a burden that had me wondering if I would be better off wishing for mine.

## Chapter 47

I parked down the street from the Ford Theater again, this time not out of caution, but because there wasn't a parking space any closer. A line at the front door and a Dodge van with the WLBT TV Jackson logo parked out front excited me. I also wondered if the world was going to be better for it.

The few audience members the night before had turned into a choice of a few empty seats. I took the last open seat in the last row and only had a moment to scan the audience before the lights dimmed. The murmur of the audience tailed off and then stopped altogether when the center spotlight illuminated Abaddon. Movement to my right caused me to turn to see someone holding a large video camera on their right shoulder, their left hand turning the lens.

"Ladies and gentlemen, welcome to the second act of Justice Delayed. For those not here last night, and that's most of you, you're no doubt here because you heard from someone or read in the Greenville Current that last night was a "surprisingly stimulating experiment in impromptu play production," as Mr. Falstaff of the Current wrote, and thank you, Mr. Falstaff, for that review."

Abaddon squinted into the front row, where Mr. Falstaff sat alongside a reporter from Jackson.

"The year is 1923 and the defendant in our case, Mr. Tucum Tutweiller, is accused of stealing land from the plaintiff, Mr. Elron Porter, an employee of Mr. Tutweiller and his father before him.

"We concluded last night with the defense attorney, Mr. Calder Ambrose, questioning his client on the witness stand. Ladies and gentlemen, the journey continues..."

The spotlight dimmed quickly, and after a moment, the courtroom lights came up to full intensity. All the actors were in place, all looking expectantly at Judge Tate like sprinters waiting for the starting gun.

The gavel cracked, followed by, "This court is now in session." Judge Tate's demeanor differed greatly from the first night. His giddiness of being in a play had turned into resentment at somehow being played. I could hear it in his voice, see it in his face and movements, and it felt satisfying.

"Mr. Miller, the court is yours."

Lon stood and buttoned his coat. He wore a different three piece suit, a lighter blue with a bright yellow tie. He conveyed professionalism and compassion, probably not a common pairing in prosecutors, I thought.

"Thank you, Your Honor. I'd like to call Mr. Faron Church to the stand."

A portly gentleman of average height and exceptional width rose from the second row and crossed the light of the courtroom to take the seat in the witness stand. Lon allowed for a slight delay while Mr. Church got his waist within the confines of the stand.

"Please state your name."

"Faron Church."

"And what is your occupation, Mr. Church?"

"I am the Department of Agriculture representative for the southern Delta counties." Faron straightened his back, proud to be an important government man.

"As such, Mr. Church, is it accurate to say your primary job is to arrange loans and credit for farmers?"

"Yes, that would be accurate."

"And this year, Mr. Church, being 1923, about how many loans and lines of credit did you issue?"

"37 according to the records."

"Is that typical, say, from 1915 to now?"

"It varied year to year, but I'd say that's a typical number."

"Out of 37, how many lines of credit or loans were to white farmers?"

Faron stuttered, "Well, umm, the records don't say white or black."

"Where did you grow up, Mr. Church?"

"Right here in Greenville, except for a couple of years with my grandparents in Holly Bluff."

"Then, as a lifelong resident, I would expect you would know the names of all the plantation owners. Is that right?"

"I suppose I do, yes."

"So, out of the 37 names on your 1923 list, how many would you say are white plantation owners?"

Faron ran a pudgy hand across his forehead.

"Well, knowing the names like I do, umm, I would say there's only one or two on the list I don't know well."

"So, there were only one or two black farmers you approved loans or credit to, correct?"

"Objection!" Calder sprang to his feet, sending his chair skittering backwards.

"The plaintiff's counsel is assuming without evidence the race of those approved, or disapproved for that matter, other than white farmers."

"Sustained." Lamar gave an appreciative nod to Calder as he pulled his chair back and sat.

Lon turned back to Faron, saying, "Mr. Church, we've established that one or two loans may have been to non-whites."

Lon saw Calder move to stand, but his objection never came.

"Please tell us the process you use to evaluate and approve applications," Lon continued.

"Well, the big thing I look for is a record of farming and collateral."

"Then, would you say the longer you've been farming and the more land you own, the easier it is to get an application approved?"

"Absolutely."

"Then wouldn't it also be true it would be near impossible for a new farmer with a small farm and a mortgage to get approval for a USDA line of credit for farm implements and seed?"

"Not impossible, no. In fact, we try hard to get new farms started."

"Can you explain then why Mr. Porter, sitting right there, had his line of credit application denied?"

Faron looked at the judge, then at Abaddon in the shadows along the wall.

"Well, no, I suppose I can't explain it."

"Would you then say someone in your position would have to deny Mr. Porter's application based on something other than the finances of the applicant?"

Faron wiped his forehead and ran his palm across a pant leg.

"If the decision wasn't based on the amount of collateral and the ability to repay the loan, then yes, there was something else at play."

"Can you speculate what that 'something else' might be, Mr. Church?"

Faron looked around the room as if searching for a lifeline. Finally, after exhaling and shrugging his shoulders, he replied, "Sounds like it might be something personal."

"Objection! The question is speculative, and the answer is the witness's opinion and not fact."

"Sustained. Keep to the facts, Mr. Miller," Judge Tate said, louder than necessary.

Lon did not reply to the judge. He walked in a tight circle, ending up close in front of Faron.

"You denied loans because what was personal was the color of the applicant's skin. Isn't that true, Mr. Church?"

"Objection!" Calder shouted, but before he could continue Lon moved towards the bench and said loud enough for everyone in the building to hear, "Your Honor, there appears to be a disproportionate number of minority applications denied compared to whites. The witness has stated as much, and I am seeking to determine the cause. This goes to the heart of the matter of how Mr. Porter lost his farm."

Judge Tate began turning red and his eyes could have burned through the shadows to ignite Abaddon.

"Overruled, but you're on thin ice, Mr. Miller."

"Yes, Your Honor." Lon returned in front of Faron, this time giving him a few feet of breathing room.

"Mr. Church, did you ever deny an application based on race?"

"I would never do that!"

"I remind you, Mr. Church, it's 1923 and you're in a position of power. Did you ever deny an application of a non-white farmer?"

Faron bowed up in the witness box. "I would never, sir!"

"Is anyone else involved in the decision?"

"No, only me."

"So, it could easily be done." Lon said as he spun around and started for his chair. As Calder was gripping the arms on his chair to rise, Lon shouted, "No further questions, Your Honor."

Judge Tate bore holes in Lon's back and reached for his gavel, but withdrew his hand as Lon sat down. He then looked at Calder.

"Your witness, Mr. Ambrose."

"Thank you, Your Honor."

Calder rose, grabbed a sheet of paper off the desk, and made his way to the witness box.

"Mr. Church, how long have you worked for the USDA?"

"Thirty-one years."

"And in all that time, have you ever had a disciplinary action against you?"

"No sir, never."

"Have you ever had any charges of racial discrimination filed against you?"

"No, sir."

"And in those thirty-one years, how many applications for loans or lines of credit have come to you from farmers?"

Faron looked up at Judge Tate, who could only stare at the shimmer of sweat on Faron's face.

"Well…I, I guess I don't have those numbers, but it would have been a lot." Faron stammered.

"And did you give equal consideration to every application?"

"Well…I'm not sure what you mean by equal consideration because very few applications are the same, but if you're asking if I treated each applicant fairly, then, yes, I did."

"So, Mr. Church, why are you even on the witness stand? You and the USDA?"

"Well..." Faron looked out at the audience, "I always wanted to be in a play."

Laughter from the audience and cast members broke the hush in the room.

Calder smiled back at the audience before continuing, "Well, I guess that goes for all of us here, but I remind you Mr. Church, the year is 1923 and with your 31 years of experience as a USDA agent and what you learned from reading about the history of the USDA, why are you on the stand?"

"Well, I suppose the prosecutor seems to think the USDA in this age is corrupt, but I can't speak to that. All I can say is I would never deviate from the process."

"Thank you, Mr. Church. That is all, Your Honor."

Before Judge Tate could speak, Abaddon came out of the shadows, saying, "Ladies and gentlemen, a brief pause for a conference."

Abaddon stopped in front of the witness box and motioned for Calder and Lon to join him. Abaddon leaned over to huddle with Faron and the lawyers and began speaking softly.

"Mr. Church, I remind you that…"

"I can't hear," Judge Tate said, as he leaned over the side of the bench, peering at the group below him.

Abaddon straightened and turned to Lamar.

"This doesn't concern you, Judge."

Lamar's face began turning red again. Abaddon could see a vein in his neck throbbing.

"This is a private conference in order to maintain your impartiality, Judge," Abaddon followed up, knowing Lamar couldn't argue the point.

Lamar eased back in his seat, teeth clenched and eyes scanning the room, looking for a release of anger.

Abaddon leaned into the trio, continuing.

"As I was saying, I remind you that you should play your character under the conditions of 1923. I'm not telling you what to say but I gave you enough history to read that you are aware of the multitude of allegations that many USDA reps of that era, not today, Mr. Church, of that era were beholden to white plantation owners, even accepting bribes to deny small black farmers loans. I only ask that you consider the realities of 1923 when answering questions."

Faron looked down before scanning the three faces peering down at him.

"Alright…alright then. I guess that's what they call acting."

"Acting true to history, Mr. Church."

"I'll keep that in mind."

Abaddon nodded, and the three men returned to their respective places.

Judge Tate looked befuddled.

"Well, I suppose it's still my place to ask, Mr. Miller, do you want a rebuttal opportunity with your witness?"

"Yes, Your Honor, I do."

Lon strode slowly to the witness box, stroking his chin while staring at the floor.

"Mr. Church, tell me about your personal relationship with the defendant."

"Well…" Faron looked over at Abaddon before glancing at Tucum, "…we're on friendly terms, not close, but we converse when we see each other in town."

"And what do you converse about?"

"Oh…just the normal things you talk about, how the family's doing, politics, how the crops are doing."

"And have you ever talked about who's applying for loans or lines of credit?"

"Well, I imagine we would have talked briefly about that…a time or two."

"I suppose the USDA considers that confidential information?"

"Well, yes, but…I was just trying to…" Faron's voice sounded as confused as his look.

"Just answer the question, Mr. Church. Is that confidential information?"

"Yes, yes, it is." Mr. Church slumped slightly in his seat, displeased with the box he backed into.

"So, did you offer that information to the defendant or did you share because he asked?"

Faron looked over at Tucum, whose stare caused Faron's eyebrows to suddenly raise.

"Well, yes, of course…he asked me and I suppose I might have shared some information I shouldn't have."

"Did the defendant ever ask you about a loan application of the plaintiff, Mr. Elron Porter?"

Faron had the feeling he was being carried along in a dialogue he had little control over and shouldn't have, since it was a play, he reminded himself.

"Yes, he did."

There was a low murmur from the crowd, heads leaning toward each other for whispered comments.

"And what did the defendant ask you?"

Faron sat up, enjoying the first feeling of the freedom to act, but trying to follow the theme of the information he had been given.

"He asked if I was going to approve the loan for Mr. Porter there." Faron pointed, feeling the excitement of being an actor.

"And what did you say?"

Faron took a moment to draw upon the information Abaddon had given him before answering forcefully.

"I told him that yes, I was going to approve the loan."

"And what was his response?"

"He said I should reconsider."

"And did you say you would?"

"No, sir. I told him I had no reason to deny him the loan."

"And what was his reply?"

Faron paused and looked at Tucum, whose eyes were squinted, his white face grizzled, and he could imagine being confronted by such a face fifty years before. He then looked over at Elron. It only took a second for him to know his answer.

"He said he could think of financial reasons that would change my mind."

"And what did he mean by that?"

"Objection. The plaintiff can't know what was in the mind of the defendant," Calder stated forcefully.

"Sustained," Judge Tate said with emphasis.

Lon didn't bother acknowledging the judge.

"What do you think he meant by that?"

"Well, I would think that…or rather, I thought he was offering me money."

Another louder murmur came from the gallery.

The crack of the gavel silenced the whispers.

"And what did you say to that offer?"

Faron thought whether his morals or those of the USDA agent in 1923 should guide the answer.

"I told him I could not accept any financial consideration, that it wouldn't be right."

"And how did Mr. Tutweiller react to that?"

"Not well. In fact, he became indignant, almost hostile in his anger."

"Did you feel threatened?"

"When he said my family would suffer if I made the wrong decision, then, yes, I felt very threatened."

"So, is that when you decided to deny Mr. Porter his loan?"

Faron's inner acting voice suddenly went silent, leaving him drifting. In seconds, he tried to envision how the possible answers would play out, but none made sense to him. His moral compass was being spun by forces from a generation ago. His way out suddenly came to him.

"I plead the fifth."

"Excuse me?" Lon looked at Faron incredulously.

"I plead the fifth amendment."

"Mr. Church, we know you denied the loan, so it's a simple question. Was Mr. Tutweiller's threat the reason you denied Mr. Porter's loan?"

"Objection. Counsel is denying the witness his fifth amendment right."

"Sustained," Judge Tate said, louder than necessary. "Do you have any other questions, Mr. Miller?"

Lon glanced in Abaddon's direction before saying, "No, Your Honor."

Judge Tate looked around the court before scanning those he could see in the audience. Those filling the seats behind the first two rows and latecomers standing along the back wall were in the dark. He cleared his throat before saying, "I have to say this is the most unusual court case I've presided over or even witnessed. The plaintiff's counsel has presented no evidence, but rather opinion, speculation, and hearsay. That may be expected considering the format of this 'trial' per se, but at this point, I have heard no substantive testimony the jury can use in their deliberations. I see there's been a marked increase in interest from the public, but I hope this, whatever 'this' is, begins to resemble a real trial more than the poor facsimile it's been."

Judge Tate slammed the gavel for effect and said, "Mr. Ambrose, it's my discretion to allow more than one examination of your client and I'm going to allow that in this case, if you wish."

"I do, Your Honor, and thank you for the opportunity."

Calder rose, buttoning and straightening his jacket. He sauntered to the witness stand, stopped six feet in front, and paused. Silence blanketed the room. Breaths were shallow and hushed.

"Mr. Church, who would you say is on trial here today? Are you, sir?"

"No, it was my understanding Mr. Tutweiller is."

"You are correct, sir, and any attempts to disparage your reputation or that of the USDA, which has done so much for small farmers, is an outrage."

Lon jumped to his feet. "Objection. I am attempting to show a relationship between the defendant and Mr. Church that supports the charges against the defendant. There is no disparagement of the reputation of the USDA on the plaintiff's part. We are merely exposing the facts of the USDA's operations."

Judge Tate looked at Lon with obvious aggravation.

"Sustained, but barely. Mr. Ambrose, get on with it and stick to the facts, slim as they are."

Calder nodded to the judge and turned back to Faron.

"Mr. Church, is Mr. Tutweiller a church-going man?"

"Yes, he is. We both attend First Baptist."

"And how does he treat his employees?"

"Oh, I think he treats his employees as well as any other farmer."

"And have you ever witnessed Mr. Tutweiller cheating a black employee or any black person?"

"No, sir, I have not."

"And do you think the charges against the defendant are without merit?"

"Objection. The witness's opinion is irrelevant to the facts of the case," Lon stated as he was rising from his chair.

"Sustained," Judge Tate said with little conviction in his voice.

"No further questions, Your Honor."

Judge Tate ran a hand across his forehead, turning to the plaintiff's table as he did.

"Mr. Miller, would you like to call a witness?"

"Yes, Your Honor. I call Mr. Brindley Davis to the stand."

A short, balding man in his 60s got up from the third row, made his way to the witness stand, and eased into the chair with a grunt.

I recognized the name, as had most of the county residents in the room, but the face had aged considerably since the last election. Either that or Mr. Davis's face on campaign billboards had been prettied up.

Lon approached the witness box while scanning a piece of paper in his left hand.

"Mr. Davis, you've been the Washington County Tax Collector since 1910, is that correct?"

"Yes, sir, that's what the profile sheet says, I mean, yes, sir, that's correct."

"So, you've had 13 years of experience running the office. Your office must run as smoothly as could be by now. Would you agree with that?"

Brindley rocked left and right and straightened his posture.

"I run a tight ship, yes, sir."

"Are you proud of the job you've done to turn your office into a 'tight ship', as you say?"

"Very much so."

"Mr. Davis, please explain to the court the process your office uses to collect property tax, that being the current year of 1923."

"Well, when tax time comes, I dedicate two employees to go through the property tax rolls and verify they have been updated with property transaction information from the last year. As they complete their review, I have another employee fill out a form stating the tax that's due, put it in an envelope, address it, and put it in a stack for stamping and delivery to the post office."

"And what is your error rate in that process, would you say?"

"What do you mean?"

"No one is perfect, Mr. Davis, even you. Certainly, there were properties that fell through the cracks that were overlooked, simply missed."

Brindley took offense as his reddening face showed. "His" office of 1971 never made such errors.

"Perhaps…maybe, I guess it's conceivable errors were made, in 1923 that is, but I doubt it. It's a very simple system, Mr. Miller."

Brindley was feeling flustered. The profile sheet of himself in 1923 said nothing about his office making errors and he was insulted that his reputation would be dishonored, play or no play.

"So, Mr. Davis, we've established that you run a tight ship with very few, if any, errors. Your office also follows a very simple system. Would you agree with those statements, Mr. Davis?"

Lon pivoted and looked at the jury.

"Yes," Brindley answered.

"Then why were there 27 cases of land repossession in Washington County from 1910 until now, 1923, all due to tax bills not being paid?"

"Uh…" Brindley looked around in confusion.

"I don't know why people don't pay; I only put them on the delinquent tax rolls when they don't."

"And what happens then?"

"If they stay delinquent long enough, I send them to the sheriff to sell the property to pay the taxes."

"And how long is 'long enough?'"

"According to the sheet you gave me, it was two years in 1923."

"And who notifies the property owner their property is about to be sold?"

"The County Sheriff."

"How does he notify the property owner?"

"I believe by mail, perhaps in person, certainly by a tax sale notice in the paper."

"So, if a person can read, he'll know he's in danger of losing his land either from a letter or the newspaper, and even if he can't read he'll get a personal visit from the sheriff or one of his deputies. Is that right?"

Brindley hesitated, glancing quickly to the shadows that cloaked Abaddon.

"I believe so, but you'd have to ask the sheriff."

"No further questions, Your Honor."

Judge Tate looked at his watch, pulled his sleeve back down before saying, "Your witness, Mr. Ambrose."

Calder rose, straightening his yellow paisley tie. He smiled at the jury and nodded and walked to the witness box.

"Mr. Davis. You testified you run a tight ship and the taxpayers of Washington County appreciate that. I know you're not told that often enough."

Brindley shifted in his seat, straightening up, smiling.

"I hear that about as often as I get a 'thank you' at home," Brindley said with a smile.

A quiet chuckle rippled from the audience.

Calder smiled, saying, "I can appreciate that, as well. Now Mr. Davis, I say this not to belittle the importance of your office, but as you described identifying delinquent property owners, it seems to me it's a simple process. Do you agree?"

"Well, yes, simple, but tedious and time consuming."

"Certainly, but simple processes are, as a rule, very low in errors, so if a property owner who is delinquent on his taxes loses his land after the process has played out, who, in your long experience, is to blame?"

"The landowner is. Every time."

Lon stood quickly. "Objection. Conjecture not based on any facts presented."

Judge Tate looked down at Lon, clearly annoyed.

"Overruled. Counselor, you're premature. Continue, Mr. Ambrose."

"So why does a landowner not pay his back taxes?"

Brindley laughed and rolled his eyes. His laugh stopped when he looked back at Calder.

"Oh, you're serious. Well, counselor, it's because they're broke. Simple as that."

"It's a simple reason, Mr. Davis, but please help the jury understand why someone wouldn't sell the farm, pay off the taxes, and move on with what's left over."

"Now that, as you described it, is not that simple. You're assuming they own their land and can walk away with cash. Most borrowed the money to buy the farm in the first place, they've tried farming and failed several years in a row, and the taxes and the loans would take every penny from the farm being sold. So, the way they see it, it's easier to just pack up and move away and let the USDA or the bank sort out the mess they left behind."

Calder stroked his chin while looking at the luster of his black leather shoes. He took several paces toward the jury before saying, "So, what you have testified to is that the fault of defaults, so to speak, lies solely with the landowner, and no one else."

Lon rose, but stopped when he saw Judge Tate's glare.

"That's been my experience, yes."

"No further questions, Your Honor."

Judge Tate looked at his watch again, exhaled, and then said, "Mr. Miller?"

"Plaintiff's counsel calls the Washington County sheriff, Buck Black, to the witness stand."

A metal chair scraped across concrete and a moment later Sheriff Black strode into the light of the stage and took his seat in the witness stand. Light reflected off the badge over his left chest and the stars on the lapels of his khaki uniform. The lower buttons of his shirt were straining to stay attached against his bulging stomach. His red face was already dotted with perspiration, and his breathing was overly heavy.

"Sheriff Black, please tell us what your role is in the tax sales of delinquent property." Lon said.

Buck dabbed a handkerchief across his forehead before replying.

"Well, I get a list of properties from Brindley every year. I give that list to the Current along with a notice stating when and where the tax sale will be held. We usually hold the sale on the courthouse steps, depending on the weather."

"So it's a live auction, as I understand it."

"Yes, we start with the amount owed and then the bids go up from there. The highest bidder gets a lien on the property."

"What do you mean 'a lien'?"

"The winning bidder doesn't own the property for another two years."

"What happens in those two years?"

"The landowner has two years to pay off the back taxes in order to keep the property."

"Is it ever shorter than two years?"

"No, not that I've seen."

"Could the county decide to not wait two years and to foreclose right away?"

"Well, being it's 1923, I can't really say, but..." Buck looked nervously around the room and wiped his forehead and cheeks.

"Yes?"

"Well, I suppose the county government could do what's best for the people of the county."

"And immediate foreclosure would be best for the taxpayers in Washington County?"

"Yea, I mean, if the land sits there for two years unfarmed, what good is that? It'd be better to have it farmed, seed bought and crops sold to generate some taxes for the county. Why should a deadbeat landowner keep that revenue from the citizens for two years while the hard-working people are paying it year after year?"

Lon froze in place, hands hooked on his suit vest, eyes boring into the sheriff. When the sheriff started fidgeting, Lon asked, "So, who exactly are the hard-working people?"

"Well...," Sheriff Black stammered, a drop of sweat dripped from his nose,

"...you know...the people who pay the taxes in this county–the people who make farming what it is."

"You mean the small mom and pop farms, don't you?"

"Hell, no. They don't mean nothing. I'm talking about the big farms that made this county more than a hundred years ago and keep it going strong."

"I see. And, Sheriff Black, you also mentioned deadbeat farmers. How many of those big farms are owned by deadbeat farmers?"

"None of them."

"So, would you say all the owners of these big plantation farms are hard-working people?"

"Yea."

"Therefore, all the deadbeat farmers are owners of small farms."

"Yea, I guess so." Sheriff Black had a questioning look on his face, unsure of what he agreed to.

"How many of the plantation owners are white, Sheriff Black?"

"Objection!" Calder rose and addressed the judge in a pleading tone. "Your Honor, bringing race into the questioning is unnecessary. In fact, it diverges from the focus on the process of property foreclosures."

Judge Tate swiveled his chair to look at Lon.

"Mr. Miller?"

"Judge, race has everything to do with this case, as I will show. Small farmers versus large farmers is at the heart of the matter and race is a driving component of each."

Judge Tate looked down at his desk for a moment before responding.

"Overruled. You're pushing it though, Mr. Miller. I'm not sure this is a road you should go down and you don't have long to convince me."

"Thank you, Your Honor."

Lon turned back to the witness stand and moved close.

"Sheriff, again, how many plantation owners are white?"

The sheriff wiped his face with a flourish, his face flushing a deeper red. He stared at Lon with contempt.

"All of them."

"And how many small farmers are black?"

Sheriff Black looked at Judge Tate, who only stared back, unable to help.

"Most of them."

Lon allowed the silence of the room to sink into the hearts of the audience.

"So, Sheriff Black, by your own testimony tonight, whites, and only whites, are hard-working farmers, and black farmers are deadbeats."

The silence was immediately broken, replaced by groans of disbelief, gasps of astonishment, and shouts of profanity.

The gavel hit the desk repeatedly, only now the crack was muffled by the outcry of the audience.

"Order! Order!"

"Objection, Your Honor! Objection!" shouts from Calder could barely be heard.

Judge Tate stared at the audience, teeth clenched, gavel held with white knuckles.

A last crack of the gavel quieted the crowd back to a murmur.

"Sustained! I won't have any more of this, Mr. Miller! Do you hear me?"

Lon looked around the room, taking in the expressions on the faces of the audience and jury.

"Do you hear me?!" Judge Tate yelled, spit flying across the desk.

Lon slowly turned to the judge.

"Yes, Your Honor, I hear you. One more question, Your Honor. Nothing to do with race. My word."

Judge Tate wiped his forehead with one hand as he set the gavel down with the other.

"I'm holding you to it."

"Yes, sir."

Lon turned back to Sheriff Black, who, by now, was showing sweat around his uniform collar. His face was a hot mixture of anger and confusion.

"Studies have shown that preconceptions in life, particularly about people of different…," Lon shot a glance to Judge Tate, "…backgrounds are passed from generation to generation if there isn't a significant event that breaks the chain. It seems things are slow to change here in the Delta. Would you agree, Sheriff?"

Sheriff Black's look of confusion vanished, leaving only a look of disdain.

"Yea, I would. That's what makes the Delta a great place to live."

"That was your one question, Mr. Miller." Judge Tate said loudly.

"One follow-up, Your Honor," Lon held up one finger without looking at the judge. He asked quickly, "Sheriff Black, I want to commend you for acting in this play that takes place in 1923. You've done a good job."

Sheriff Black's demeanor didn't change. If anything, his face turned a deeper red.

"But tell me, sheriff, who was the actual sheriff of Washington County in 1923?"

Sheriff Black stammered, "Wait one second, dammit. Judge…?" Buck beseeched the judge anxiously.

Judge Tate gave a fake chuckle, ground his teeth while staring at Lon, and finally said, "That's no secret, Buck. Folks can look it up if they don't already know it. Answer the question; the last question from Mr. Miller."

Sheriff Tate hesitated, then his shoulders slumped.

"My father was."

The audience, those few who already knew and the rest who didn't, erupted again. The shouting echoed off the cinderblock walls and concrete floor.

The gavel cracked repeatedly, to no avail. Those who couldn't hear the judge's profanity knew he had had enough when he stood up in a flourish and stormed off the stage.

Abaddon hurried into the center of the courtroom and signaled for the overhead lights to come on, which immediately began to quiet the audience.

"Ladies and gentlemen, if I could have your attention."

Some in the audience began waving their hands at their neighbors, signaling them to hush. One by one, people took their seats until all eyes were back on Abaddon.

"Ladies and gentlemen, what we've just witnessed is the fact that history is never far away. In fact, it's sometimes still living, and human shortcomings will always be with us. Revelations exposed have been unscripted, as advertised. And although tonight was short, it was a necessary step in the process of fairly and honestly judging the defendant. It also sets the tone for what I expect will be a most interesting Act Three. Thank you for coming and I hope to see you all tomorrow night."

Abaddon left the set quickly and exited through the storage room door Judge Tate had used a minute before. Members of the press in the front row surged toward the two lawyers. Tucum waved off an approaching newspaperman and quickly made his way out the front. Without missing a beat, the newspaper reporter cornered Mayor Campbell before he could get out of the jury box. Being a politician, he quickly warmed to being quoted in the paper.

"Mr. Mayor, what did you think of tonight's performance?"

"Well, it surprised me for sure, just like everyone else. Racism has no place in this town. I won't tolerate it and the citizens won't tolerate it. It was clear neither will Judge Tate, the way he stormed off."

"Should there be repercussions for the sheriff?"

"I can't speak to that. I think he owes everyone an apology, but beyond that I think the sheriff will have to decide that himself."

"What effect do you think this will have on the reputation of Greenville and Washington County?"

"None at all. We're not racist here. We welcome all and we treat everyone fairly. Our legal system doesn't recognize color. Judge Tate will confirm that."

"What do you say to people who might have a hard time believing that?"

"Don't let the past stain the present. This is a great place to live, for everybody. Come see for yourself."

## Chapter 48

Kim woke to the chirps of birds in the holly tree outside their bedroom window. Rubbing her eyes, she looked to the other side of the bed and was relieved to see Lon on his side, eyes closed, a soft snore coming from his open mouth. She slipped out of bed quietly, wrapped herself in her fleece robe, and gently closed the bedroom door behind her. After putting a pot of coffee on to brew, the memories from the night before paraded through her mind. She retrieved the Sunday paper from the front landing, eager to read the media reaction to the play's second night. She sat on the couch, rolled the rubber band off the coiled paper and let it unfurl in her lap. Her eyes widened in surprise to see the prominence given to 'Lon's play', as she called it. The Sunday headline was in bold print:

**Race Slander Shuts down Greenville Play**
by Andrew Falstaff

Kim's eyes raced to the text below the headline.

The second night of the most unusual play held in Greenville, Justice Delayed, ended with loud revolts from the audience in response to Sheriff Black's statements calling black farmers "deadbeats" and white farmers "hard-working." When confronted by this reporter in the dim light outside the theater, Sheriff Black would only say, "It's a play. I was acting." When reminded that it was a mock trial that was unscripted, letting him say anything he wanted, the Sheriff only shook his head and hurried to his car…

Kim set the paper aside to think for a moment. She felt something impactful was happening, but she couldn't quite grasp the significance of it. Lost in thought, she jumped when Lon's hand caressed her shoulder.

"Sorry I scared you."

Kim put her hand over Lon's. "No, it's my fault. I didn't hear you open the bedroom door. Grab a cup and have a seat. It's almost 7:00 and I want to see if we're picking up the Jackson news."

Kim turned on the 15 inch black and white Zenith TV that had belonged to her mother. A larger color TV had been on the list since they set up house in Greenville, but there was never leftover money at the end of the month to even amount to a down payment.

Audio interspersed with static came through first, followed by the gradual emergence of a hazy image of an austere TV stage with one reporter behind the desk, a large WLBT logo behind him.

"Good morning, Mississippi, I'm Jeff Holloway, and this is your Sunday news. It's going to be a beautiful day with mild temperatures and Barry Swenson will give us all the details, but first here are the headlines.

"There's somewhat of a controversy brewing in Greenville coming out of what's called a play, but is unlike any play anyone in this area of the country has heard of. Delayed Justice is the name and to put it simply, it's a play without a script. The leads have been given background details of the characters they are playing, but beyond that the lines they say are up to them, which makes what happened last night all the more remarkable.

"The Washington County sheriff, Buck Black, apparently had a moment of brutal honesty in his acting, again, without a script, when he called black farmers of 1923 deadbeats. The question folks in Greenville have of their sheriff is did his words come from his attempt to actually play a white sheriff in 1923, who ironically was his father, or do his words reflect what's in his heart in 1971? What's even more puzzling is his doubling down on racist remarks by calling white farmers hard-working.

We had a news crew there and here's what Sheriff Black said."

The video began with a wide view of the stage before zooming in on Sheriff Black giving his damning testimony. Angry shouts dominated the audio when the video ended.

"This controversy has gotten the attention of TV and newspaper media around the region with reporting of this story from Montgomery to Biloxi, Memphis, and Baton Rouge.

The play continues tonight at 7:00 at the Ford Theater and we'll be there to cover it for you to see what other controversy might be stirred up.

"In other news…"

Kim got up from the couch, turned off the Zenith, and looked at Lon with a curious smirk as she came back to the couch to wrap an arm around his shoulders, folding her legs onto the couch, knees at his side.

"What have you gotten into, Mr. Famous Prosecutor? Are you off to Hollywood after this?"

Lon chuckled. "Of course. Should we start looking for a mansion in Beverly Hills?"

"It has to have a pool, and color TVs throughout."

Lon leaned over and kissed Kim, pulling back to look her in the eyes.

"You know I wish I could."

Kim took in a breath and turned to look out the front window and the azalea blooms that stood upright inches above the bottom window frame. The lightness she had felt so briefly passed with a whisper.

"Did you have any idea the play would go in this direction?"

Lon spent several moments looking at Kim, an expression of complete seriousness on his face.

"Not this specifically, but yes, I thought it might go in this direction."

Kim pulled back. “How, without a script?”

Lon exhaled and took a long sip of coffee before answering.

“Can we please postpone this conversation until the play’s over?”

“Why? What are you keeping from me?”

“Kim, please. It’s just best that we not talk about it now. Not until it’s over.”

The feeling of the playful moment and the closeness she had felt to Lon suddenly slipped away, replaced by confusion and diminished trust. She got up and went to the front door, hot coffee on the side table forgotten. After stepping onto the landing and closing the door behind her, she crossed her arms and stood there for minutes, staring at nothing, wondering if she was looking at a lifetime of disappointment.

## Chapter 49

LJ entered Ruth's and immediately felt a comfort befitting a decades-long place of refuge. Despite open tables at the front, he walked around the corner and was relieved to see his table by the kitchen empty. Within a minute, Ruth plopped down a menu and silverware wrapped in a paper napkin.

"Well, stranger, I'm glad to see you have a few minutes to come see me in between stirrin up every hornet's nest in town."

LJ looked up with a feigned hurtful look. "Who, me?"

"Yeah you, you varmint. You got this whole county talkin like we just woke up to somethin that's always been there."

LJ sat back and said in a lowered voice, "Is that bad?"

"Bad? I didn't say it was bad. It's the best thing that's happened since…well…I can't remember…but I tell you what, people needed a good wakin up. Everybody goes about their business every day, sayin "Hi, Sheriff Black, how are you?" and, "Good morning, Mr. Mayor", "Judge Tate", and the rest of them, pretendin they somebody they ain't. I'm glad you done ripped the band aid off so everyone can see that old wound ain't healed one bit; it's only been covered up, and barely at that."

"Hmm. Ruth, you have a talent for putting into words what others can't."

"I just says what I sees, Mr. LJ. And don't put on you don't, neither. Otherwise, you wouldn't be here, would you?"

"No, ma'am, I guess I wouldn't." LJ smiled. "But since I am, I'll have today's special and don't tell me what it is. I like it when you surprise me."

"Oh, then you in for a heapin of 'like' today," Ruth said before turning serious. "You seen the mayor?"

"Today? No."

"He in here a little while ago lookin for you. Said you ain't at your hotel and to tell you to be at Judge Tate's at 1:00 if I see you."

LJ thought for a moment. "Did he say anything else, like what it's about?"

"Nope. Guess that's part of the surprise." Ruth winked, picked up the menu, and got her hips moving toward the kitchen.

## Chapter 50

The ten foot tall door opened slowly. “Hello, April.”

A faint smile emerged on the frail girl’s face. “Hello, Mr. Marshall. Please come in.” April said, barely above a whisper. She stepped back, pulling the white door with both hands grasping the edge. When LJ stepped into the massive hallway, she gently closed the door with only a whisper of sound.

“How are you, April?”

April stood at attention, both hands clenched in front of her, eyes downturned.

“Better, thanks to you.”

“How’s that?”

“Mr. Tate’s been some upset about your play and he hasn’t had any time for me.”

“Have you decided?”

April wrung her hands and looked up at LJ with pleading eyes.

“Mr. Marshall, I just don’t know…”

“LJ, is that you? Get in here, right now!” Lamar Tate’s voice boomed from the library to fill the hall.

LJ looked down the hall, then looked at April.

“I’ll be by at 5:30. Please be there, April. Please, you can do it.”

Without waiting for April to escort him, LJ strode quickly down the hall and into the library. He paused at the door when he saw his meeting wasn’t just with Tate. The judge sat behind his massive desk, cigar smoke hovering above his head like a sickly halo. At either front corner of the desk sat Mayor Campbell and Sheriff Black. LJ didn’t have to wait to be told to sit in the middle chair.

Lamar sat puffing on his cigar, spewing smoke from both corners of his mouth. The intensity of his stare was obscured by his squinting from the smoke, but LJ could feel it just the same.

"I've had all types of…people…here on my plantation, but none that have pissed me off more than you, Mr. LJ Marshall, you and your sidekick. This bullshit you started is ending right now."

Lamar leaned in, put his elbows on the desk, and pulled the cigar out of his mouth.

"Now here's what you're going to do. When you leave here, you're going to call every TV and newspaper that reported on your hit job and you're going to tell them the play is canceled because of a lack of interest from the public. You're going to tell them your concept didn't work and you and everyone else you brought in are leaving town. And, hear me real good, y'all are going to be out of my town and my county before the sun goes down and I never want to see your sorry asses again."

Lamar brought the cigar to his mouth, breathed deeply, and blew a wave of smoke across the desk nearly to LJ.

"Did you understand me or do I need to repeat myself?"

LJ looked at Mayor Campbell to his left, whose hatred was almost as palpable as Lamar's. He looked at Sheriff Black to his right, who glanced down at the floor.

"Well, at least the lawman has some sense of shame," LJ thought.

LJ grabbed the arms of the chair and sat up straight. He cleared his throat and said without the courtesy of formality, "Lamar, that would be a damn shame if I did that, because we'd both be sorry."

Lamar took the cigar from his mouth and squinted at LJ with suspicion.

"How the hell you figure that?"

"Well, I'm going to miss your shining moment of bringing the trial to an end and you're going to lose your election."

Lamar gave out a laugh. "Ha, that's a good joke, but you see, there's no way that's going to happen. I'm running unopposed." Lamar sat back and took a smug draw on the cigar.

It was all LJ could do to stay calm. After a deep breath and a long stare, he answered, "Right now I'd put my money on anybody beating you. Hell, even your girl, April, could whoop your ass. You see, Lamar…actually, no, you don't because your arrogance blinds you…the smell of racism the sheriff let loose last night has put a stink on all of you."

Without breaking his stare at Lamar, he could see heads on either side of him turn.

"Welcome Lamar, gentlemen, to the life of a black in the Delta. You assume every black person is a nigger until they prove otherwise. When they prove useful to you, and loyal, and subservient, then, and only then, will you call them black. Well, now gentlemen," LJ looked to either side before returning his stare to Lamar, "you are racist through and through until you prove otherwise. You see, we look at you whites in power in a town or county as all being in cahoots. If one's rotten, you're all rotten, else why wouldn't you clean your own house?"

LJ stood to leave, "Lamar, y'all quit this play and you'll only confirm what every black voter and a lot of white voters now think about you. And if that's your decision, let me know when Miss Legare can have a leave of absence to campaign. I can't wait to get it started."

LJ turned and confidently walked out of the oppressive smoke and antiquity of the plantation library into fresh air and the freedom to settle old debts once and for all.

## Chapter 51

I got the call to be at LJ's motel room at four o'clock. I didn't have to be told it was urgent, since this would be our first team meeting in the daylight. The time for secrecy was over, which was just as well. A sheriff's deputy was sitting in his cruiser in the trash-littered parking lot of the abandoned gas station next door. I gave him a wave when I got out of my car and had forgotten about him by the time I got in the room. We had bigger worries.

"I don't know," was how LJ answered my question of whether the play would go on tonight.

"My meeting with Tate didn't end well. Abaddon tasked Calder with getting the mayor and judge to the courthouse for a meeting at 6:00. We have a proposal that, hopefully, he'll see as a way to save face with the voters. We'll see if they show. If not..." LJ said, letting those words hang in the air.

The possibility the whole long and complicated web would come undone hit me like a gut punch. Much like your life flashing before your eyes just before you die, the whole journey to this point scrolled quickly through my mind's eye, starting with my brother getting killed, seeing Tucum for the first time and hating him until he became my tutor and best friend, to being set on this path from a conversation in Sammy's bar, learning about moot court from law students in the Greenville library, to seeing a civil rights lawyer in Jackson whose college friend at Texas Southern University was now a Broadway producer, who then enlisted, as I would learn later, one of the first black Hollywood directors. After that, I became a bystander and watched as God brought his people together, the people in this outworn and sad Delta motel room. If God didn't finish what he started, I would have some choice words for him. Until then, I'd do what I did best-keep praying.

LJ continued, "Abaddon and I think that if Tate shows up tonight, we need to accelerate the schedule and bring this to a close. Charlie, that means you need to bring our witness, but get someone to stay with him until one of us comes out to get him. I don't have to tell you how critical it is that you get him to the theater."

"No, sir, there some things I don't understand, but that ain't one of them. We'll be there, don't you worry."

LJ followed with, "I'll pick up my witness and meet you at the parking spot at six o'clock. The two of them can stay in my car."

I nodded and shifted on my feet from sudden nervousness. What I had been pretending would happen for so long was actually about to happen. What should have been excitement surging through my body was instead exceptional fear.

"Abaddon, you want to add anything?" LJ asked.

Abaddon glanced at everyone in the room before saying, "We're expecting a big turnout tonight and we want everyone to at least hear what's said. Tucum is running wire and power for speakers to the storage room behind the curtain. We're putting as many chairs in there as we can find and there's a lot of room for standing. In case we have more press show up, I blocked off the first three rows of seats for them. Lon and I agreed on how he's going to streamline cross examinations to accommodate a compressed schedule. Other than that, we've done everything we can think to do.

"One last thing, I think it's best for me and LJ to say goodbye now. Regardless of how this ends, the press will turn their attention on all of us, but perhaps more so on us two, since we're the unknown wild cards in all this."

Abaddon paused and looked at each of us before saying, "I didn't know what to expect when I told LJ I'd do this, but I'm glad I did and I'm so very glad I met you all."

I choked on Abaddon's sincerity. His intelligence and ability to manipulate others were a given, but there hadn't been time to see another side of him. His crisp but gentle language to us now, soft eye contact, and out-turned palms reflected a heart that could compassionately connect with others. Then I realized these two men who had pulled this all together would disappear back into their far-off lives, back to their real names, and if tonight was a failure, the world would never know what they had at least tried to accomplish. I also realized the rest of us wouldn't be so lucky.

## Chapter 52

I drove slowly and stared in amazement. Two nights ago, I could have parked in front of Ford's Theater. Tonight, cars and vans with colorful television decals splashed across them had been in the front spots for hours. It was over an hour until the start of the play and already there was a line of three dozen people waiting at the front door. I parked two blocks away, told my passenger to wait for LJ, and walked slowly around the corner to the back of the theater. The western sky was pink with edges of orange, the air was turning cool, and birds were chirping excitedly before nightfall hushed them. Anxious excitement spread through my chest with every step, and I wondered what I would feel when the night was over.

I was reaching for the back door when it opened suddenly and Tucum stepped out wearing shorts, worn out tennis shoes, no socks or shirt, looking worse for the wear from the afternoon's work.

"Hello, my brotha from anotha motha," Tucum greeted me with a smile.

"Tucum, you sho don't look like you gonna be in a play tonight."

"I'm headin to the truck right now to get some decent clothes. They say this doesn't quite meet the standards of this here production."

We both laughed. "Hell, it don't meet the standards near about anywhere," I said. "You got the back room set up?"

"Better than any playhouse in New York City, Paris, or maybe Greenville, Mississippi. It'll do."

"You seen Tate?"

"Nope."

"How about LJ and Abaddon?"

"Them neither."

"Shit." A big dose of excitement left my body. After a moment, I realized Tucum wasn't aware of how tenuous tonight's performance was. I didn't want to be the one to tell him all his work today might be for nothing.

"Well, my stinky friend, go get prettied up like the big city star you is!"

Tucum laughed and looked at me with a smirk.

"I been called lots of things, but pretty ain't one of em."

I needed that diversion to settle down. One thing was for sure. No matter what happened tonight, I would still have a good friend in Tucum tomorrow. When it came down to what made a good life, that was all I needed.

## Chapter 53

Lamar shut the door to his office next to the courtroom in the county building. Being Sunday, there was nobody to stare at the peculiar group that had walked straight to the judge's chambers.

"You only got a few minutes of my attention. You better talk fast," Lamar said gruffly as he plopped into his leather chair.

LJ and Abaddon looked at each other before LJ started, "Judge, I apologize for being short with you. I was caught up in the moment and I want to say I'm sorry."

Lamar leaned into the desk and began fidgeting with a black Waterman pen.

"'Sorry' doesn't fix the damage you two have done. Unless you can convince this whole town the sheriff was just reciting a script you gave him, you're just wasting my time."

Abaddon spoke up. "That might convince some, but I think most people would see through it. In fact, it might make things worse. What we recommend is for you to speak to the press and the audience before the play starts, expressing your disgust of racism and apologizing to those who were offended. We've taken the liberty of drafting a statement that you're free to edit as you like."

Abaddon stretched over the desk, handing a sheet of paper to Lamar, who glanced at Abaddon, pursed his lips, and sat back to read the statement.

Lamar passed the paper over to the mayor, then looked out the second-floor window at the light green spring buds emerging on the trees.

After a minute, Lamar looked at the mayor and asked, "You think that's a good idea?"

"Yeah, if you put your charm into it, Judge, you can convince the Devil he needs to buy a heater. You can't leave this hanging the way it is. I say give a heartfelt apology and let's move on," Mayor Campbell answered.

Tate thought for a moment.

"Move on to what?" he asked as he swung his chair back to look at LJ and Abaddon.

Abaddon answered, "To the end of an experiment that didn't work out as we thought it would, Judge. We hoped to keep the play going longer, but we'll end it after tonight if you wish. You have my word. A few more witnesses, the jury will convene for a few minutes and then pronounce Tucum innocent or guilty, and the public will be none the wiser that we shortened the play. You all can get back to your lives and frankly, after the emotional statement I'm sure you'll give, Judge, you will probably be in better standing with the public than before all this."

"Or at least not any more disliked," Mayor Campbell said as an attempt at a joke.

Tate thought for a few more moments, the silence of the room broken only by the tick of an antique clock on a sidebar.

"After tonight, am I ever going to see you two again?"

"No, sir," Abaddon answered immediately.

"Not a chance," followed LJ.

"Those are the right answers," Tate said as he pushed back from the desk.

"Let's get changed and finish this shit show of yours," Tate said as he stood and motioned everyone to leave. On the way out, he poured himself a shot of bourbon.

"Here's to better days ahead without those niggers in my town," Tate toasted as he knocked back the shot in one motion.

## Chapter 54

I had taken a middle seat in the third row when the doors opened for the press. I was skeptical that two rows were needed for them, but not only was I wrong, I sat next to a sure enough good-looking young reporter all the way from Birmingham. She wore a dark knee-length skirt and a white blouse that highlighted her amber skin. High heels and a slender frame made her seem like an apparition. A small gold necklace and gold bracelet said class without screaming it. In my world, she was the picture of elegance.

I nodded to her when she sat down and told her, "Ma'am."

She said good evening and rifled through a large handbag to produce a writing pad and pen.

"You with a paper?" I asked, curious because I had never met a black reporter, and a female, too.

"Yes, I am." She stuck out her hand. "Felicia Evans, Birmingham Times."

I reached up to remove my hat before realizing I didn't have one on.

"Charlie…Charlie Neely." I stammered. "Nice to meet you."

"Who are you with, Mr. Neely?"

"Well, Ms. Evans, I like to think I'm with God most of the time. Truth is, I don't know if he feels the same."

Felicia laughed, and that put me at ease.

"Well, I'm sure he's with you more than you know. What I meant was, what paper are you with, or are you television?"

"Neither, ma'am. I'm just an interested observer, like the rest of the folks."

The doors opened and the noise in the room rose with scuffing of moving chairs and low conversations as patrons flooded in.

"You must know somebody to get an early seat, Mr. Neely. Am I perhaps sitting next to a Greenville dignitary?" Felicia asked, as she tilted her head and looked at me with a playful smile.

"Oh, no ma'am, I'm no dignitary. I'm just Charlie Neely, that's all."

Our small talk went on for a minute and she put me so much at ease, as if we were the only two people in the room. It was the best sensation I had felt in months.

The crack of the gavel brought me back into the world, but the tightness in my chest that had moved in and wouldn't leave was suddenly gone, replaced with a calm reassurance that the outside world of possibilities, including female companionship, was waiting when this chapter of my life ended. I glanced over at Felicia and smiled. She smiled back.

Looking around, I saw every chair was filled and at least two dozen people were standing along both walls. I was turning back when I recognized one person I didn't expect to see. I gave Cleve McDowell the slightest nod, and he returned the gesture. We both then turned our gazes to the courtroom, but my thoughts lingered on my fateful meeting with Cleve in Jackson that put all this in motion.

Judge Tate set the gavel down and slowly scanned the room, beginning with the press in the first three rows.

"Ladies and gentlemen, before we begin tonight's act, I need to apologize first to the citizens of Greenville and Washington County and secondly to all the media types who are visiting our fine city. Racial comments were made last night that I want you to know do not represent the values and sentiments of our citizens. I was insulted and ashamed, as were thousands of others who enjoy a good quality of life here. We all get along and we're all family here."

Up to that point, the room was hushed, but Tate's last comment brought on a brief murmur and muffled coughs.

"As both a responsible citizen and as your chancery court judge, I want to assure you I will continue to fight against racism in any form. I don't allow it in my home or in my courtroom."

That brought on more chatter in response, louder this time. Felicia glanced behind us and then looked at me quizzically. I could answer only by shaking my head.

The gavel cracked again to open the court, and I suspected, mainly to silence the crowd.

"This Court's now in session. Does the defense want to cross-examine Sheriff Black?" Lamar asked, knowing full well the sheriff was miles from the River Theater.

Calder stood buttoning the jacket of a flat black suit, much subdued from the previous two nights.

"Not at this time, Your Honor."

Tate quickly locked eyes with Lon and paused for a moment with a look of trepidation.

"Does the plaintiff want to call a witness?"

"I do, Your Honor." Lon rose and stood ramrod straight before glancing back at the audience. He slowly buttoned the jacket of his lightly textured suit, which couldn't have been more different from Calder's. Lon wore the suit that identified with the South. A seersucker suit was and is the suit worn by white men in warm weather to look stylish, distinctive, and well-off. It's also a suit never seen on a black man.

I leaned over to Felicia and whispered, "He sho don't look like he's on the black man's side, wearin that."

She rolled her eyes in agreement. I had caught a whiff of her perfume and was lost in a daydream when I heard, "I call the plaintiff, Mr Elron...."

"Just a minute, Your Honor!" Abaddon hurried onto the set, went to Lon, and whispered in his ear before turning to the audience.

"Ladies and gentlemen, it's common in plays for actors to change from one night to the next with understudies filling in for an actor who cannot perform. It's also rare, but not unheard of, for cast members to change during a performance, as is about to happen."

Abaddon gave a nod to the gentleman he enlisted to play the plaintiff. Without ever having to say a word of the script Abaddon had given him, Mr. Elron Porter, an actor in the Greenville Little Theatre, rose from the plaintiff's desk and walked off the stage.

Abaddon quickly nodded to Lon before retreating out of the light.

Lon cleared his throat and stated in a loud, clear voice, "Your Honor, I call the plaintiff, Mr. Charlie Neely, to the stand."

A low murmur moved through the back of the room like a gust of wind.

Lon had brushed past me earlier and had told me in a whisper he would put me on the witness stand. I knew it would happen at some point, but that time had seemed too distant to worry about.

It was suddenly time to worry.

As I stood, I saw Felicia's eyes, now squinted in confusion, which didn't ease my panic. I scooted sideways down the row of chairs and white folks scrunched back in their chairs to give me room. One older black man at the end gently slapped my arm, saying, "Go get 'em, brotha."

Stepping into the bright lights of the courtroom was harsh. I was squinting as I sat in the witness chair and was surprised when I looked up to find I couldn't see much beyond the lawyer's tables. It suddenly looked and felt as if I was in a real courtroom with no gallery. My heart raced with fear of right now and where we were going back to. I frantically tried to remember everything Lon and Abaddon had told me, but I mistakenly looked up at the judge. He was almost out of his chair to stare down at me over the side of the desk. He looked like a blind man hearing a match strike, and all he could do was wait for the smell of smoke to let him know the fire was not far behind. I saw hate in his eyes, but I also saw something that likely no one had seen before on Lamar Tate's face-fear. He was frozen in place as he tried to comprehend what was happening. He was too slow to stop it, though, as Lon moved quickly to stand a few feet from me.

"Mr. Neely, please tell the court who you are and what you do for a living."

I looked over at the jury and saw all eyes were on me, and the mayor's were full of hate. I had been carrying a burden hidden from others, hell, I tried my best sometimes to keep from looking at it myself. Now, the time for hiding was over. It was time to trust in the Lord. I just wished he'd keep my heart from trying to jump out of my chest.

"My name's Charlie Neely. I's born and raised here in Washington County. Except for a trip to Vietnam, I ain't ever left."

A low snicker came from the audience, and Lon smiled at Charlie.

"Very well, Mr. Neely, but I remind you the year is 1923."

"Oh, right, sorry bout that. I'm just a bit nervous, that's all."

"That's quite alright, Mr. Neely…"

Getting that admission out seemed to begin to calm me.

"…what do you do for work?"

I looked at Tucum. He gave me the slightest of nods, so slight no one else would have noticed.

"Farmin. Least I used to."

Lon moved closer and angled toward the jury.

"Used to? What happened to get you out of farming?"

I took a deep breath and looked up at Judge Tate. "My land was stolen from me."

Sounds of people shifting in their chairs and whispering came from the audience. The judge looked in their direction with a scowl and the sounds trailed off.

"Mr. Neely, please tell the court how that happened."

I glanced at the little I could see of the audience, the first rows shrouded in shadows that went down to darkness in the back.

Now that I was talking, I wanted to talk to every one of them and ask them to tell my story to their families, their friends, even strangers. I wanted those I could see, members of the press in the front rows, to hear me clearly and hear me speaking for all those who were now forever silent. History is ever-repeating, generations gaining and losing, but dammit, it was time to hear about some good people, hard-working people who lost and didn't deserve to.

"Yes, sir. Well, I was born on the Tutweiller Plantation in 1887, oldest of seven brothers and sisters who was born after me. My momma and daddy worked for Mr. Tutweiller until they passed in 1914 and 1917. They both sick at the end and…"

"Excuse me, Mr. Neely. For the understanding of the audience, are you referring to the defendant right there, Tucum Tutweiller, when you say your parents worked for Mr. Tutweiller?"

"No, suh. I'm talkin bout his daddy, Mr. Irwin Tutweiller."

"Right, well, continue on, please."

"So, Mr. Irwin treated my parents real good when they started dying, bringin in doctors and havin his maids help me and my siblins take care of them, especially durin harvest time when we all be in the fields."

"So, you respected Mr. Irwin?"

"Yessuh, I did. Very much. He was a good man, best I can tell."

I realized my mistake when I saw Lon's look.

"I mean, Yessuh, he was a good man…to my parents and me."

"And how did Mr. Irwin treat you after your parents passed?"

"Real good. He took care of us better than other plantation owners treated their people. He made sure the young 'uns got some schoolin, made sure we was all fed. We was happy workin for him."

"And what was your job on the farm?"

"Well, for years I worked in the fields like everybody else, but he started givin me other jobs too, kind of being the overseer of the field hands and workin with the foreman to make sure everything ran smooth. I learned a lot workin with the white foreman."

I paused for a moment, feeling myself slipping into the role, and it was feeling damn good.

"The foreman didn't like workin with a nigger that close, though." I said, glancing toward the jury.

The crowd murmured and the press people started writing in their notebooks fast as hell.

"Objection, Your Honor. This racial speculation is just that, speculation that has no bearing on this case," Calder stood pleading to Judge Tate.

Lon spoke before the judge could open his mouth.

"On the contrary, Your Honor. The jury needs to understand the racial realities of the day in order to understand the seriousness of the charges against the defendant."

Judge Tate had so little expression on his face I wondered if he had been beaten down or he was about to finally explode.

"Overruled." He said, firmly, but with diminished volume. He sat back in his chair and intertwined his fingers, deep in troublesome thought.

"Continue, Mr. Neely, please," Lon said.

"Yea, he didn't like it at first, but over time he saw I was a big help to him. I made his job easier and bein a black man, I wasn't a threat to take his job from him. At least, not until Mr. Irwin asked me if I would be the Assistant Foreman."

"Well, that must have been quite an honor."

"More like an honor that would get me killed."

"How so?"

"Now I'd be second in line to the foreman and he saw that as a threat, sho nuf."

"A black man being a foreman was unheard of, correct?"

"Yessuh, with everybody and them except Mr. Irwin. He was different from any white man I knew. Seemed like the only rules he followed were ones written down. If he was supposed to do somethin just because somebody said that's the way it's done, well, he might, and he might not."

"And how did people take to his behavior?"

"It depends on which end of that behavior you was on. Me, I admired him for bein his own man and I appreciated him for treatin me as a man, and not just a black man. It didn't go over real well with the whites though."

"Who in particular?"

"The foreman, for one. He told Mr. Irwin he was givin too much responsibility to me, that no nigger was smart enough to do his job."

"Anybody else on the plantation feel that way?"

"Oh, yeah. Mr. Irwin's son, Tucum Tutweiller. That man right there."

I pointed at Tucum and suddenly I wasn't looking at my friend. Who I saw was a privileged, rich, nigger-hating white man from 1923.

Tucum didn't surprise easy, but his eyes got big so I knew whatever came over me was written on my face.

"Did Tucum take his resentment out on you?"

"He couldn't. Not as long as his daddy was alive."

"So, did you work as the assistant foreman?"

"No. Never got to that point. When I told Mr. Irwin I didn't think his son, or the foreman, would put up with it, he asked me if there was another job I would take."

"And what did you tell him?"

"I told him my dream was to have my own farm and if there was any way he could sell me a piece of land and finance it over time, I would be willin to pay him in crop or money."

"And what was his answer?"

"Said the only way he could do that was if I still worked part time for him."

"So, he was willing to sell you some acreage for…"

"A hundred acres," I broke in.

"He was willing to sell you a hundred acres for some flexible terms. That is highly irregular, wouldn't you say?"

I glanced at Calder half expecting him to jump up like a cricket and object, just because he was craving attention like a moth to light.

"You right. It sho was."

"And why did Mr. Irwin give you such good terms, you figure?"

"Well, he knew me real good, knew my parents, and we was all loyal to him. But he became more like a friend than a boss man to me and I think he felt the same. Like I said, he was a good man."

"He was such a good man and friend that he sold you one hundred acres of his plantation, and a fine piece of ground at that."

"Yeah, I didn't expect that. Kinda expected to get some low land that flooded now and again."

"And how did the defendant act about the business arrangement his father made with you?"

"Oh, he was madder than a…," I had to search for the words I had rehearsed but they didn't feel right when I remembered them, "…I guess I can't rightly compare it to anything I had seen before. He never threatened me, even when Mr. Irwin wasn't around, but he looked at me like he could taste revenge on the tip of his tongue and he couldn't wait to get a whole mouthful."

"Objection, Your Honor. Witness is speculating on the defendant's intent with no proof." Calder had jumped so fast he startled most in the gallery.

Judge Tate leaned forward, elbows on the table, and looked down at Lon. "Counselor, what little patience I walked in with is leaving the room with every word I don't see a point to. Get with it."

"Yes, Your Honor. Bear with me and it will all become relevant."

"Mr. Neely, moving ahead quickly then, I suppose your hundred acres were and still are a successful farm. Am I correct?"

"Started that way, sho nuff. Mr. Irwin would have been happy for me too if he hadn't died."

"And that's when your troubles began?"

"Not too long after, yessuh."

I paused but continued when it was clear Lon would not lead me on with another question.

"As soon as Mr. Irwin was in the ground, Tucum there, his son, came by my shack and fired me. Told me I had one day to get off the property. Also, told me I had to pay the land note in cash. He wouldn't take no crop as payment."

"So, did you have the cash?"

"The crop that year had been good; very good. I told you that was some good ground Mr. Irwin sold me. I had some of the money, but not enough. The money I had saved to plant that next spring went to the note instead.

"I assume you had to get a loan for the planting seed, then?"

"Yeah, one would think it, huh? It didn't happen, though. The USDA turned me down and I couldn't even get an appointment at the bank."

"And why was that?"

I looked over at Tucum, and he stared back.

"Because of that man, right there." Our stares broke when I pointed at Tucum.

Calder jumped like a scalded cat. "Objection, Your Honor. This line of…."

Judge Tate held up a palm towards Calder, silencing him.

"Overruled," Judge Tate said with a sigh. "I think all these people came out tonight to be entertained with a make-believe story. Let's let them."

I looked at Judge Tate. He looked like a worn-down channel cat that was giving out from the fight, but I knew there was a pot of hate boiling inside. We needed to strike fast before he called an end to the entire production.

Lon continued rapidly. "But Mr. Neely, you were able to get seed that year, correct?"

"Yessuh, I was. Had some good friends who loaned me the money."

"Black friends?"

"Good ones, yessuh."

"And you had a good crop that year?"

"Yessuh. Better than the year before."

"So good that you were able to pay Mr. Tutweiller here the cash payment for the land?"

"Yessuh."

"And what was Mr. Tutweiller's reaction?"

"He was madder than a springtime moccasin. Told me my cash money didn't make no difference. That land belonged to him and he was gonna get it back."

"And did you believe him?"

"I believe every white man's threat. I believe they mean it at the time, anyways. Whether they gonna do it or not, hell, only God knows."

I was in a trance, like it was just me, Tucum, Lon, and the judge. Calder broke the spell.

"Objection. Only God knows where this subjective and speculative discussion is going, Your Honor."

"Sustained." Judge Tate peered at Lon, his bushy gray eyebrows furrowed in agitation. "Counselor, even God is losing patience. Do him and us a favor and wrap up your questioning. God says you have two minutes."

Lon glanced at Judge Tate but didn't acknowledge him before asking me, "Mr. Neely, you were an experienced farmer. You knew how to farm, how to work hard, and you made enough money to pay your land note. So," Lon turned slowly to face the audience, "how in heaven's sake did you lose your farm?"

"Taxes, suh." I answered.

"Taxes? Surely you paid your land taxes?"

"Didn't know I wasn't."

"How was that?"

"I was never told I owed taxes. Found out later I shoulda gotten a notice from the county tax office. Never did. Guess I thought Mr. Tutweiller was payin the taxes since I thought he legally still owned the land while I was payin it off."

"But that's not how it works, is it?"

"That's what they tell me now."

"So, who was to blame? You, the county tax collector, or Mr. Tutweiller?"

"I guess we all was in a way. I'm just a farmer, Mr. Miller, and I was to blame for not knowin the legal stuff about land, but the other two were to blame for being in cahoots to cheat me."

"And how did they do that?"

I looked around the courtroom and looked most of the jurors in the eye before answering.

"Well, like I said, no one ever told me I owed taxes. And after my land was stolen, there was this group from up north that came through the county askin us colored what problems we was havin. The one I talked to spent a day at the Greenville paper lookin for a notice printed in the paper that said my land was going to be sold off. Never could find it."

I paused to take a deep breath and glance up at Judge Tate.

"They broke every law there is about takin someone's land. Tucum Tutweiller told me on the day he showed up with the sheriff to take my farm that he controlled the USDA and had the bank dancin to his tune. He made me feel a fool thinkin I could fight the white system. Turns out it happened to more than just me."

I saw the gavel arcing down a split second before the crack echoed through the room, causing most everyone to startle. Several jurors exchanged glances and all the press were writing frantically in between glances to see Judge Tate's reaction. I didn't have to look up to the judge to tell out of the corner of my eye he was glaring down at me. I imagined his hate was falling on me like acid rain.

Judge Tate raised the gavel in the air once more while he stared around the room. He slowly let it down to come to rest on the desk without a sound. He brought his hands together, intertwined his fingers, and seemed to study the wrinkles of his fists.

"This all…this whole production," he scanned the room and the lights above, his eyes squinting almost to a close, "was clearly written…I say written," Judge Tate paused and looked toward Abaddon, "to depict the plantation owners of the 1920s in a bad light, all based on conjecture and baseless allegations. Now, in the world of theater in New York, this format might be all the rage and if I thought like a New Yorker, I might actually like it. But, Mr. Thomas," the judge looked to the shadows where he knew Abaddon perched, "and Mr. Marshall," he looked over the audience where LJ likely was, "I'm not a New Yorker, never been there, never want to go there. I'm from right here. This is my home. This will always be my home. Us large farm owners are God-fearing people who treat our employees right and we don't appreciate outsiders coming in stirring up people with make-believe stories about the past. What may or may not have been done in the past is just that-in the past. It's over and done with and has no relation whatsoever with today. Now at the end of your so-called play, and that end is very near, I can assure you, you both are going to explain to all the press you enticed here under false pretenses, that everything they've heard these three nights has been pretend. And I don't deal in pretend, gentlemen. I live in a world of facts. And the fact is, you have a brief time to bring this to a close."

Judge Tate sat back in his chair, looking satisfied, as if he had done a great service clearing the air.

Suddenly, Abaddon walked into the light to where Lon stood and whispered in his ear. Lon nodded several times before Abaddon walked over to the bench, pressing against it to get as close to Judge Tate as possible.

The judge leaned forward, matching stares with Abaddon. In a hushed voice, Abaddon said, "Judge, I don't have to remind you there are newspaper and TV people here from a half dozen states and media outlets run their stories all over the country. I would hate for you to end this play early because you're annoyed it's not going the way you thought it would. If we don't end it our way, judge, the press will end it a half dozen ways to their readers, and I don't think you'll look good in any of them."

Judge Tate's forehead folded like a crimson mountain range.

"Who do you think you are, coming into my county threatening me?" Lamar yelled in a whisper.

Spit flew from the judge's mouth onto Abaddon's suit.

"You got no business coming into my home insulting our way of life when you don't know the first thing about it. Niggers around here have disappeared for less, Mr. Thomas. You keep that in mind. I'd hate to see harm come to you before you got home. I'm not sure where exactly in Chicago that is, but I have people working on that."

It took a lot to rattle Abaddon, but that statement made him blink.

"Be careful, Mr. Thomas. Be very careful."

After a moment, Abaddon broke his stare, turned and nodded to Lon on his way back to the shadows.

Lon turned to Judge Tate.

"Your Honor, I hear the impatience in your voice, so in order to bring this case to a close tonight, I propose we do the following. Defense can cross-examine Mr. Neely if they so desire or they can decline to save time. The plaintiff has two last witnesses to call and I will make their examination brief, at which time the defense can decide whether they want to cross-examine. If not, we'll both make our closing arguments to the jury. Since we've come this far, it would be an injustice if the jury didn't have the opportunity to adjourn and take one vote on the guilt or innocence of the defendant. Once they announce their verdict, the producer and director will give their closing remarks to the audience and the press. All that can be done in the next hour, Your Honor, and justice will have been served."

Judge Tate looked at his watch for several moments before looking up at Lon.

"Alright then, bring this, as you say, to a logical close. And counselor, this gavel will hit the table sooner rather than later."

"Yes, Your Honor, thank you."

Lon turned and looked at Calder, then back to the Judge.

After an awkward silence, Judge Tate picked up on Lon's cue and said, "Mr. Ambrose, do you want to cross-examine Mr. Neely?"

Calder had to restrain his legal training in saying, "No, Your Honor. In the interest of time, I decline."

"Very well then. Mr. Miller, call your witness, please." Judge Tate put unmistakable emphasis on 'please'.

Lon spoke immediately. "The plaintiff calls Mr. Otis Clarence to the stand."

Hearing his name made me pause while leaving the witness chair. In the dimness of the gallery I saw the shape of a small, hunched over individual coming slowly down the aisle, helped by a larger, upright person. It snatched me back to the memory of Mr.

Larry's hundredth birthday at Sammy's, the night the first light of truth revealed my family's past. It seemed like a dream long ago, but now here he was, shuffling past the rows of press people, with LJ holding his left arm.

I hustled off the platform that held the witness chair and grabbed Mr. Larry's right arm to help him up. The ornamental railing attached to the platform was there to resemble a real courtroom, but it made for an awkward time for me and LJ as we shifted positions around the railing and chair, but nothing was working. Poor Mr. Larry must have felt like he was in spinning storm winds.

"When I turned a hundred, I didn't overnight become helpless, goddammit. You niggas get off me!"

LJ and I looked at each other and let go of his arms. Mr. Larry put one hand on the railing and the other on the chair, stepped up on the platform, twisted slightly, and plopped down in the chair, all in one slow but steady motion.

"Sorry for the language, Judge. I don't like to be fussed over, that's all." Mr. Larry said as he glanced up for a moment.

"Not at all, Mr. Clarence. I hope I can say the same when I'm your age."

"Oh, you gonna wish people never fussed with you, and a lot sooner than that."

Judge Tate tilted his head, his eyebrows furrowed in confusion. He opened his mouth to ask something of Mr. Clarence, but thought better of it.

Judge Tate cleared his throat and said to Lon, "Counselor, the clock's ticking."

Lon glanced at Judge Tate while he cinched his tie, but again did not acknowledge him.

Lon approached the witness stand, and putting one hand on the railing, said in a kind voice, "Are you comfortable, Mr. Clarence?"

Otis was scrutinizing the room and didn't immediately answer.

"Mr. Clarence?"

Otis finally looked at Lon, "Oh, I hardly goes by my name. Been called Mr. Larry for years."

"Alright, Mr. Larry. As I explained to you earlier, Mr. Charlie Neely, whom you know, has accused Mr. Tucum Tutweiller, that man there, of stealing his land through an illegal land tax deception. This being 1923, that would put you how old, Mr. Larry?"

Mr. Larry worked his mouth around, "Hmm, well, I suppose I was a young man back then, around fifty."

Light laughter fluttered from the audience.

"'Back then', Mr. Larry, being now, remember 1923, how do you know the plaintiff, Mr. Neely?"

Mr. Larry shifted in his seat with a grimace, "'Scuse me tryin to keep all this straight. You jumpin back in time like bad memories of my first two wives."

Lon smiled, "Yes, sir, I know it's confusing, but it's 1923 and how did you come to know Mr. Neely?"

Mr. Larry looked at Lon, his watery eyes the color of egg yolk, before answering, "We all plantation workers at one time and we all got our own plot of ground at one time or another. We all be in the same boat so if I don't knows somebody personal I knows their name, and prob'ly knows somebody in their family personal. Now, I knows Mr. Neely personal for many years. We had cousins marry back in the day, so we related far down the railroad track."

"And you know Mr. Tutweiller well, also?"

Mr. Larry ran his hand over his bald head and put a finger to an ear to wiggle out an itch. Looking back up at Lon, he answered, "Son, I'm a hundred years old and feel like I's old as the dirt under my fingernails. If I was gonna be an actor, it would have happened years ago when I had the patience to pretend."

Mr. Larry looked around the room before looking up at Lamar Tate.

"I don't have many days left and none of 'em are gonna be spent pretendin bout nothin. Sorry if I can't keep up with who's who and what year they be in in this here play, but let me tell you what I do know. I knew Charlie Neely's father in tha year 1923. He was a good man, a hard-workin man, just like most of us. He deserved better than he got. All he wanted was his own piece of ground to farm, and he had it for a short time. He was a happy man then, and a grateful man."

Mr. Larry hung his head. The room was silent in anticipation. When Mr. Larry didn't move again, Lon stepped toward him and stretched out his hand to touch his shoulder. Before Lon could close the gap, Mr. Larry snapped his head up, turned to look at Judge Tate, and spoke loudly enough to cause some to twitch.

"I knew you, too." Mr. Larry slowly raised a wrinkled hand and pointed. Lamar recoiled as if an arrow had pierced his chest. His face showed confused alarm and defensiveness.

"Heart blacker than a hog liver. A nigger-hater thru and thru."

Judge Tate fumbled for the gavel as the room erupted in shouts. Lamar finally got a grip on the gavel and slammed it hard on the desk.

"What is this? What kind of…? Lon Miller…Abaddon…what kind of bullshit is this?!"

Abaddon came quickly out of the shadows.

"Please, please, Judge, Mr. Larry seems to be confused, which is to be expected of someone his age. Just give me a minute with him."

Abaddon didn't wait for Lamar to reply, but instead stepped over to Mr. Larry and leaned into one ear, whispering, "You're doing fine, Mr. Larry. The judge thinks I'm setting you straight, so just nod a couple of times."

Mr. Larry stared ahead and nodded.

"I'm not going to tell you what to say or don't say. I told you this is your chance to tell the truth if you want to and there are a bunch of folks sitting out there who are going to hear it and they're going to tell the world what happened to black folks not long ago. Don't be afraid to follow your heart, Mr. Larry."

Mr. Larry's head snapped back to look at Abaddon before leaning into his ear.

"Ain't fraid of dying and standin before God. I surely ain't fraid of saying the truth here on earth."

Abaddon stood straight and smiled, giving Mr. Larry a pat on his hand before walking off the set.

Judge Tate pulled back the sleeves of his black cloak and leaned over the desk to say in a scolding tone, "Has Mr. Thomas got you back on track, Otis?"

In response to being called Otis, and not 'Mr. Otis' or 'Mr. Larry' or Mr. Anything, Mr. Larry waited a moment before looking up at the judge.

"I ain't never been on a straighter track than this one, Lamar."

Judge Tate could only stare, couldn't even blink. He finally fumbled with the gavel before simply waving it at Lon.

Lon paced in a circle in front of Mr. Larry, stopping to face the audience.

"Mr. Larry, what do you know first-hand about injustices done to black farmers having their land taken from them?"

From my seat, I could see Tate's face turn red and his knuckles go bone white as his hand strangled the gavel.

Lamar came out of his chair to lean over and threaten Mr. Larry. "Now listen to me, I will not have you spouting any more lies about me, you hear me?" Lamar was sweating profusely, drops flung off his face like heavy dew.

Mr. Larry slowly looked up, staring straight ahead. His hands clutched the railing in front of him. As he struggled to stand, Lon stepped forward to grab an arm, but a look from Mr. Larry stopped him. Lon slowly backed away as Mr. Larry stood up straight, the hundred-year-old stoop nearly gone.

"My momma used to tell us chilluns God loved us and our sufferin be matched with the same amount of peace and reward in heaven. I too likes to think bad things folks do on earth will be matched with punishins in Hell. If I be's right, Lamar," Mr. Larry turned and looked at the judge with a hatred I didn't know a kindly old face was capable of, "then you gonna burn for stealin Charlie Neely's daddy's land. This ain't been no trial about Tutweillers, you stupid bastard. You be gettin judged here. Finally!"

Lamar jumped up, his robe flailing as if in a strong wind.

"And you gonna burn right along with yo brothas for doing wrong to yo workers, starting with what you done to Miss April!"

Mr. Larry was shaking his fist at Lamar, and he suddenly looked twenty years younger.

Lamar swung the gavel down like a wild man until the handle shattered, but the splintering sound was drowned out by the cacophony of shouts from the audience.

The press people were simultaneously looking at each other, furiously jotting words in notebooks and staring at the mayhem in the court. Cameramen were jostling for clear shots of Judge Tate's meltdown.

Lamar threw down the stub of gavel handle left in his hand and screamed, "Liar, liar," pointing at Mr. Larry, whose look of hatred had been chased away by a look of serene satisfaction.

"This shit is over. Don't believe these lies!" Lamar screamed at the press people. He then looked over to the side of the room, "Abaddon, I'm going to sue your ass for libel. I'll see your black ass in a real court!"

Lamar spun around and missed the one step down from his raised platform. He simply disappeared from view, the sound of his falling smothered by the ruckus that had only gotten louder. When he stood up, his forehead was bleeding. He wrestled the gown off his arms like a windmill caught up in bedsheets. The black gown went up in the air and landed at Mr. Larry's feet in a clump. Mr. Larry gave it a shove with one foot to keep it away, as if it bore a disease.

Lamar pulled furiously at the curtains behind the set, finally pulling one down with a ripping sound. He pushed open the door into the storage area that was now full of overflow patrons. Angry shouts caused him to slam the door and run back onto the set. Seeing no way out but through the front door, he staggered through a storm of thrown programs and insults to the front door. Several reporters jostled along behind and alongside him as he hustled across the street without looking.

All the shouted questions melded into one scream that reverberated in his head. As he fell into his car seat and slammed the door, he was spinning in a world he had never known. The mouths of the faces in his windows were opening and closing furiously, but he wasn't hearing a word or making sense of anything. He mindlessly started the car and hit the accelerator, causing the tires to screech and the mob of press to jump back. As he sped down the street and through a red light, he realized that for the first time in his adult life, he wasn't in control of everyone around him.

I was numb to what happened, trying to digest it, and I stayed in the theater too long. The press had immediately swarmed on Abaddon, LJ, Lon, Tucum, and Calder. Abaddon and LJ patiently took questions and gave thoughtful answers. Lon bloomed in the spotlight and was in the focus he had been trying to get to since he opened his practice in Greenville. Tucum didn't have the patience for idiots. He hung in longer than I expected, but when a reporter from Memphis asked him if all whites in the Delta were racist like Judge Tate, he gave a typical Tucum response, "Are you fuckin kiddin me?" When he turned in disgust to get the hell away from the press, I waved to him from across the room, but he probably couldn't see past the steam coming from his nose.

That's when they turned on me.

There were seven or eight surrounding me, way too close. If I could have pushed through the cinder block wall against my back, I would have done it and kept on going until I couldn't hear another question yelled at me.

"Mr. Neely, was the play your idea?"

Those words shocked me. After all the secrecy, I realized the whole thing was over and out in the open, for better or worse.

"I ain't the only one in the play, am I?"

"Does Judge Tate owe you a hundred acres?"

"Hadn't thought about it. I wouldn't turn it down, I guess."

"What did Mr. Larry mean by saying Judge Tate does wrong to his workers?"

I took my time answering that one.

"I think what he meant to say was, Judge Tate and a lot of other plantation owners do wrong to their workers."

"Who is Miss April?"

"She works for the judge. Takes care of the house and such."

"What's her last name?"

I hesitated, wondering if it was my place to answer that.

"Y'all gonna find out from somebody. It's Legare."

"Does her family know how Judge Tate's treating her?"

"She don't have no family no mo."

"How can we get an interview with Miss Legare?"

"Stay in town a day or two. If she wants to talk, she'll find you."

I can't say how long the questions went on. It seemed long enough for the moon to set and the sun to rise, but it couldn't have been more than a few minutes before I felt panicked and pushed through the circle of press toward the front door. I started jogging when I was through and out on the street. I heard footsteps behind and turned to see who it was.

"Mr. Neely, please. Please, just another minute."

After all the yelling, her voice sounded soothing, welcoming, and trustful. I slowed to a walk, and she came alongside.

"My truck's a block away, Miss Evans. When I get in it, I be gone."

"I get it. You must have felt like a cornered dog."

I turned, slowing my stride as I stared at her.

She blushed. "I'm sorry. I wasn't comparing you to a…"

I stopped under a streetlight nestled in the branches of a wild pecan tree, the leaves sending down dancing shadows all around us.

"No offense taken, Miss Evans."

She looked up at me with eyes big as an owl's.

"I got a question for you. What you gonna write about what just happened?"

She glanced down at her notepad.

"Well, I uh…"

"That ain't gonna sell papers."

She smiled faintly before taking a breath.

"What I'm going to write is that I witnessed something that was supposed to be one thing, turned out to be another, and how it all came to be is a mystery I'm going to try hard to figure out."

"Sometimes things be simpler than you think."

I started walking again, slowly.

"Mr. Neely…"

"Charlie."

She looked up at me. I could tell she wasn't comfortable calling people she didn't know well by their first name. Sign of a good upbringing.

"This wasn't the impromptu play it was advertised to be. Was this designed to end the way it did?"

"How's that?"

"With Judge Tate being exposed as a privileged son willing to do anything to keep blacks from getting ahead, and perhaps worse. Hopefully we'll hear that from Miss Legare."

I stopped again, this time next to my truck. I grabbed the door handle and, after a moment, turned to look at Felicia.

"Do you think it was a good thing, turnin out the way it did?" I asked her.

"Well…yes. Shining the light of justice on any wrong is a good thing."

I gave the door handle a tug and the truck door creaked open. I put one foot on the floorboard, smiled at her, and said, "Well, then, Felicia, it don't really matter how we got in that light you talkin bout, at least to me. What matters is that light's shinin and there be a cockroach runnin to get out of it. Now it's your job to make sure he don't get away."

I hopped up into the seat, started the truck, rolled down the window, and before pulling away, looked over at her and gave her a smile and a wink. She smiled back.

"Felicia, I sho enjoyed meetin you tonight and I normally would ask you to join me for a cup of coffee, but my tired head's spinnin and I'm not up for talkin right now. If you still here tomorrow though, maybe we can have that coffee."

"I'd like that."

I drove home feeling good, calm, fulfilled, and finally no longer feeling the weight of having to do something; something for me, but more for my father. As I drove, I tried to see him smile, but I could never quite get to it. By the time I was old enough to hold on to memories, all the smiles he was born with were gone. Just the same, I hunched forward over the steering wheel and looked up through the cracked windshield to the full moon shining a white light like it was brand new.

"That was for you, daddy," I said to the moon, and the stars, and even the darkness.

I leaned back, put my elbow out the window into the cool night air and we both made our way home in long overdue peace.

## Chapter 55

The next morning, I pulled around the back of Tucum's and parked under his old red oak, feeling foolish as soon as I killed the engine. There was no need for secrecy anymore, but it seemed second nature.

His back door was open and the screen door unlatched. I stepped into the kitchen, giving a yell, "Hey!"

"Hey, back at ya," came from down the hall.

I sat at his breakfast table, which was also his lunch and supper table. At one time, back in the day, I imagine the yellow table and shiny yellow padded chairs sold as a breakfast table to rich folks. Now, time had turned it into just a table; a tired table with little future left. I thought, "Damn, if I don't know people like this table." I ran a hand over it to see if I could feel a sense of history.

Tucum rounded the corner, hair wet, and combed down to his bare shoulders, wearing only old shorts that supported his tanned belly. He sat down opposite me, spread his hands out on the table, and looked at me before speaking.

"How ya doin, my brotha?"

"I'm doing ok, Tucum."

"You answered too damn quick. This ain't any old cracker stranger sittin over here, so let me ask you again. How ya doin?"

I had been up most of the night tryin to grab onto what all had happened and what it meant. I had no answers, but I hadn't asked myself those three simple words.

"I think I'm ok, Tucum, but the fact I can't say fo sho has got to mean I ain't."

"Well, good; some honesty for both of us. That's alright, Charlie. You ain't supposed to be ok after last night. I know I ain't and if I ain't you damn sure better not be."

I looked at my friend, who had a way of pulling the truth out of a magic hat.

"We're on unplowed ground now, Charlie. I was so busy helpin you and Abaddon and LJ, I didn't stop to think about how it might end; whether it was gonna be good, bad, or neither."

"Now that the shit hit the fan, what do you think?" I asked.

"I was up like you was last night, and I wish I could say one thing or another for sure, but the best I can say is Judge Tate's in a dangerous place and I'm happy to see him there. The worst I can say is he's a rattlesnake, and he's got a whole den of rattlers loyal to him. They believe in revenge like me and you believe in sayin our mornin prayers. They will bite, Charlie. It's a question of who and when."

We stared at each other, two somber faces framed with worry.

A car door slamming out front made me jump. Tucum spun around to look out, reaching for the shotgun in the corner behind him. He relaxed before his hand got to it.

"Abaddon," he said as he got up and walked to the front door.

"Come on in, Mr. Thomas. Charlie's back here."

"Oh, good. The two people I wanted to see."

I stood up as they entered the kitchen.

"Charlie, it's good to see you. I wouldn't have felt right leaving without saying goodbye."

We shook hands and Tucum motioned for us to sit.

"Why you leavin so soon? Don't you want to stick around and see the end of the shit you started?" Tucum asked.

"Well, yes, I want to, but thanks to all the interest in the media, I think I'll be able to keep up with it in California."

"California? I thought you was from Chicago," I said.

Abaddon looked at me, then Tucum.

"It's not important. What's important, Charlie Neely, is that you, you and LJ, figured out a way to tell the world some things the world had decided a long time ago to ignore. Where it goes from here, well, I certainly don't know. What I do know is that it can't be stopped now. I also know I was proud to play a small part in it."

"Small, my ass," Tucum jumped in.

"I'm not being modest. The play really came alive on its own. I was thrilled to have a front-row seat. But now I think it's best I disappear as quietly as I appeared. I'd be lying if I said I wasn't concerned about Lamar and his friends being mad enough to retaliate. I wish I could make sure you two are safe, but other than praying for you, I'm completely helpless."

"We appreciate that, Abaddon. Really do," I answered, trying to sound upbeat. "Prayers done some mighty things and last time we spoke, the Big Guy said he's still hearin 'em,"

Abaddon looked at me for a moment.

"Are you worried, Charlie?"

"Hell, I was doin alright until I get here and first Tucum tells me to be scared and now you tellin me the same thing."

Abaddon reached out and grabbed my shoulder.

"I don't mean to scare you, Charlie. You can't live like that. But you can learn to live cautiously. Keep friends like Tucum close. Make sure someone's got your back, at least for the next few weeks, a couple of months maybe. Once their anger cools off, you'll be alright. I'm sure of it."

Having Abaddon say that made my jitters settle. I'd lived with the play for so long that another couple of months looking behind me would not be the hardest thing I've done.

Abaddon turned to leave, but stopped and turned back to us. "Did you get the word LJ is holding a small press conference this afternoon in the theater?"

"Nope. What for?" Tucum asked.

"Miss Legare wants to make a statement."

Tucum and I looked at each other and, at the same time, said, “We’ll be there.”

## Chapter 56

Abaddon was right in calling it a small press conference, especially compared to the gaggle of press that had been in the theater less than twenty-four hours before. One row of a half dozen folding chairs was set up and three were occupied. One of the three reporters was Felicia Evans, and I gave her a nod when our eyes met. Tucum and I stood off to the side with Abaddon and Lon, not wanting to say the wrong thing the press might hear, so we said nothing.

After a minute, the door to the back room opened and Miss April Legare stepped out, escorted by LJ. She stopped to look over who was in front of her and 'scared' was all over her child-like face. LJ put his hand on the small of her back and guided her in front of the reporters. There was no need for a podium or microphone. LJ intentionally did not invite more reporters to make it less intimidating to April and to keep it from leaking to Lamar and his friends.

LJ and April stood six feet in front of the three reporters. LJ gave a smile to all three and began.

"Thank you for your coverage of our trial. I wish you all had been here the first night, but to your credit, you knew a good story when you heard about it and we appreciate the coverage your companies gave us. If the trial had continued, we would have called one more person to the stand, the witness who stands before you, Miss April Legare.

"Speaking in public is not something April is comfortable doing, and speaking about something personal and upsetting is even more difficult. Even so, April was prepared to take the stand, and she was extremely disappointed when she didn't, so much so that she asked me to call you here this afternoon so she can give you a statement."

LJ turned to April and whispered a word of encouragement. He stepped back but stayed close enough to give her a reassuring hand on her shoulder should she need it.

April pulled a folded paper from the pocket of her plain white and gray dress. It shook as she unfolded it and shook even more as she held it open. She glanced quickly up at the reporters, but just as quickly back to the paper.

She cleared her throat. "I done worked for Mr. Tate my whole life. Can't remember a time I didn't. My parents died when I was a young girl leavin me by myself. Had a few cousins living on the plantation like us, but none of them would take me into their shacks already overfull with folks. The only one who helped me was Mr. Tate. He took me into the big house. Gave me my own bedroom. Had my own bathroom, too…inside."

April looked up at the reporters to emphasize how amazing that was, though seeing the reporters looking at her unnerved her again and she looked down and continued reading.

"Those were the best days of my life. Mr. Tate's sons didn't like me bein in the house but they wasn't mean about it. They just wasn't friendly, that's all. Mr. Tate was real friendly, real nice, up until I was around thirteen."

April stopped and took a deep breath. She looked at the reporters again, this time slowly, and then turned back to Lon. Lon made a motion of putting his hand over his heart, followed by a nod. April sighed and went on.

"That's when he done first raped me."

For under a dozen people in the room, there was an impressive response of noise. A couple of "Oh, my Gods" and an "Oh, shit" from Tucum, and a lot of shifting in seats and shoes, everyone either writing or looking at each other. I knew this was coming, but I still couldn't make sense of what it meant. We had embarrassed Lamar last night with the hope it would cost him the election, but this…this was way beyond that. I felt somehow this would change my life, and not for the better.

April's reading of the rest of her statement was overtaken by rapid-fire questions from the three reporters. She handled it for a minute, but LJ saw her wilting and stepped in.

"That's all for now. Everything will come out in trial, I assure you."

"Have you filed charges?" One asked.

"We're going to the police station right now," LJ answered as he, now joined by Lon, steered April to the front door, one hand on her forearm and the other on her back. When they got to the door, LJ stopped and turned back to the reporters who were picking up their bags, deciding their next move.

"Please follow us. I'm sure your readers would like to hear how the police appreciated April coming forward."

I couldn't tell if the reporters detected LJ's sarcasm, but they immediately rushed to the door. I felt better for April's safety knowing they would be at the front door to interview her when, not if, she made it safely out of the police station.

We had that cup of coffee later at Ruth's. Felicia got insights no other reporter would. I got a reminder my life would be different with a woman in it. I knew she wouldn't be Felicia; the woman across the table was educated, ambitious, and loved the hustle of the city. I was none of those and never would be. Despite that, she gave me hope and excitement for the future, and that's something I hadn't felt in years, or maybe never.

# Chapter 57

I gave a few interviews over the next couple of weeks, but those calls stopped as quick as a passing July shower with all the attention turned to the lawyers involved in Lamar Tate's prosecution and defense. That was more than fine with me. Falling back into my routine of work at Sammy's helped to ground me again. I even welcomed the quiet of my trailer. My mind was free to examine what had happened, how it evolved, and what it all meant. I began sleeping again, no longer burdened by worry about the play.

After a couple of months, the worry of reprisal had also left me and I felt almost anonymous again, too inconsequential for anyone to bother with. I was just Charlie again, living a peaceful life, until the whoosh of igniting gasoline woke me at three in the morning.

Yellow light flickered outside the windows on either side of the camper door. A thought of Christmas lights entered my groggy mind and then vanished when I realized they were flames racing up the side of the trailer. I began hearing pops coming from the wall of the trailer and knew the siding or something in the walls was being cooked by the heat. I also knew the fire would cook me in short order. It happened so fast I barely remember wrapping a blanket around me, burning my hand on the doorknob, and diving through flames. Landing in a shallow puddle put out the flames on part of the blanket. I dropped the rest of it and immediately felt the skin on my face burn from the intense heat coming off the camper. I ran until the only thing I felt was the cool night air, and stood there watching the camper, my home, be consumed in a deadly fireball. I stood in a trance until the camper walls, what was left of them, collapsed inward and the flames began subsiding. It wasn't until then that I saw flames on the back wall of Sammy's beginning to creep up from the ground. That was enough to break my shock. The garden hose that brought water to my camper was much shorter now with half of it being turned to burned rubber and smoke. What was left was enough though to wash down Sammy's and put the fire out. I stood there for I don't know how long keeping Sammy's wet, even as the camper flames died down to mostly smoke. Now Sammy's was all I had to call home and I would have stayed there for days washing it down if that's what it took to save the last thing in my life that gave me purpose.

A week later the fire marshall confirmed it was arson, and even though I already knew it, being made official shook me. I had been a fool to think a black man could instigate the takedown of a powerful white man and the white man and his friends would just roll over and take it.

I felt bad for Tucum because when he took me in to stay as long as I needed, he also took on the risk of having me under his roof. He didn't seem to mind all that, but his patience with the phone calls from the media around the country was wearing thin. I tried to stay closer to the phone than him so I could save the caller from a more than likely unwelcome greeting.

On a Friday morning, a week after the fire, I had just hung up after talking with a reporter from the Milwaukee Journal Sentinel, of all places, when the phone rang again. "Hello, Charlie," sounded so familiar, but I had to think for a moment to place the voice.

"Abaddon, is that you?"

"It is, Charlie. I'm calling to see how you're doing."

"I'm fine, Abaddon. Livin with Tucum for the time being. Well…you must know that since you called here. You heard about what happened at Sammy's then?"

"I did, Charlie. It was in the paper out here."

"All the way out in Los Angeles?" I still wasn't sure where Abaddon lived, but this would confirm my guess.

"Sure was. And in more than one. You're known to a lot of people, Charlie, and in a good way, I can assure you."

"Those fellas that burned up my camper, and tried to burn me in it, sure know me too. I guess the Tates didn't take this whole thing as good as I hoped they would."

"No, I was afraid they felt like they had to retaliate, but I hear things aren't going well for them."

"Yeah, like what?"

"Nobody will work for them. Since Lamar was charged with raping April, I hear most of the workers living on the property have moved away. Day laborers won't even work for the Tate boys."

That news made me feel bad for not keeping in touch with my Aunt Luretha and I told myself to take a drive out to the plantation, as hard and maybe dangerous as that would be.

"You be hearin more news two thousand miles away than I am right here in Washington County, but then I been tryin to keep away from anything havin to do with them evil people."

"I don't blame you, Charlie, but if you can stand one more mention of them, I also hear the Tate boys are thinking about selling out and moving."

"You shittin me? Like for good movin?"

"Well, I can't say for sure, but with the money they can get for the plantation, they could live anywhere. I suspect they would want to move where they can impress people with their wealth."

"Lord, I will drop to my knees the day that happens. Abaddon, I don't know who you talkin to, but keep talkin to them and you let me know what else you hear."

"You can count on that, Charlie. And you stay close to Tucum. I think the boys who tried to kill you might think twice of trying again with Tucum by you. I know I would."

I hoped that truer words were never spoken.

# Chapter 58

Several weeks went by without a call from Abaddon, and I was frustrated. He didn't give me his phone number, so all I could do was wait and see if he had any news of what the Tates were doing. What I got from the customers in Sammy's were opinions and hearsay. There was talk of some big corporation buying the farm and that could be true, seeing that it seemed to be the way farms were being gobbled up, but who knows if anybody in Sammy's knew the truth?

Me and Tucum drove to the Tate Plantation late one night to hear what Aunt Luretha had to say, but my shack, or rather her shack, was empty, as were the rest of them. My guilt at not having kept in touch with her doubled.

A month later, I was in Tucum's kitchen having a meal before heading to work at Sammy's when I answered the phone.

"Hello, Charlie. It's Abaddon."

"Well, Abaddon, I've been hopin you would call."

"Why? Has something else happened?" Abaddon's voice was suddenly concerned.

"No. I was thinkin you might know more about what's going on here than the old men in Sammy's."

Abaddon chuckled. "Well, your customers are the news experts, especially with some spirits in their bellies, but the news I have for you is that I'm coming to Greenville next week and I want to come visit you and Tucum."

I hesitated a moment. "You comin here? I…I didn't think that would ever happen, what with all the…"

"I'm not staying long; just one night. By the time the wrong people hear I'm in town, I'll be gone again, at least that's the hope."

“Well, it be great to see you again and I won’t even bother askin why you comin. You’ll either tell me the truth or you’ll give me a line out of a play.”

Abaddon laughed. “I’ll tell you the complete story Tuesday. In fact, if things go as planned, I’ll show you, too. Tell Tucum to clear his social calendar Tuesday and tell him I’ll be there for breakfast. Deer sausage and a farm egg omelet would go a long way to starting off what should be a very satisfying day for all of us. See you then, Charlie.”

## Chapter 59

I had been nervous all morning about what the day would bring. Tucum had been shirtless and barefoot, seemingly oblivious to the outside world. I felt my heart spike when a new car pulled up and Abaddon stepped out. Joy in seeing him again was fighting with fear that his return would reignite the curse of revenge.

I met him in the front yard, him having to step carefully between a truck tire and a mud puddle, and me around a car battery and jumper cables on the front steps. We shook with firm grips and earnest smiles.

"Abaddon, I didn't think I'd ever see you again."

"I thought the same thing, Charlie. You're looking good, my friend. How are you doing after the fire?"

I started to answer, but then a wisp of smoke from the kitchen slid under my nose.

"Let's go inside, Abaddon. Tucum's busy in the kitchen and we can talk over breakfast."

The smell of deer and hog sausage was powerfully good in the kitchen. Tucum gave Abaddon a bear hug. Abaddon didn't let on any discomfort of hugging shirtless, and a tad sweaty, Tucum, nor should he have. We were all brothers now, having gone through a different sort of combat together, but one that bound us to each other just the same.

"I got your request for breakfast and I am more than happy to oblige, my brotha," Tucum said, smiling at Abaddon. "Have a seat at the best table in this here establishment and you'll soon be eating the finest breakfast this side of the Yazoo River."

Abaddon and I pulled out chairs and took our seats at Tucum's yellow table. Tucum pulled three plates down from an open shelf above the stove and began fixing plates.

"So, Charlie, back to my question; how are you doing?"

I opened my mouth to answer with a standard, shallow, and insincere response we all fall back on. After a deep breath, I got honest.

"I'm scared, Abaddon. Scared for me and now scared for Tucum, too."

Tucum's bare back was to us and he didn't bother turning around to throw in his opinion.

"Fuck em, Charlie. It'd be worth dying with you in a shootout as long as we could take a few of them motherfuckers with us."

Abaddon's eyes widened just enough for me to see Tucum's remark confirmed to him he was definitely no longer in L.A. He was back where talk was real, loyalty mattered, and genuine friends were to die for. Abaddon looked at me, smiled, and settled back in his chair.

"I have missed you two, I really have. I had no intention of coming back here, at least not until enough time had passed for it to be safe, however long that will take."

"We ain't there yet, are we, Abaddon?" I asked.

"No, Charlie, not by a long shot, but something has happened that is going to speed up that process, I believe."

"What's that?" Tucum asked as he set plates on the table, steam coming off the grits like hot asphalt after a summer shower.

"Well, that will be answered after we enjoy this beautiful breakfast. Charlie, would you lead us in a prayer of thanks?"

I did and there was a lot to be thankful for—the two friends I sat with being the last blessings I thanked God for and closed by asking Him to help us remember our plans in life take a backseat to what he has planned for us.

I hadn't a clue how he would remind me of that in a couple of hours. He had surprised me countless times since coming home from Vietnam, but nothing prepared me for what he had in store that day.

## Chapter 60

"What's the dress code for where we're going?" Tucum paused at his bedroom door looking at Abaddon.

Abaddon started to laugh, but realized Tucum was serious.

"Hmm, well, Tucum, I suppose it's as casual as you feel, as long as a shirt and shoes wouldn't be too much to ask."

"A shirt and shoes it is, then." Tucum disappeared into his room and I whispered to Abaddon that he should have specified a clean pair of shorts. When Tucum came out, though, he looked more than presentable, wearing the best shorts he had along with a polo.

"If this ain't good enough, then y'all can go by yourselves. I don't break out my good clothes for just anyone," Tucum said with a hint of a smile.

"I could take you almost anywhere in L.A. wearing that, Tucum. I'm honored you consider me worthy of your formal attire."

Tucum laughed, tilted his head and squinted one eye toward Abaddon, saying, "Cut the shit and let's go see this surprise that brought you all the way from Tinseltown."

By the time we set off in Abaddon's rental car, it was warm enough for air conditioning, which made it easier to talk. I had questions, and I wasn't gonna waste this opportunity.

"Abaddon," I asked from the backseat, "you ever gonna tell us your real name?"

Abaddon didn't turn his head. He didn't answer, either, until we had passed through a thousand acre field of cotton plants.

"I want you two to remember me as Abaddon, if you don't mind. The Klan knows me by sight, but I'd feel better if my real name wasn't written on their hit list. Not just yet, anyway."

Tucum answered before I had a chance, "That's fine with me on one condition. Where the hell did you think up the name 'Abaddon'?"

Abaddon laughed, “And that’s from a guy named Tucum?”

“Hah, fair enough.” Tucum looked over at Abaddon, smiling.“You show me yours and I’ll show you mine.”

Abaddon hesitated a few moments before saying, “Abaddon means ‘The Destroyer’ in Hebrew and I thought that reflected my mission as director of your play, Charlie,” Abaddon tilted his head to look at me in the rear view mirror. “It wasn’t until later I learned that in certain texts it’s also another name for Satan, but at that point there were people here who considered me that, so I was ok with that aspect of the name.”

We rode in silence for a minute, probably all of us lost in reflections of the destruction we had brought to the Tates, Sheriff Black, and, to a lesser extent, Mayor Campbell.

“Your turn and I’m guessing your name might be a tad light-hearted compared to mine,” Abaddon said as he looked over at Tucum.

“Well, I ain’t Satan, but when I was little my family might have thought I was related to him. I couldn’t stand to be left behind when someone left the house. Didn’t matter where they were goin, I wanted to come with them. They heard ‘I want to come, I want to come,’ so much they started calling me ‘to come’ and that turned into ‘Tucum’.”

Abaddon was turning at a four-way intersection of dirt roads and he waited until he straightened the car on the road to look over at Tucum.

“I love that story, Tucum. Do you mind if I use it in a movie one day?”

“As long as you pay me the millions it’s worth, or buy me lunch. Either one will work. But since you brought it up, are you really a movie director?”

“I am, and a producer. I do some scriptwriting, too. And no, I’m not exactly famous. I’m well known in L.A. but not so much anywhere else yet. But all it takes is a movie with a character named Tucum to be the breakthrough film I need."

We all had a good laugh at that.

"Tucum, don't forget about us little people." I exclaimed from the back seat.

"Oh hell, Charlie, I'm taking you with me!"

I lost my interest in the banter when I realized where we were.

"Abaddon, you're getting too close to the Tate Plantation for me. Where you takin us?"

Abaddon looked up at the mirror, saying, "Charlie, do you trust me?"

"Of course I do, Abaddon, but I damn sure don't trust the Tates."

"I don't either, Charlie."

We drove on in silence. A few minutes later, the long line of oaks straddling the Tate drive came into view across a sea of corn stalks. My stomach tightened, but I held my tongue. Leaving the paved road we slowed to a stop on the gravel drive and stared at the white monstrosity of a house at the end of the oak tunnel.

"Thought you said you don't trust the Tates," Tucum said without looking at Abaddon.

"I don't, but they're not here," Abaddon answered as he took his foot off the brake and tires began to crunch the gravel.

Tucum and I didn't say another word, trusting in Abaddon, but unable to shake the feeling of looming danger.

As we passed the muddy road to the worker's shacks, I stared at the one I grew up in and I felt like I was looking at a lifetime of emotions inside an eggshell. It was there to crack open if I wanted to or to let lie for another day. I turned and looked ahead.

Abaddon entered the circle around the fountain counter-clockwise, so our doors opened to the brick walk.

"We're here gentlemen. It's time to see reality, face to face."

Tucum snapped his head back to look at me. I could almost hear the cursing in his head. I opened my door, and he followed my lead a second later. Abaddon came around the car and started along the walk to the house's steps, where he stopped and looked back. We were standing by our open doors, as if we couldn't leave the protection of the car.

"Charlie, Tucum, remember…trust. Follow me."

Abaddon stepped up to the porch and walked to the front door, where he waited for us.

I exchanged a glance with Tucum and we both eased our doors closed, shutting off that escape.

Each step was timid, but my scanning of the porch and floor to ceiling windows found nothing alarming. We stopped next to Abaddon at the front door, confused thoughts racing through my mind.

We watched as Abaddon put a hand in a pocket and pulled out a ring of keys. He flipped through several before shaking one loose and handing it to me.

"It's only right you do the honors, Charlie."

Nothing made sense, and I wondered if I was foolish in trusting Abaddon. I just knew one of the Tate boys was going to fling the door open and put a shotgun in my face.

"Do…do what?" I finally got out with a stammer.

"Well, Charlie, be the first to open the front door of my house."

I felt like I was frozen in a nightmare, and the movement to slide the key into the lock was not my bidding. The click of the lock snapped me out of it.

"Go on, open the door." Abaddon's immense smile told me to quit imagining demons that were no longer there. I swallowed hard, turned the doorknob, and pushed the massive door open. We stood there for a while, Abaddon smiling at us, and Tucum and me with our mouths open.

"You bought this house, Abaddon?" I asked, dumbfounded.

"Me and some rich friends, Charlie. We bought the whole plantation."

Tucum and I looked at each other, then at Abaddon, then at each other again.

"I can't believe the Tates sold to you."

"Oh, I'm sure they never would have. They sold it to a corporation, but the corporation is owned by us. The closing was yesterday afternoon and our lawyer represented us. I was here only because I wanted to bring you two here today."

Abaddon let all that sink in for a moment before saying, "Well, we don't have to wait out here on the porch. Let's go in!"

We stepped into the foyer and other than the grand chandeleur, the rest was empty. There were no Tate family portraits, none of their furniture, and no ghosts that I could feel. We walked the length of the hallway, through the French doors and onto the back porch, which mirrored the layout of the front.

"Have a seat, my friends." Abaddon motioned toward four rockers in a line. We sat for a while looking at corn, soybeans, and cotton as far as the eye could see. None of this made sense.

"So, let's take this real slow. How…well, that can wait…why did you buy this plantation? You're not from here. It don't make sense." Tucum asked, echoing my thoughts exactly.

Abaddon eased back in his chair and took in the view before answering.

"When I came here, I thought I was coming to a place that had moved well beyond the horrible history of the Old South."

"Just cause somethin's in a history book don't mean it's gone," Tucum interrupted.

Abaddon looked over at Tucum and gave him an appreciative nod.

"You are so right, as usual. I was ignorant, Tucum, and shocked. It felt good doing my small part to bring a racist tyrant to justice, but I realized there's so much more to be done. The more I talked about the Delta in L.A. the more appalled and interested my friends became.

"It was Lon Miller who gave me the heads up that the Tate boys were having trouble and had no future ahead for them. I talked to my friends about the opportunity to change one farm in the Delta with the hope others will follow. Two of them with deep pockets bought in, so we sent our lawyer to talk with the Tate boys and, skipping through the details of the negotiations, here we are."

"You said you want to change the farm. In what way?" I asked.

"Charlie, sometimes you can't wait for the old ways to slowly slip into history. We're determined to rip the grip of the past off the present and build a better future for the good people of the Delta."

The looks on our faces caused Abaddon to pause for a moment.

"Yes, I guess that sounds too much like a political slogan, but we mean it."

"How are you gonna change what time hasn't hardly been able to budge?" Tucum asked with his usual skepticism.

"Well, Tucum, I have to admit we haven't thought of every detail. Some details we don't even know we have to think about, if that makes sense. We do know we want to go fully mechanical in picking cotton. The technology of pickers and strippers is evolving and we want a plantation where you never see a human picker in the fields. We're out on a limb financially and we have to make this farm profitable, but we also need to break the mold of workers barely getting by on what they make. Our plan is that every employee will be an owner and will share in the profits. We're hoping that will create a home people feel invested in instead of just a place to labor day after day. And who knows? We might just shoot movies here, including your story, Charlie."

I laughed, but stopped when I could see that Abaddon was serious. I was uncomfortable with that idea.

"What you know about farmin, Abaddon?" I asked, searching for familiar ground.

"Hardly a thing, Charlie."

"Your partners know how to farm?"

"They know less than me."

"Then how you gonna farm it?"

Abaddon leaned over to look at me. "Oh, we're not going to farm it. We're going to leave that to the plantation manager."

"You done hired somebody already?" I asked, impressed with Abaddon's efficiency and secretiveness. A rumor like that surely would have circulated through Sammy's.

"Not yet, but I have high hopes he's going to take the job. And it would be a personal favor to me if he did. You see, he's a dear friend of mine."

I creased my brow tightly. Abaddon gave a laugh, seeing my confusion.

"The dear friend is you, Charlie. We want you to run the place for us."

I was speechless and numb and hardly heard Tucum explode.

"You have got to be shittin me! Charlie Neely, you're gonna be the top nigger…," Abaddon and I both turned and looked at Tucum, "...the top dog on the plantation you grew up on, livin in a slave's shack and workin your ass off for hardly nothin. You gonna let him live in the big house, Abaddon?"

"Absolutely, and anyone else he wants to live here with him. I want to keep three bedrooms for me and my partners when we visit but the rest are for you to do with as you please, just as long as you don't turn it into another Sammy's," Abaddon smiled at me before getting his rocker going.

Without looking over at me, he said, "Oh, and the same goes for hiring, Charlie. You're well respected now and I think people will come to you in droves, asking for jobs. They'll know you'll treat them fairly and with respect since you know what being in their shoes is like. I want you to be fair in your hiring. Be open to everyone, even somebody who is almost downright allergic to shirts and shoes. People like that are some of the finest, smartest, and hardest working individuals you'll ever meet, even if their language is a bit crusty."

I turned away from Abaddon to look at Tucum and I swear his tanned face was turning red.

"Can you imagine, Charlie, me and you runnin the Tate Plantation and livin in the big house?" Tucum asked.

I squinted real hard at Tucum as he wiped his eyes and looked at me.

"Who said you gonna stay in the big house?" I asked as seriously as I could, like an actor in a play.

His hand froze in mid-air and seeing the hurt coming on made me drop the facade and laugh, joined by Abaddon and then Tucum, too.

The plantation porch echoed with long overdue laughter for quite some time.

## Chapter 61

The smoke spiraling lazily up from the grill disappeared into the deep blue of the twilight sky. Tucum was twirling a toothpick in his mouth. I was simply savoring the taste of the marinade on the venison steaks. Our plates were still on the table, emptied in time to pull on flannel shirts and sit in the backyard of the plantation to listen to the crickets and watch the day surrender to the Delta night.

"Sometimes I still can't believe we're here, Charlie."

"Me too, and I think it's the same for the employees. It's taken over a year, but this place has shaken off the Tate stink one hundred percent and what we got now feels like a big and helluva better family."

I paused as a cloud passed over my contentment.

"What you hearin the white folks sayin about us and the farm?" I asked.

Tucum took his time twirling his toothpick before answering.

"It's all good, Charlie. As good as it gets."

His voice sounded off. I expected him to say more, but I resigned to be happy in the moment and not push it.

"We gonna have good crops this year, Tucum."

Tucum smiled and answered, "Abaddon and his partners are gonna be pleased. They'll put some hefty money in their pockets. I know I've done well workin here and I want to tell you again, Charlie, I appreciate you hirin this old fat boy. It's given me a real purpose and sure has helped my disposition."

I thought for a moment about joking about Tucum's previously sour attitude, but thought better of it.

"Hirin you was an easy decision, Tucum. This farm wouldn't run without you. And you know you're welcome to move into the big house anytime you want."

"Hah, thanks, but I ain't a big-house kind of guy. I'm right at home in my nine hundred square feet. But if the Klan ever burns it down, I'll be right over."

We both smiled, feeling secure enough now to joke about the KKK. As far as I knew, time and our rise in stature in Washington County had sent that threat back into the shadows. Life was good, and we sat in silence, savoring it.

"You never told me what the occasion is."

"What?" Tucum had been in a full-belly stupor.

"You said you wanted to have supper on this special occasion."

Tucum looked over at me with a look that called me stupid.

"You know where you were two years ago?"

I thought for a minute and then looked quickly at Tucum. "It was around this time I met with Cleve. How'd you remember that, Tucum?"

"Because I remember I was huntin squirrels in Panther Swamp by myself while you were visitin 'a sick friend', you lyin son of a gun."

"Damn, Tucum. That was the start of it all, wasn't it? There been a lot of water under the bridge since then."

"Yep, a lot of water. That would have been a dry riverbed had it not been for you, Charlie Neely. Yes, sir, Charlie, somebody needs to write a book about what you done."

I chuckled. "Shit, Tucum, somebody can write all they want. Ain't nobody want to read about dumb Charlie Neely dreamin up some crazy play."

Tucum shifted in his seat to stare at me, serious-like.

"Don't ever call yourself dumb, Charlie. If you're dumb, then I don't even measure up to be a dumbass. You a man I look up to, Charlie, and don't you ever forget that. If you do, I'll kick your ass all the way to Vicksburg, you hear me?"

I laughed, a satisfying laugh from the heart.

"You won't have to hurt yourself tryin to kick my ass, Tucum. I won't ever forget you're my friend, don't you worry about that. A peculiar friend, but still the best friend I can hope to have."

We looked at each other, our faces reflecting the bright orange of the last brilliance of the sun cutting long ways through the sky. We both chuckled instead of laughing. The full laughs were happening inside, where they were savored as memories time and again.

The comfort of the chair, the serene backyard ringed with tall corn turning brown, and the deep colors of twilight caused my muscles to relax and my mind to wander.

A year and a half ago, Lamar Tate was the epitome of a rich southern racist. He controlled people as a birthright, to do what he wished with them. Now he's under the control of the Mississippi Department of Corrections, and will be for the next fifteen years.

Even though the play ended before the case went to the jury, the speculation of the outcome if it had was that the mayor was going to ensure it was a hung jury. In his case, speculated racism was as good as being proven and his political future was on rocky ground.

Sheriff Black was persona non grata in most of the county, especially in the black population. His quote from the trial about blacks being deadbeat farmers got quoted so often and for so long in the national press as being typical of the attitude of whites in the Delta that the pressure from state leadership caused him to resign. His replacement was a deputy with enough education, experience, and dark skin to quiet the national media.

When April filed rape charges against Lamar, Lon Miller announced his candidacy for chancery court judge. With Lon getting notoriety from the play and the trial putting stink on Lamar, Lon won in a landslide. It wouldn't surprise me if he runs for mayor of Greenville in a year, and it's probably his for the taking. Lon told me winning the election probably saved his marriage now that he had a respectable job. It helped when Kim was hired by the Current as a reporter shortly after Lon's election victory. I'm happy for her, but I'm not crazy about the Current's owners only seeing her qualifications when she became the Judge's wife.

April Legare became a celebrity. When Lamar's trial started, Greenville was once again the host to a throng of reporters, this time from the entire country. April was the centerpiece of most articles and TV reports, and rightfully so. She became the face of young vulnerable innocence corrupted by the dark soul of a southern white plantation owner who controlled her and most of Washington County. After the trial, April had many calls from people around the country offering her a home and an education. She took less than a day to pack a suitcase and get on a bus to Detroit. I heard she was living with a rich black record producer and his family and getting a high school education. Hers was the most unexpected, and frankly, the happiest, outcome of the entire undertaking.

People feared for my safety in the days and months after the trial, but I feared more for Cleve. Unlike Abaddon and LJ, who appeared out of the mist and disappeared just as thoroughly, Cleve had no secrets. And though his name had yet to be connected to the play, I felt it was only a matter of time. Everyone knew or could easily find out where he lived in Jackson and where his law office was. And if he didn't earn enough hatred for his role in producing the play, he was April's lawyer and won the guilty verdict against Lamar Tate, putting him in the crosshairs of the Klan. Cleve thought he was bulletproof, and maybe that confidence kept him safe. All I know is he will always have a special place in my heart for believing in the stranger who made a cold call to his office and proposed a crazy idea most would have laughed at.

The recollections finally brought on the feeling I could close that chapter of my life. In that moment, I felt a peace I hadn't felt in the last two years, and probably never had in my life. If I died right then I would at least have one good thing to tell God I did with my life.

"You've had a while to think on it, Charlie. Was it worth it?"

Tucum broke the silence as subtle as a dinner plate crashing on the floor. I took my eyes off the western sky and peered into the corn at the back of the yard, the individual stalks disappearing into a solid dark wall.

"Tate's in jail, so yeah, it was worth it."

"You ain't mad you ain't gettin nothin out of it?"

"Like what?"

"Like the hundred acres should have gone to you."

"Huh!" I sent spit flying into the dry grass between us.

"That be nice, wouldn't it? Be nice if Miss Cicely Tyson came with the land too, but that ain't gonna happen either."

"You don't think you deserve it?"

I moved my butt to the right and leaned on my left elbow to better look at Tucum.

"The way I see it, Tucum, is the sins of the father go to the grave with him. Wouldn be fair for the son to have to carry sins he didn't commit. Same thing with someone who was done wrong. That wrong goes to the grave of the man it was put on. It ain't passed down to the son, though there's lots who think it does."

Tucum did his own shifting now. We looked like bookends holding up something weighty between us.

A gust of breeze rippled through the cornstalks, sounding like a gentle wave on the beach. Tucum stroked his white goatee, which meant he was deep in thought.

Tucum finally let go of his goatee and spoke, "I've been paying for the sins of my father, and the fathers before him, all my life. I was carrying a burden I thought was a birthright. It seems so obvious now that treating people badly just because they're darker than me makes no sense. I guess every boy is born wanting to be like his father. You got to take the bad with that, too."

Tucum looked over at me, his face tensed, and he continued, "I'm ashamed I followed my father down that road of hate. Fightin alongside my black brothers in Vietnam made me see how wrong that was, but when I got back, I don't know, Charlie, it's like I slipped right back into a life that was too big for one person to change. But I'll tell you, my friend, you done changed me and I will be forever grateful for that."

I gave Tucum a sincere nod of appreciation and answered, "I'm a simple person, Tucum, but I ain't stupid and you know I ain't as naïve as I looks. I know how the human heart works and I know souls can be bright or dark. We all gots to deal with the same good and evil while we're here on Earth. Some knows mainly good in life, some knows mainly evil, and folks won't understand why until God tells them on Judgment Day.

"People say life ain't fair, and it sure don't look it, but if I think on it too long it makes me confused and mad. I gets to be like them that can't live their life because they tryin to relive some bad from their mother and father's lives, their grandparent's lives. Hell, they'll keep going back until they find an injustice that fills them with hate. That ain't me, Tucum. Hate and injustice should never be a couple, at least not in my world."

Tucum gave me a nod.

"Hate ain't you either, my brotha." I followed with.

"Amen to that, brotha. Amen to that."

At that, we both rolled back onto both butt cheeks and returned our eyes to the night sky. A handful of stars had emerged to chase another day into history.

Tucum finally broke the silence.

"I asked a preacher once what was the best gift we could give to God. He said it was to be grateful for the things he gives us and don't resent the things he don't. Charlie, I'm grateful the Tate family was shown for what they are. I'm grateful you did that, Charlie; amazed and grateful."

My eyes suddenly blurred with tears determined to find my cheeks, and I was thankful for the twilight darkness.

"When we get old we'll have somethin to talk about, won't we?" I asked.

"Yes, we will. Yes, we will. But until then, let's pretend those days are so far around the corner they're in the next county. How does that sound?"

"Sounds like music, Tucum."

"Well, alright then. In that case, let's start tomorrow with a young men's squirrel hunt."

I leaned over and grabbed up my tea glass. Sweat dripped onto my shirt and pants as I swung it over to clink glasses with Tucum.

"May we have many a good hunt together befo we can't get up from these chairs no mo," I said to Tucum from my heart.

I felt more grateful in that moment than I may have ever felt, and I told God. I didn't hear him answer, but I know he did, in his own way.

## Chapter 62

The cool morning air, the crispness of sound in the forest, the blue of the sky, all made the change of seasons official. The intense heat and humidity that made the summer months a test of endurance were gone, replaced by days best spent in woods beginning to show color; not New England color, but color nonetheless.

The western sky was brilliant with stars, and the eastern sky was showing the barest hint of lightness when we turned onto the east levee of Panther Swamp. I drove slowly down the levee road, windows down to bathe in cool air we hadn't felt in six months or more.

"God, this temperature been a long time comin," Charlie said to me.

"Like an old friend you ain't seen in too long," I answered.

Grass grew high on both sides of the road, dropping steeply to thick, dark woods. The truck headlights illuminated the eyes of several deer just above the grass line. A nice buck ran across the road yards in front of the truck, too fast for either of us to count the points of his rack. We agreed that was a nice one and I'll bet Charlie hoped at that moment, like I did, to see him again in gun season.

Being a weekday, we didn't see another soul. No trucks parked on the levee, and three miles down the levee road, an empty parking lot waited for us at the base of the levee next to a water diversion canal.

We both paused after getting out of the truck to listen to the expansive sound of nothing. After a minute, the first bird chirp rippled through the trees, announcing the soon-to-come light of day. We both wanted to stay motionless, that to move a boot would be to send the sound of gravel out to shatter the stillness and ruin the morning. But the morning wasn't staying motionless, so I moved first to keep up with it. I split a box of 12 gauge shells into the pockets of my jacket, grabbed my shotgun, closed the truck door, and walked around to the other side. Charlie was standing there, one arm on the opened truck door. He was staring up at the trees and at first I thought he might have seen an early-rising squirrel jumping through limbs, oblivious to the threat below.

"I'm going to miss this," Charlie said without moving.

I hesitated for a moment.

"What do you mean? You goin somewhere?"

Charlie turned around and looked at me, there now being just enough light to see each other's faces.

"Eventually we all are, Tucum. I guess I've been thinkin a lot lately about how quick life is."

"Hell, boy, you soundin like an old man. You can tell me that crap in another thirty years."

Charlie laughed. "I hope so, Tucum, I truly do. Maybe I'm finally gettin old enough to appreciate things a little more."

"Well, we're both gettin older standin here. Get your shit together and let's go kill some squirrels," I said to prod Charlie to get moving.

"You go ahead, Tucum. I won't be far behind. I'll find you when you shoot. Just leave one or two for me, will ya?"

"No promises, Charlie. I got my heart set on fryin us a pile of squirrel tonight, but just maybe I'll intentionally miss one or two." I winked at Charlie. He smiled in return.

"You do that, brotha. I'd be much obliged," Charlie answered.

"See you soon," I told my friend. And with that, I crossed the footbridge across the canal and started stalking into the deep woods.

## Chapter 63

Three hours later, I reached my limit of squirrels when a big male dropped from high up a towering white oak, snapping leaves off as it fell. The thump it made hitting the thick carpet of leaves on the forest floor was a sound I will never tire of. As I slipped the squirrel into the game pocket in the back of my jacket, I looked behind me, hoping to see Charlie coming through the woods. I had been looking behind me for a while; looking for Charlie and listening for a shot, but there was no movement among the trees and the woods remained quiet. I told myself everything was ok but doubt grew as I headed for the truck.

I started off scanning the ground for a coiled moccasin or rattler but as I neared the footbridge I gave up and stared intently through the trees, hoping I'd see Charlie fiddling with a shotgun that wouldn't fire, or dealing with some other problem that had kept him from hunting.

The footbridge came into view, but not Charlie. I paused at a tree next to the bridge, confused by what I saw on a limb. I grabbed it down, then hurried across, expecting to see him sitting in the truck. I imagined hearing him now, complaining about an old boot sole that had fallen off or a twisted ankle.

No amount of pretending could keep my heart from tightening when I saw the passenger truck door open and the truck empty. I sprinted to the truck, dead squirrels jostling my back. Charlie's shotgun was gone and his box of shells was open with a few shells left in the bottom. There was no sign of Charlie.

I cussed while I thought about what I should do. I finally reloaded my shotgun with three shells and blasted them into the air and followed with long bursts of the truck horn. The natural sounds of the forest were the only answer that came. Pacing and yelling consumed the next hour. I hated leaving to get help if Charlie came dragging himself out of the woods, too injured to yell, but I finally decided I would never find him on my own if he was out there unable to move.

I tore up the side of the levee in first gear, tires slinging gravel like fire hoses. Traveling too fast down the levee road, I glanced over at the empty passenger seat. What a fool I had been. I had lied to Charlie the night before about what I was hearing. Talk wasn't at all good; in fact, talk was dangerous amongst the worst of the worst in the county. We thought the Klan's attempt to burn him alive in his trailer was the end of their retribution, but Charlie living in the former Tate Plantation house and making the farm successful had rekindled hatred. I had hoped it was just talk, but now I feared the worst.

# Chapter 64

At first, it was just one sheriff's car with two deputies that showed up. They were halfway listening while I told them every detail of the morning. Mainly they were walking around the parking lot, scanning the ground, and occasionally looking into the trees. They didn't give me confidence.

My frustration was about to turn to anger when three trucks came off the levee and parked in a row next to my truck. Two more deputies and a guy in a Fish and Wildlife Service uniform got out of two of the trucks. A guy in hunting clothes and snake boots got out of the third truck, a coiled leash in his hand. He opened the dog box in the bed of his truck and commanded a Walker Hound off the tailgate.

"Mr. Tutweiller?" One of the new deputies approached me.

"I am."

"Your hunting buddy's lost?"

"I hope so. I mean, I hope he's just lost, but I doubt it. He knows his way through these woods better than me."

"Not to worry, sir. This fella's dog could smell a fart in a windstorm. We'll find your friend. He got out the passenger side here?"

"Yea. He was standing right here when I left him."

The deputy turned to look back.

"Scott, start here. The dog should get a good scent from the seat."

It was afternoon by now and warm. I feared that somehow the warming earth would burn off scents, but I was relieved and encouraged when the dog smelled the seat and around the ground on that side of the truck and then made a beeline for the footbridge. The dog strained at the leash, pulling his handler across the footbridge. I pictured the dog racing through the woods to find Charlie sitting against a tree with some minor medical condition. For a couple of seconds, I thought it would turn out good, and we'd have that squirrel fry after all.

The dog came off the footbridge and stopped at the first tree, the one with low branches I had paused at on my way out of the woods. His handler took the leash off and the dog circled the tree several times, nose sweeping back and forth over the brown leaves. After every circle, he would stop for a moment at the side of the tree facing the footbridge. He made one last circle, stopped at that spot, sat down, and looked at his handler.

"He came to this spot alright, but no farther."

My stomach coiled in a knot. "What do you mean? He ain't here, so where did he go?

"He must have walked back to the truck. That's the only line of scent there is."

"Well, if he ain't here and he ain't in my truck, where the hell could he have gone?"

"Could he have gotten into another vehicle?" One of the deputies spoke up.

The handler thought for a moment while staring at the footbridge.

"I suppose, or…"

He walked to the footbridge, the dog and the rest of us following. Halfway across, he stopped and looked over the railing. We did the same, some on one side, the rest on the other.

Another deputy spoke. "Would he float?"

The meaning of his question hung in the air, and the thought made me nauseous.

The dog handler spoke first. "Not necessarily. They often will sink pretty quick and then it could be days before they come back up."

"That's if a gator don't eat him," someone said. My head was swimming too fast to notice who.

What he said was a likely possibility. I had seen bona fide monsters in Panther Swamp more than capable of eating a grown man.

"Should we cut some open and see if we find any of him?" someone asked.

The Fish and Wildlife Service man answered immediately,"That's not gonna happen. They're federally protected in the refuge."

"They're more important than people?" I said in a tone verging on madness.

"Here they are," He answered and turned to me. His face changed when he saw my rage.

"I don't make the rules. I'm sorry," he mumbled and turned away to stare at the water again.

## Chapter 65

The next morning, the call for volunteers brought more people out, but by early afternoon most had left, saying they had to leave for this or that reason. I thanked them for coming out and I didn't hold their leaving against them. I could feel hope slipping away and I was sure they felt it after only a few hours in the woods and no sign of Charlie. At sunset, I was the only person left in the parking lot.

The day after fewer volunteers showed up and the day after that, there were only a couple of game wardens and a deputy sheriff on his day off. That day we ventured so far into the empty woods it sucked the last drop of optimism from me. After that day, I knew there would be no other days that would bring out any volunteers but me.

I stayed until well after dark, hours after, one by one, the men mumbled something to me about being sorry they couldn't do more and left. I had never felt so alone. Charlie had been a part of my life, off and on, since I was a boy and he became the biggest and best part too late in life.

Clouds had moved in during the afternoon and now, sitting in the pitch black with the window down, the smell of rain was heavy. I hardly noticed. My mind was years away, remembering all the things Charlie said that made Charlie Neely who he was. The thought we would never spend another day together, never share a meal, never talk again, finally let the buildup of tears release. He was gone; one way or the other, he was gone. Reaching behind the seat, I pulled his jacket to my chest and more tears followed. I sat there, alone, alone in my truck, alone in the vastness of Panther Swamp, and alone in the world, until there were no more tears. I wiped both cheeks with the back of my hand and wiped my hand on my pants, not wanting to wet Charlie's jacket. I knew I would treasure that jacket for the rest of my life, the jacket that Charlie left for me as a sign, hanging in the tree on the other side of the footbridge. I thought back to our pig hunt a lifetime ago. Charlie had left a shirt hanging in a tree over his dead pig and had never returned to get either. I hadn't thought about it in so long, but his words came to me clear as crystal.

"I'll leave it to be somethin curious for someone to ponder. They won't know it marks the spot where the woods disappeared another creature and didn't leave a trace."

I didn't show the jacket to the guys who came out to search. It would have made no difference to them. They were looking for a body, not a jacket. But it mattered to me. It mattered because I knew Charlie's disappearance was no accident. Before whatever happened to Charlie, he had time to hang his coat in that tree, a last message to me in a story I may never know the ending of.

The finality of that thought caused me to start the truck. Putting it in gear was like closing the door on a hallway I had been walking in most of my life. Charlie once said he was sick and tired of hearing people tell him to pretend something or other never happened. Charlie chose to pretend things happened and then he did his best to prove it. As the truck crested the top of the levee and the engine stopped straining, I did too. I took Charlie's advice. I would pretend Charlie wasn't a victim of revenge and I would pretend Charlie had slipped away to live a life somewhere else without fear. I would also pretend Charlie would show up at my door one day asking for his jacket and we would pick up our friendship like this never happened. Until then, I had my memories in my head and Charlie's jacket in my hands.

I finally reached the end of the levee road and, before turning onto pavement toward home, I put the truck in park, turned off the lights, and cut the engine. My tears had dried and my grief was slowly being overtaken with gratefulness for what had been and what I would pretend would be.

I looked out the truck window into the edge of the dark woods and imagined I could see the faint outline of Charlie Neely. He was smiling. There was no pretending in that smile, either.

I smiled back, started the truck, and drove on, leaving the deep and mournful blackness of Panther Swamp behind…and perhaps Charlie too.

Three Nights in 1923 is a fictional story as are the characters. Three of the fictional characters, however, share their name with three actual people: Cleve McDowell, Tucum, and Charlie Neely.

Cleve McDowell was the first black American to attend the Ole Miss School of Law and was the roommate of James Meredith at Ole Miss. The story of being expelled, receiving a law degree in Houston, and returning to Mississippi to practice is true.

Tucum Tutweiller is based on a real-life south Delta native named Tucum. He is one of the most interesting persons I've known and has become a dear friend. Everything good in Tucum Tutweiller is based on the real Tucum. Everything bad in Tucum Tutweiller is fiction…maybe.

The disappearance of Charlie Neely, the seed that sprouted this story, is regrettably true. According to the Yazoo Herald,

"Charlie Neely, age 67, was last seen standing by his truck near the ten-thousand-acre Panther Swamp Wildlife Refuge at 7:30 a.m. on October 25, 1996. He had gone to the refuge to go squirrel hunting. Neely told his hunting partner to go into the woods alone while he finished putting on his hunting gear.

Neely's partner went into the woods as instructed, but Neely never caught up with him. When his partner returned to the truck at the pre-agreed time four hours later, Neely wasn't there. His partner blew the horn to let Neely know he had returned, then went into the woods to look for him, but couldn't find him.

He has never been heard from again and an extensive search turned up no indication of his whereabouts. He had been hunting since he was a child, and his children stated he always practiced safety measures such as staying on the trail and setting a return time in advance.

When the ten-day search for Neely yielded nothing that would indicate his whereabouts, police stated they thought he could not be in the area they searched. His hunting partner passed a polygraph test and was ruled out as a suspect in his case. One person allegedly told several people he had killed Neely, but this individual has not been named publicly or called a suspect in his case.

His case remains unsolved."

www.ingramcontent.com/pod-product-compliance
Lightning Source LLC
LaVergne TN
LVHW050615100826
845148LV00011B/1592

* 9 7 9 8 2 1 8 8 5 6 7 1 7 *